A Different Manger

JAMES E BURK

To Evan
Have a good read
Jim

ISBN: 978-1-927059-17-3

DEDICATION

IN

Memory of my Father, Delos Burk, who told such vivid stories of adventure, risk and overcoming in real life he instilled in me an urge write stories of a similar vein.

My mother who began reading to me as a toddler and for being hardworking, resilient, adaptable, and hospitable. My model for the pioneer woman and for many of the women appearing in my stories.

CONTENTS

ACKNOWLEDGMENTS

Geneva, my wife, and strength of my life.

Martin, Sandra, Mike and Linda and all those other friends who stayed with me through the writing process and provided encouragement, corrections and changes that helped with both content and readability.

For Doug McDougall of Medicine Hat, Alberta who took the author's picture for the back cover.

Syria
Capernaum
Ptolemais
Lake
Kinneret
Nazareth
Galilee
Caesarea
Great Sea
(Medditteranian)
Jordan
River
Trade Route
Samaria
Trade
Route
Joppa
Arimathea
Judea
Emmaus
Jericho
Jerusalem
Bethany
Bethlehem
Herodium
Azotus
Machaerus

THE SHEPHERD

1 The Tower of the Flock

But you O Bethlehem, Ephratah, who are too little to be among the clans of Judah, from you shall come forth for me one who is to be ruler in Israel.

Micah 5:2: circa 700 bce

Only partway up Migdol Eder's slope I met Caleb already coming down. *What's going on,* I thought. Shepherds of the holy flocks never abandon watch before passing over the ram's horn.

"Have a good sleep," he sneered, slapping the horn onto my palm without missing a stride. No mention of conditions so far, just the jibe. I'd never slept on watch and he knew it.

Should tell Eliezer, I thought. *We've never faced greater hazards than right now.*

I'd observed the crowds flooding the nearby roadway. Some here to celebrate the Festival of Booths; others to prey on any unsuspecting shepherd or celebrant.

Festival of Booths! As regret filled my mind I turned away from Bethlehem towards Jerusalem, its walls etched against the night sky, its golden dome glinting in the moonlight. Inside the temple courts Jews from many nations were coming to worship. *Worship!* A privilege I'd never enjoyed as an adult. Never been allowed to enter the temple. Never worshipped Jehovah in the inner court, and never would while I remained a shepherd. Shepherds and lepers both banned.

But I wasn't here to dream. My duties as watchman required vigilance. I began circling the summit, eyes searching the pastures and surroundings for possible dangers; thoughts flashing back to the shepherd boy, David. A shepherd who'd led his flocks on similar pastures before gaining the throne.

Dodging through scattered hewn stones remaining from the ancient crumbled tower, still known as Tower of the Flock, I mounted a rough, stone platform for a more panoramic view of the valley below.

The moon shone, nearly full, spilling shadow among the streets and houses of Bethlehem. As a boy I'd lived in that town. Attended Beth Sefer in the local synagogue, and roamed its streets until my father's death and sale of our home. I wondered if the new owners would purchase the willow packets with which to build the temporary shelters symbolizing our past nomadic heritage? Would they have taken those willows to the roof of our house and woven them into temporary shelters as homage to the sacred festival?

A remembered sense of childish joy swept over me. A memory of sharing such a shelter with family and glimpsing stars through openings in the woven branches. Most of all though, I remembered father's stories and quotations from the words of Moses. Through those stories I'd developed a yearning for Israel's future Messiah who would destroy our enemies and establish Israel's pre-eminence among earth's kingdoms.

Then my eyes lifted towards the single, most dominant blot on Bethlehem's landscape; Herod's fortress, the Herodian. My father had died, conscript labor in the mammoth task of flattening that hilltop. Now, Herod's dark creation perched above Bethlehem, a giant, hellish monster, whose silent stare served constant reminder of Israel's slavish state.

Messiah will remedy that! I thought.

Laying the ram's horn on a large boulder, I stretched and realized I'd been too much dreaming. Not a good habit for a watchman. And with that thought I began another circuit, eyes switching focus from sheepfold to the nearby road, the visible portion of our pastureland and the inn that marked a boundary between pastureland and city.

The last of the itinerant Levites had passed through the inn's doors hours before. These Levites had come from all over Judea to assist the priests in dealing with the influx of worshippers.

No stragglers remained on the road below, which only a few hours previous had been filled with would-be worshippers seeking shelter during festival.

Worshipers? The very word brought deep sadness. While others worshipped in the temple, covered their sins with the blood of sacrifice, I possessed no means for covering my own.

I held out my hands, pale blue in the moonlight, the unclean hands of a shepherd attached to an unclean body, which, if daring to trespass on temple grounds would lead to death by stoning.

Then, looking up at a shining moon surrounded by shimmering stars, my melancholy evaporated in night's beauty. For certain I missed sharing in festivities of the moment, but duties involving oversight of Jehovah's flocks seemed Jehovah's will for me.

Under the illuminating sky I looked out on rolling hills surrounded in mysterious shadow, on the pattern of houses and streets in Bethlehem town, and on to the profiled walls and towers of Jerusalem. I breathed the pure air, inhaled the beauty and repeated a thought often running through my mind, *so much better to be a shepherd here than tending sheep among profane ruffians in the wild lands of Judah* as I'd done for my five years following Beth Sefer.

Below me, moonlight highlighted each paving stone laid by Roman engineers and that sight returned me to not-so-beautiful thoughts. *Romans.* Bile rose in my throat. *When will Messiah come? How much longer can my people wait?*

Even the unmanageable crowds of the moment could be blamed on the Romans and their desire to squeeze more taxes from an already overburdened nation. Emperor Caesar Augustus had ordered a census where each family would return to their city of origin. All descendants of the great king David had been ordered to Bethlehem for their official head count.

I could not help but think of words from my namesake Micah. Over twenty generations before my time he'd declared that Bethlehem, insignificant Bethlehem, would be the birthplace of Messiah, Ruler and Savior of Israel. Should Messiah come soon he would certainly put an end to Caesar and his Romans.

What if Messiah were born this night, on my watch? I shivered at the thought. Would I even know?

A shadow on the moonlit roadway caught my attention, a shadow that grew as it passed from Bethlehem's shadow. My pulse quickened when it continued along the Roman road paralleling our pasturelands until it paused near the Inn of the Levites.

Foolish people travelling at night. Those lurking in the shadows would as easily plunder a stranger as steal a sheep.

I straightened, wet my lips, and reached for the ram's horn as the moving shadow separated itself from the road and moved into the sacred pasturelands. The moonlight now illuminated a man leading a donkey with a rider balanced on its back.

The urge to race down the hill and direct the man back to the road passed as the intruders paused at the inn. I knew the innkeeper, a brusque, no-nonsense type. *Good*, I thought. *He'll send them on their way.*

The man knocked on the door and the sound of his voice carried faintly through the night. A muffled voice answered. The door didn't open. *Good*!

But the man didn't turn back towards the road. Instead his steps took him towards the lambing stable.

"Stop them Jehovah!" I prayed. "Stop them lest they defile the sacred space intended for your lambs alone."

I saw Eliezer, our lead shepherd, exit the stable, lamp held high, and expected to hear his stern voice ordering these trespassers on their way. Instead, the lamp moved towards the intruders as the man dropped the donkey's lead rope, and eased its rider to the ground.

A lady! A lady, stumbling as her feet touched ground.

My heart nearly stopped when Eliezer took one arm, the man the other.

Eliezer touching a woman. No! No! It could not be.

Stunned, I watched Eliezer join the stranger in assisting the lady through the entrance of the lambing stable.

My panicked eyes locked on the space meant only for sacred newborn lambs. I waited, watched, unaware of passing time. My mind flashed back to a few hours previous when I'd assisted Eliezer in the birth of a lamb from one of my own ewes. My fingers felt again the wetness of afterbirth on the newborn's wool as I performed my first search for any defect making it unfit for temple sacrifice. Finding none I assisted Eliezer as we washed the newborn, wrapped it in cloth and placed the newborn in the hewn stone manger giving protection while it gained the strength needed to suckle.

But anger, disgust, and fear disappeared as stable, town and pasturelands dissolved in a burst of light. The sky bloomed, consuming and brilliant; birthing a moving form, a form defined in light of such piercing intensity one forgot the world of light in which it moved. A form floating over our pastureland.

Facedown, shaking hands held to my eyes, there came a voice of such crystalline purity I felt a soothing peace drive fear from my shivering body.

Were they audible words, or thoughts impressed on my soul? I don't know but they rang clear as a bell. "I bring good news, news meant for all peoples everywhere. A Savior, Messiah, is born today, right here in Bethlehem, David's city. You will find the baby wrapped in strips of cloth and lying in a manger."

At the sound of those words I half uncovered my eyes to a vision of sky swirling with life, and music and voice. One voice? A thousand? But words I would never forget. "Glory to God above all and peace to His creation and to all those with whom He is pleased."

Then, light and voices receded, leaving pregnant silence behind. Peering out through parted fingers, eyes still half blind, I saw only moon, stars, and darkness. Bathed in euphoric memory, I lay still while savoring words of the celestial vision. A vision, quickly fading, as doubts crept in.

Could it really be? Had I, Micah, seen Messiah's mother and father! No! That could not be. Fragments of Torah, the Prophets and Midrash flashed through my mind. Messiah's mother would be a virgin. There could be no father.

Rolling onto my knees and looking downslope I saw shepherds standing frozen and still under the open stars above the sheep-fold. As still as Lot's wife who'd turned from being a frightened human to pillar of salt.

I bolted down the hill and joined a group no longer frozen. A milling, clamoring group. Questions tossed about. Answers no one listened to. Loud bleating from the sheepfold compounding the confusion.

Thaddeus' rough voice over rode the din. "Quiet! We have heaven's instructions, *Go! See! Tell!*

Even those not seeing Eliezer usher a man and woman into the sacred lambing booth as I had, knew the way. The, birthing stable for sacrificial lambs. I followed behind the others, my mind buffeted by scripture, rabbi's teaching, heaven's explicit words, and evidence of my own eyes.

In spite of heaven's words, doubt nipped at my heels. I hesitated at the stable's open entrance, my view blocked by shepherds arriving before me. When bodies parted for a moment, I glimpsed a tall stranger standing beside the polished, white stone of the manger.

I forced my way forward until the whole scene came to life. A young woman, younger than me, lay on the stable floor with Eliezer's cloak around her and an infant in a manger beside her.

When the tall man leaned down, I noted grey highlights showing on hair and beard and heard the scorned accents of Galilee.

I slipped between two other shepherds and stared down on the baby lying in our sacred manger. A tiny hand and arm slipped from under swaddling cloth. A mouth opened, and I heard a cry, much like a bleating lamb.

That cry struck like a hammer and we twelve fell to our knees as one. We had waited so long. Waited and hoped for the Messiah who would deliver us from our oppressors. Now, here he lay. Not what we'd expected. Not what we'd hoped for, but we all knew Jehovah's plans were not ours.

Eliezer moved towards the stable opening, intruding on our ecstatic moment. We followed until a short distance outside the stable we formed a semi-circle and awaited his leading.

Lifting his eyes skyward he raised his arms and repeated the words from heaven's messengers; *A Savior, Messiah has been born for us today in the city of David.* "Thank you, great Adonai, for blessing us, your unworthy worshippers; blessing us with words from heaven and granting us first sight of the One who will be our Great King."

Our arms mirrored Eliezer's in silent worship. Only Caleb's arms remained inert and motionless.

Eliezer's voice brought us back to the moment. "Yonder couple are indeed man and wife, Mary and Joseph from Nazareth. But," he paused, "many miracles surround this baby's birth beyond even what we've seen this night. Joseph told me how Adonai touched Mary's body and the baby grew within her. He told me how he'd wept when first learning of her pregnancy and how he'd begun arranging a secret divorce, until Jehovah's messenger came in a dream and explained a miraculous conception.

Eliezer paused, sucked air, shook his head, and in words, nearly too faint for hearing, said, "How can this be, two men, neither with proper cleansing, participating in a baby's birth? A baby, any baby, but Messiah!"

He shook his head again before speaking. "Joseph and I assisted in the birth. I cut the cord. Messiah cried like any baby. We washed his little body, wrapped it in the cloth intended for our next lamb and lowered him into the manger just as the heavens erupted in light and music. We looked out to see the skies full of life, hear music such as we had never heard, and then those words. This baby is indeed the promised Messiah!

Leaving our flocks behind we entered Bethlehem in a tight group, exuberant and inspired; then spread out to follow the command of angels. "Go and tell."

I entered the familiar street leading to my former home troubled by a haunting question. Why are all still sleeping? Did the tumult in the skies not waken them?

I beat on several doors before one opened. The man answering showed little interest in my report. Shocked at this blatant rejection a tear trickled down my cheek.

One tear became many as doors opened, eyes examined my shepherd's cloak, heard my news, and turned away. Finally, those tears robbed me of sight and choked off further words. Overcome with a sense of futility my thoughts turned to my unattended flock and I faced away from Bethlehem town.

With leaden feet and guilt of a traitor I retraced my steps towards Migdol Eder. Thaddeus, the shepherd I most respected, exited a side street as I passed. His expression reflected the same feelings as my own. Looking toward the pasturelands I saw Caleb well ahead. He had to be even more disillusioned than I or hadn't bothered with door knocking at all.

Nearing the stable Thaddeus broke the silence. He waved a clenched fist and shook his head. "I knocked first on my uncle's gate, a man obsessed with Messiah, or so I thought.

"After blurting out news of what we'd seen and heard, my uncle spoiled whatever prestige I'd given him in the past. *You're just a shepherd,*" he said.

A spasm ran through Thaddeus' body. "And he's from the blood-line of Aaron just as I. Then came my uncle's next words, more cutting than the first. *God would never deliver the message of Messiah through the lips of an unclean shepherd. I swear by the temple, I've never heard such nonsense. Please tell no one else.*

A real sob broke through his tight lips. "I will never forgive nor forget my uncle's next words, more demeaning than everything before. *Your presence renders my dwelling unclean. Now I must bring a priest for cleansing and excuse myself from the temple for seven days. Go!*

Entering the shepherds' fields, we saw ahead the birthing stable, dark and silent, but more sacred than ever before. We detoured wide, tip toe, hardly daring a breath. Upon reaching our nook under the rock overhang, Thaddeus slumped in silence.

Off, nearly hidden in shadow, Caleb sat, head in hands. I stirred embers into flame and waited.

Avner, the next shepherd to arrive walked with brisk steps. "Did you hear the buzz?" he asked.

Thaddeus' head jerked. "What buzz?"

When I knocked on the door of my first house, I found it full of guests preparing for festival. They broke into singing before I'd even finished my news. Together we scattered throughout the whole neighborhood; *Messiah*, the word on every tongue."

Thaddeus turned his eyes my way, blood red in the firelight. "Didn't hear that, did you?"

The next shepherds arrived in a clump, their gloom, similar to my own. The last shepherd to arrive described a positive, though muted response.

I felt sorrow for those bringing this good news; good news cancelled and swallowed in the dark pit of futility and despair from those sharing the same message.

Why had we failed in delivering the angel's message? The thought repeated itself over and over as I sat by the fire, head buried in my hands, wrapped in the gloom of my fellows.

Through those dark shadows emerged an image of the baby Jesus. An infant wrapped in similar cloth to the lamb I'd helped inspect and wrap just the previous day. A lamb whose kicks and squirms came vividly to mind along with the satisfaction coming as it relaxed in my cradled arms. I'd been first to inspect, my hands touching every part of its body. Together with Eliezer we'd washed it, wrapped it and placed it in the same manger now occupied by Messiah.

Had Eliezer washed Messiah? The thought seemed like sacrilege.

Dropping the comparison, I turned my thoughts back to the lamb I'd helped wash and wrap and the way its head lifted from within the manger; the bleat as it sought its mother.

I bowed my head in prayer and sought Jehovah, not with words, but with thoughts too jumbled for recall.

When my eyes opened, they fell on the birthing stable, just visible in the half-light of dawn. The only sign of life, the donkey munching on a pile of hay, a sight so ordinary as to give a lie to the miraculous message of the night before. The echoing bleat of a ewe gave further reason to believe this to be just another day on the pastures of Bethlehem.

That single bleat roused me to action and I headed for the large fold that penned my flock as well as that of the other eleven shepherds.

An expected stirring answered my call from among the combined flocks in the large enclosure. A call reminding me of the difference between present duties and that of watching sheep in the wilderness. There, my fold would be wherever I could find a cave or windbreak. And, only occasionally would I cross paths with other shepherds.

Here, my fellow shepherds were as committed to God's service as I. When on our present pastures, we greeted each other with a psalm or blessing, never curses. Here my flock rested at night within a roomy cave, expanded by a fencing barrier. We fed our sheep in bountiful pastures, and watered at a flowing stream.

Pride, the ewe who'd lambed the previous day and always came first at my call, rested this day in an enclosure near the birthing stable. Today, the ram, Alon, came first to the gate. Alon, the oak, aptly named considering his dominant horns, strong neck, and muscular shoulders. He paused. I spoke his name, ran hands over his body, gave permission for him to go and turned to the next animal within the flock's hierarchical power structure.

As each animal reached me it paused and allowed my hands to run over its head, my mouth whisper its name and my fingers check for injuries.

A voice called and I turned to see Thaddeus, our leader of the night before. He was a large man, shaggy browed, curly haired and bearded. Large nose and ears dominated his face; eyes, nearly hidden due to a permanent squint from long sun exposure. He possessed greater strength than any man I had ever known.

Not the kind of man one would expect to be an expert in Torah. Typically abrupt and usually aloof, we had nevertheless become friends in spite of my short time as a shepherd of the sacred flocks. I'd found him to be calm, thoughtful and unmatched in practical knowledge of the Scriptures.

Strange, I thought, how so many outside our profession equated unclean hands with unclean minds. We had more time than most to contemplate life's meaning and to go over and over the words of Torah we'd memorized in Beth Sefer. Also scraps of scripture did come our way. We even had a scroll containing all the Psalms. A treasure we passed from hand to hand. No greater treasure existed among us. Even the itinerant Levis added to our store of knowledge, arguing and debating as they did whether a shepherd happened to be in listening distance or not.

As Thaddeus' approached, I saw over his shoulder the hill known as the Tower of the Flock. Near here, according to the first book of Moses, our ancestor Jacob had buried his beloved wife, Rachel. Near here, according to some scholars, Jehovah would reveal his Messiah. My namesake, Micah had mentioned this place. *Bethlehem Ephrata.* A strange pairing of names. *Bethlehem*, "House of Bread" and *Ephrata,* "Fruitful." Maybe something to do with Jacob whose twelve children had provided names for each of our tribes.

Those thoughts fled as Thaddeus walked past, his face a chiseled stone mask.

2: Puzzles

Isaiah 40:29 He gives power to the faint, and to him who has no might he increases strength.
From Isaiah's vision: circa 740 bce.

That night, sitting before our evening fire, eating flat bread from the inn and meat roasted over the fire, we twelve sat, heads down, each lost in thought.

The tail of the Big Bear constellation tracked across the sky and occasionally I lifted my eyes towards the stable of Messiah's birth. The donkey no longer remained tethered where it had been that very morning. I remembered tip-toeing by it the night before. Now I felt that even the stable had developed overtones of holiness.

There will soon be a shrine there, I thought. Maybe even another temple.

Overwhelmed with lethargy, I barely registered Thaddeus stirring beside me. Remember," his voice hardly more than a whisper. Then almost a shout, "Remember! Remember the words of heaven. *The message I have for you is one of great joy and is a gift belonging to all peoples everywhere."*

"Do you not remember those words? A message of great joy for all peoples."

I could feel his eyes pass over our huddled shadows before he continued, "God's very messengers spoke those words, but how do we respond?"

Silence hung over us, as heavy and enveloping as the darkness in which we sat, until Avner responded, his voice, high and nasal. "As though we'd never seen or heard the events of this night. As though we'd seen no baby in a manger."

Yigal's voice, a monotone of despair responded, "Maybe we're part of a collective dream or victims of evil spirits sent to make us targets of mockery before the whole world." These words from a man I'd come to regard as unshakable as the walls of Jerusalem.

Thaddeus spoke again. "We twelve, thirteen including Eliezer, are the only ones reporting the sights and sounds of the evening. We are the only ones responding to divine spirits announcing a newborn baby in a manger.

"No man since Adam is more privileged than we. Yet what do we do?"

Silence fell over us again, until Avner's voice broke into singing. A song of King David.

> "PRAISE GOD!
> PRAISE HIM IN HIS TABERNACLE;
> PRAISE HIM IN THE HEAVENS OF HIS POWER!
>
> PRAISE HIM FOR HIS MIRACLES;
> PRAISE HIM FOR ALL HIS GREATNESS!
>
> PRAISE HIM WITH THE SOUND OF THE SHOFAR;
> PRAISE HIM WITH THE LYRE AND HARP!
>
> PRAISE HIM WITH THE TAMBOURINE AND DANCING;
> PRAISE HIM WITH STRINGS AND HORNS!
>
> PRAISE HIM WITH A LOUD SOUND;
> PRAISE HIM WITH LOUD AND CLEAR SOUNDS.
>
> LET EVERY LIVING BEING SING PRAISES TO GOD!
> PRAISE GOD!

The psalm shone light into my gloom, but brought no certainty.

Sleeping mats rustled on straw as my fellows prepared for sleep. Feeling no similar urge, I stood and walked from under the rock overhang and looked upward into what seemed a living expanse. A moon that moved, the Great Bear in its nightly rotation, and among the sparkling host a few wandering lights. No angels but a marvel all the same.

Dropping to my knees I raised my hands toward heaven and prayed. Prayed Jehovah would speak and explain his expectations of me. Of us.

When no voice spoke or angelic beings brought insight, I turned my eyes to the stable; sat, watched.

I continued sitting, eyes open, half asleep, until the call of thirsty, hungry sheep brought me fully awake. Lifting my eyes toward the fold I saw Caleb already there. *What demon wakened him,* I thought. *He's always the laggard.*

Waiting until he and his flock were well on their way to the watering place, I looked around to see if any of the more senior shepherds were on their way. Seeing none, I proceeded to follow Caleb.

In spite of the proofs from the night before, evil spirits troubled me through the day as I led my sheep from one choice bit of pasture to another. The voices were many. Many and persistent. *You are delusional. Your dreams of Messiah are but self-serving fantasies, and what if you did see something, no one will believe the words of a shepherd, especially one so young.*

With such thoughts whirling through my mind, I set out to find another shepherd who might remove my confusion.

I sighted Avner about the sixth hour as he watered his flock at still waters upstream of the morning location. Seeing me, Avner led his flock away from the stream, gestured with his staff and the flock lay down as one.

After settling my flock, I moved to join him.

"Avner," I started, and paused, unsure of my next words.

He turned his shaggy head my way. After searching my face for several seconds, he lifted his eyes and pointed skyward. "I saw heaven move. I heard angel's voices. I remember every word. That baby is the Messiah of God. Whatever that will mean."

I raised my hands. "But why? Why would Jehovah's messengers talk to shepherds? Why would God invite us to be first to see His Promised One and first to tell the world? And why were we so rejected if God wants His Messiah known?

Bushy eyebrows lifted, "Do you question Jehovah?"

I persisted. "But now Jehovah has but a few shepherds to spread news of Messiah's birth. And we've been far from successful so far. It's mad!"

A bleating ewe from Avner's flock interrupted and he walked over to an animal with her fat tail tangled in a thorn bush. Large hands, tender hands, took a few pricks and scratches before assuring painless release for the helpless animal.

One "thank you" bleat from the ewe and she rushed back to her flock.

Avner stood, examined me, eyes angry at my questioning and disbelief. "Do you believe? Do you believe we all suffered an identical illusion? Of course you don't. Think of Queen Esther, whose one obedient act preserved our nation. We may be the Queen Esther for our time."

I almost laughed at the picture of two ritually unclean shepherds, a little odorous, dressed in sheepskin and standing next to beautiful Queen Esther, wife to the most powerful man on earth.

Avner sensed my skepticism and scowled. "Jehovah makes no mistakes, and you, Micah, and I, are part of His bigger plan. Do not fight Jehovah's call." He tapped his forehead. "As children we spent six years or more filling our minds with the words and actions of Jehovah in His dealings with Israel. We've never had a better chance to explore that knowledge and apply our learning, not just recite the words of others.

"Possibly minds such as ours, less cluttered by Pharisaical legalisms, will bring forth better insights? Maybe we will help tell the world? After all Jehovah chose to bring his Messiah into the world in the ritually unclean space of a stable with two men as attendants. Why? Why not a palace with nursemaids and guards? Why?"

A moment after bowing my head and taking several deep breaths I felt faith flood through me as a cistern fills with the rain of spring.

That peace brought a smile to my lips and I looked up at Avner. "Our campfire time tonight will be an active one, will it not?"

With the flock following, I moved on to other pasture with thoughts of the evening whirling in my mind. *Get together tonight and share thoughts of Messiah through the words of Scripture. What can I bring to such discussion? Will the older shepherds pay any attention to my ideas, anyway?*

I recalled my first day at Beth Sefer as a timid five-year-old. An old man with few teeth introduced himself as Rabbi Korah. His first rant scared us half to death. "I am not here because I want to be," he whined. "I have always taught from the Scriptures in the Hebrew language. Here, I must use the Pentateuch and the Greek language since none of you in this village know Hebrew."

By the end of six months we could not even recite one hundred words from the first book of Moses and the leaders of our synagogue sent Rabbi Korah on his way.

The vision of our new teacher, Rabbi David, on his first day with us, resurrected itself in my mind. The leader of our synagogue had towered over our new teacher as he introduced him. "Boys," he said, "You have a new instructor, Rabbi David, a recent arrival from Alexandria in Egypt, the very city in which 70 Jewish rabbis translated the Hebrew Scriptures into the Greek."

Rabbi David waited for the synagogue leader to depart before making a circuit of the room, stopping first at me. "What is your name?" he asked.

"Micah," I answered with eyes to the floor.

"Micah," he seemed to savor the name, and I felt more important than ever before in my life.

After going to each student, Rabbi David opened a scroll to the first words of Scripture. He read, *In the beginning God.*

His eyes touched each of us. "Repeat those words."

Since Rabbi Korah had already gone over the same words many times, we answered in the same singsong voice we'd learned from our late teacher.

"Again." This time our unison improved.

Rabbi David gave a slow headshake. "You are not little monkeys," he said. "Those words just repeated are the very words of God as given to our great teacher, Moses. The words are holy. They have value. Each word of the Torah must become your personal treasure. A treasure you share with fellow Jews.

"Yaakov," he addressed the oldest and shiest boy in our class. "You try."

Words stumbled from Yaakov's lips. I listened, ready for the kind of blistering criticism we'd grown used to. Instead, Rabbi David's words were kind and thoughtful. "Thank you, Yaakov," he said, before uttering words I remembered as though they were yesterday. "Each word from your mouths must make its exit clearly and full of emotion. Words, covered with the honey of emotion will stick in your memories and last a lifetime."

By the age of seven I could recite much of Moses' book of beginnings. Most of those in my age group could recite more and Rabbi David found me a mediocre student. I knew my Greek as well as any of the others, but the rabbi despaired at my inattention. Should a portion of scroll intrigue me, that I could memorize and recite with enough passion to draw the ears of other students, but many passages I ignored.

When at the age of thirteen many students moved on to advanced studies in Beth Midrash, Rabbi David called me aside. "I cannot recommend you for advancement," he said. "Your future role is not that of a rabbi, nor even that of a scholar." A soft smile took the sting from his words. "You listen only when you want to, and your stylus, too often, busies itself with drawings or with poetic fantasies, rather than the words of Scripture. In many ways you are my best pupil." He paused after emphasizing the word *my.* "You do belong to the tribe of Levi and a normal path would lead to your becoming a priest, a scribe, or to special service in the temple. But your path lies elsewhere.

"Jehovah bless and keep you."

And that had been my last contact with Rabbi David.

But neither Rabbi David nor I anticipated my next step in life would be that of a common shepherd in the Judean wilderness. Not a bad path in many ways. I spent hours comforting myself and flock with the sounds of a flute. I spent other hours reciting Scripture to this some-time attentive audience, using all the tricks of elocution learned in Beth Sefer.

During those five years my father died and my mother and grandfather took refuge with other family members.

After five years tending sheep in the wilderness, Rabbi David's hand reached out to me again. The sacred flocks grazing in the consecrated pastures between Jerusalem and Bethlehem required another Levite as shepherd. Rabbi David remembered me.

I'd heard people talking about shepherds in general. "Not much better than common thieves. Moral reprobates. Don't let your daughters or wives anywhere near them." But for those of us tending the temple flocks, nothing could be further from the truth.

Though blocked from participation in temple rituals, we sought truth with greater diligence than most in Judah, and regular interchange deepened our understanding of texts memorized during early years in Beth Sefer.

In my months since becoming a shepherd of the temple flocks, I'd internalized more scripture than absorbed in all those years of formal instruction. Now looking forward to lively interchange this coming evening, I watched the sun advance across the heavens at the sluggish pace of a hobbled donkey.

That evening, around our fire, and taking my usual place beside Thaddeus I waited for the anticipated discussion to begin. No one spoke and when my eyes passed over my fellow shepherds I saw men with heads hanging, avoiding eye contact, avoiding discussion.

Collecting my bowl and half bread loaf, I stood, shook my head and walked into the night. Anger roiled through me. I wished for an intruder on whom I might exercise my staff. None appeared and anger gave way to something else. The same nagging questions. What were we to do, mere caretakers of sheep? Why had the angel come to us?

My doubts returned. The newly born Jesus had been just like any normal baby. His parents, poor. From Galilee even; Bethlehem not even their home and with a questionable story of divine impregnation.

We would never erase the little baby and his manger from our minds or conscience. But, could we call him *Messiah?*

3: Backlash

The proud have hid a snare for me, and cords; they have spread a net by the wayside; they have set traps for me.

King David; circa 960 bce

On the evening of the tenth day following Jesus' birth, I visited Eliezer at his temporary stable a little removed from the one in which Jesus entered our world. Not even Eliezer had visited that stable since Mary, Joseph and the baby departed. The manger, in which Eliezer laid the baby, remained where it had been and a new manger filled a corner of the new shelter. Its rough-hewn stonework a sacrilege

Now, with ewes giving birth on a regular basis, Eliezer busied himself with increased birthing rituals.

I washed before entering the stable.

Eliezer spoke over his shoulder as he continued adding fresh straw to the new manger. "We receive a temple delegation tomorrow evening. I am surprised it has taken so long. You will need your flocks penned early. Tell the others."

I had visited for nothing more than his reassuring presence and, feeling anything but reassured I walked over to the new manger, and ran my hands over a varicolored, rough surface.

Eliezer placed a single finger on an opposite corner. "Not the same is it? No history here. That manger in which we laid Messiah received the blessing of the priest, Ezra, nearly 500 years ago. It survived the ravages of the Greek King, Antiochus Epiphenes, and has remained in these pasturelands since Ezra's blessing."

He paused, his smile sad. "Best go tell the others."

News of the upcoming visit left us all unsettled. An emotion picked up by our flocks during the day.

Unsettled could not describe my reaction on nearing the fold the following afternoon. Tents, mules, couched camels and a large tent filled most of the space between roadway and fold. The camels still carried riding saddles.

As I led my flock to water I noticed six of my fellow shepherds standing near the fold. After watering my flock and leading them into the enclosure, I joined the other shepherds standing outside.

Each additional flock entering the fold increased the restiveness of the animals within. Our twelve rams began intruding on each other's space. Head butting started. We then had the unpleasant task of tethering the rams outside the fold, agitating the ewes even more. And, agitated sheep meant agitated shepherds.

Avner, carrying his lyre, entered the fold and I followed with my flute. The sheep settled a little.

From inside the fold I was able to see activity within the large tent. Several richly dressed individuals stood with arms raised in prayer. I saw lips move on the man facing me. When darkness fell Avner kindled our cooking fire and soon the smoke drifting through the fold carried the aroma of roasting meat.

From within our visitor's tent, flames from several oil lamps spilled light through open flaps and painted moving shadows on the tent walls.

We watched as a servant brought Eliezer to the tent and had him stop about three paces distant from a carpet serving as barrier between tent and unclean visitors. The men inside the tent now sat on stools. Voices carried as faint murmurs only.

Eliezer stood outside the tent for only a short time before returning to his temporary stable. Those of us waiting took turns visiting the fold to check on ewes about to give birth.

Surprise caught us when Caleb received the first call for questioning. He remained outside the tent much longer than Eliezer.

"Not good," Baruch spoke from the shadows.

I exhaled, realizing I'd been holding my breath.

When Caleb returned, he took a position as far from the rest of us as possible.

One by one we, the unclean, stood outside the sanctified space and the occupants within.

When I stopped in front of the tent I found myself facing a young man standing beside a small table with someone I took to be a priest seated behind.

"Your name?" The young man's terse voice startled me.

"Micah," I answered and a scribe sitting near the tent's wall put quill to parchment.

"Your training?" a question came from the shadows.

"Beth Sefer," I answered and watched the priest's lip curl.

"You were on watch the night of this reported phenomena were you not?" A man in the rich clothing, prayer shawl, and long tassels, common to the wealthiest of Pharisees brought the next question.

"I was."

"And you abandoned your watch?"

"Yes, but..." I paused at an upraised finger.

"That will be all. You may go said the seated priest.

Turning away I noted the scribe dip his quill in water and wipe it clean.

I returned to our sheltering overhang, collected my flute and went into the sheepfold, blind and deaf to the world around me. Unaware even when the sun rose over the horizon.

Consciousness returned only when Thaddeus touched my shoulder. I lowered the flute, mouth so dry I wondered what sounds, if any, I'd been creating.

Thaddeus' words were as stunning as the interview of the night before. "Why were you playing such joyful music through the night. The sheep rested and most of us slept. I didn't even hear our questioners leave."

I looked out towards the birthing stable past the spot where camels had been couched the previous evening. They were indeed gone.

Servants busied themselves dismantling the tent. Several mules stood packed and ready to leave.

That evening as Eliezer read the names of those on watch I realized I would be on watch with Caleb again. He had second and I the third and last.

After Eliezer returned to his station, Thaddeus took me to one side. "You slept not at all last night. Allow me to take your watch."

"Thank you, but maybe stars and night air will clear my head."

My heart beat a little faster as I started up Migdol Eder's slope for the last watch of the night, wondering what to expect from Caleb this time. He'd been avoiding me, and I him ever since the exchange on our last adjoining watches. *Strange fellow,* I thought. *Hasn't tried making friends with the other shepherds. Maybe thinks he's better than us with an uncle serving in the temple. Hope he's more civil this time.*

I'd barely finished the thought when I saw Caleb leaving his post on the summit. Reaching me, he slapped the horn into my outstretched hand, speaking over his shoulder as he passed. "You're late. Hope you stick to your post this time."

Shock froze me in place for a moment; then I started after him. Started and stopped, memories of two other shepherds fighting. Eliezer had sent them on their way the very same day.

Nevertheless, Caleb's taunt kept me in a foul mood as I paced my circuit on Migdol Eder's height. On this night starlight and the faint glimmer of a waning moon cast not even a shadow. Then I sensed a spark in the darkness below.

Can't be," I thought, *just a star's reflection.* But that imagined spark suddenly exploded in a sheet of flame racing up the rear wall of the stable.

Before I could even get the ram's horn to my lips that flame illuminated two mounted, shadowy forms disappearing into the darkness.

I gave a single blast of the ram's horn and plummeted down the hill, my only thought, Eliezer.

I found Caleb and Thaddeus already at the temporary stable that stood well away from the flames. Caleb knelt with Eliezer's blood-soaked head in his arms. My legs crumpled and I fell to my knees beside Caleb, tears flowing.

I continued kneeling as other shepherds gathered.

In the glow of coals from the ravaged stable Thaddeus signaled quiet. "The flock;" his voice broke. "The flocks remain our sacred duty. We must tend them first."

"Micah," he turned, eyes reflecting the red coals of the burning. "You will alert Rabbi Jonathan in Bethlehem. The temple lambs require a trained servant of God to manage their care. Until that occurs each new lamb will be unclean."

Caleb, still cradling Eliezer, raised his head. "I should go. Micah may have failed in his duties as watchman and be an unfit messenger."

A dark haze settled over my vision and my head whirled. Thaddeus examined Caleb, contempt showing.

"We have no time for blame or guesswork." He turned to me and pointed. "Go!"

The sixth day of the week following Eliezer's death meant Sabbath would commence as the sun dropped over the horizon. With it being the day before Sabbath we tried to follow the traditions of the rabbis for the evening meal. We washed as best we could, enjoyed our food, sang the appropriate psalms, drank the wine, and quoted prescribed prayers. We did little work after sunset; though each shepherd checked his flock before sleeping and then alternated regular checks through the night.

On the morning following Sabbath I pastured on a slope looking over the stream and out to the roadway. Nearing the third hour with the sun mid-way to zenith I caught sight of several mule-drawn wagons moving south out of Bethlehem.

As they neared the pasture lands my gut clenched when the horse-drawn chariot leading the procession turned off the roadway and stopped near the lambing stable's burnt out remains. The man stepping down from the chariot, radiated authority. A cloak of white linen covered his undergarments and almost obscured long, blue fringes dangling from a prayer shawl.

Those accompanying the wagon were clearly gentiles with no requirement for ritual purity. They began loading the ashes and unburned remnants of the birthing stable onto their cart as other transport added to the congestion building between sheepfold and road. Building materials filled each cart. This time, though, Hebrews accompanied each wagon and I recognized Samuel, the most skilled craftsman in Bethlehem.

I watched the first laborers hoist the cracked remains of Messiah's manger onto their cart and drive away. They treated this precious reminder of Messiah's birth as though it were dung. The sight brought tears.

While these laborers erased all reminders of the previous stable, Samuel circled the space he'd chosen just a few cubits from the burn marks on the ground. The master builder signaled, and other individuals grouped about him. The man in white linen joined and I saw the priest's arms rise and the faint sound of his voice. The group answered; their chorus echoing a psalm's soft rhythm.

The priest dropped his arms, stepped back, and Samuel took a measuring rod from an assistant.

A growing sense of foreboding increased when I glanced back at the road. Six men on horseback were raising a dust trail on their way down from Jerusalem. I'd seen temple guards but twice before; often enough, though, to identify them at a glance. They, too, turned into our pasturelands. One of the horsemen spotted me, kicked his horse into motion and stopped alongside. "Water your sheep and pen them now. The other shepherds will be doing the same."

Just finished with penning my flock, two wagons of fodder stopped near the fold. The drivers unhitched their mules and led them away. I stayed with my sheep, gentling them as best I could.

Maneuvering until I had a clear view of construction activity, I noticed the man I'd guessed to be a priest standing near the horsemen. Taller than I. Perfectly proportioned. A reminder that not only were sacrificial lambs to be perfect, but priests and Levites serving in the temple must also be of noble appearance.

The priest spoke to the lead horseman, his words clear and succinct. "Collect shepherds and flocks. There will be no debate. Punish any reluctance."

At this time of day the flocks were well spread out, but the first flock arrived within the hour. Each shepherd followed the same pattern. Take sheep to water and pen them in the fold. Then each shepherd remained with his flock as I had done in an effort to calm nervous animals unused to any break in routine.

When Caleb arrived, the priest met him, had a brief discussion, and Caleb led his flock back into the pasturelands.

As Caleb left, the priest turned toward us, flanked by a guard in elaborate armor. The other guards fanned out behind him.

The priest moved up to the walls of the sheep-fold, looked over and spoke loud enough we each heard. Nodding toward the guards, he said, "These, Jehovah's servants, will lead you to another pasture." And then in words dripping contempt, "your animals have been too long in unsanctified space to be of any use to the temple."

4: Cast Out

But you priests have turned from the path God set for you. Your instructions have caused many to stumble.

The Prophet Malachi: circa 400 bce

Anguish enveloped me as I looked over the barren pastureland to which we'd been delivered. The barrier surrounding the fold, a mere collection of rocks, dirt, branches and thorn bush. A barrier defining an area far too small for our flocks. No stream, just a well; its protective stone wall of un-dressed stone the only visible evidence of ongoing care.

An acacia and two fig trees stood near the well, obvious beneficiaries of occasional watering. Our exhausted flocks seemed to have picked these trees as their base and lay in rough groups according to their shepherd.

Two wagons carrying dry fodder had been following us and now began dropping their loads near the feeble barrier. The flocks stood as one and rushed the fodder before the wagons even emptied. We fought to turn them back as a few began tossing fodder into the fold.

When one of the rams jumped the barrier into the fold, I turned and ran to the well, stumbled over remains of a broken winch and picked up a bucket attached to a long rope. The rope slid through my fingers until the bucket struck water. Grunting with effort I hoisted the full bucket upward and balanced it on the well casing until I caught a breath.

Water-scent filled the air as I tipped the bucket and let its contents cascade into a shallow stone trough, diverting some of the animal's attention from dry fodder to life-giving water.

And that began the story of the next few days. Days in which I wondered whether we, or our sheep, would die first.

Adding to our difficulties, Avner arrived in camp one evening, carrying a sheep carcass and nursing a damaged arm. One of his ewes had fallen into a crevice and in his rescue efforts he'd gashed an arm. Though the ewe still lived its leg was broken, so he'd killed the animal for its meat. This left us with one less ewe and one more orphan lamb.

That same night three shepherds abandoned both flocks and fellow shepherds.

Two days after that abandonment three temple guards rode in with a final message of doom. "We need but two men to drive these animals to Egypt. A caravan leaves in four days. Prepare the flocks."

"Can't be done," Thaddeus stated matter of fact, following the messenger's departure. "This is the furthest I've ever been from Bethlehem, but I've heard tales about that journey to Egypt. I suppose our overseers expect the Red Sea to part for us as it did for Moses." He gave a sick, weary smile, "And I don't think sheep do well on manna. Any of you with more optimistic words?"

No one answered.

"Well, then, we can draw lots to see who goes, or we can abandon the sheep and let them die right here rather than one at a time in some God-forsaken desert. We'll decide in the morning. If angels really exist, we need them now."

Those words from Thaddeus drove away any of my last flickering hopes. To this point he'd shown no doubts, a pillar of strength for us all.

Thaddeus, Avner and I woke next morning to find ourselves further abandoned. No other shepherds. No, *Adonai bless and keep you.* Just gone.

A few weeks previous we'd been thirteen men including Eliezer; each shepherd responsible for thirteen mature animals. Each flock containing twelve ewes and one ram. The last of the ewes had lambed while still in our original pastures. These new lambs had arrived without inspection or washing.

Even with the impossible ultimatum facing us, we were still shepherds. We still had sheep in our care, and buried within us a commitment to give our lives for these animals rather than leave them to nature's random forces. There remained enough forage that each animal could have a mouth full each day for the next three, with further survival depending on barren pasturelands offering only random sprigs of grass.

Once again I wandered over to the well, a welcome bit of good news in this desolation. We'd found good water about ten feet down. However, the winch still straddling the well casing offered but a devil's tease with its broken handle.

Touching a loose strand on the sun-bleached rope, I wondered how long this fragile support could survive a constant lifting of the heavy, ironbound pail.

Returning to the warmth and companionship of the fire, my thoughts focused on my two friends. Were they contemplating the same question hanging over me?

Only two shepherds were to accompany the flock to Egypt and we were three. I didn't know how to ask the question, so just blurted out, "Are you both going with the flock?"

Their eyes met. "Of course."

I took a deep breath. "Well, me too, and I won't expect payment. I'll just feel safer. It seems each one of us who heard the angels and viewed Messiah may be marked for the grave, and not by Herod." Then I added with a shrug, "Fear aside, Avner has an injured arm; you're my friends and you need another man."

A brief smile flashed across Thaddeus' face.

That night we slept among the flock, waking and settling animals where necessary.

Sheep, absent their familiar shepherd are objects to be pitied and while the three of us slept among our own flocks outside the over-crowded fold, those animals inside, lacking a shepherd of their own, moved about in frequent unsteady waves.

We three met the next morning near the fragile barrier serving as gate. We could have no orderly plan for watering and pasturing all our animals, but we had to do something. We hoped and prayed for a miracle.

As usual, Thaddeus assumed the lead. Impatient at the best of times, he seemed more abrupt than ever this morning. "We'll divide the animals into three flocks. Micah, you water one third of the animals while Avner and I pasture the rest. I'll leave before my flock takes water. Avner will help you water his flock, and you will give water to your own grouping last of all. The animals in my care will return at noon for water then go out to pasture again. When Avner returns he will take your well-watered flock while you finish watering and penning them.

I used my shepherd's staff less gently than ever before as we separated our animals into three rough groupings.

Thaddeus led his thirsty flock away with a little starting help from Avner and I; then we watered those animals Avner would lead to pasture.

Left alone with all my flock and over twice as many other animals, I began the arduous task of watering. Before opening the gate of the battered fold, I filled the trough with water, then opened the gate to the frantic sheep. This began the most arduous task of my life. Drop the bucket into the well, haul up the heavy contents, fight off thirsty sheep, empty the contents and then return to the well for more.

When Thaddeus returned near the sixth hour, I helped pen his animals, gave my special call and began walking away from the fold with my flock leading the way. With direction established I stepped to one side leaving them to follow Thaddeus.

Staggering with exhaustion, numb from the exertion of the morning, and mouth parched with thirst, I filled the bucket, balanced it on the well casing, pressed my face into the cool water and drank.

After lifting my dripping face from the bucket, I looked down into its mirror-like contents. My own eyes looked back, as though giving life to the bucket. They seemed to speak for this disembodied, impersonal, taunting object. *You're done, finished. Drop me in the well. Lay down and sleep.* I jerked erect, banishing the hypnotic image and looked down on the sun-bleached relic. Water dripped through a poor seal between shrunken wooden slats. Metal bindings sagged.

In spite its decrepit state I felt a need to answer back. "You pitiful excuse for a bucket, I won't listen to you. Just hold together for another day." The sound of my own voice gave me enough strength to lower the bucket one more time.

My strength seemed to give way as I drew the next bucket- load. Groaning with effort I turned towards the watering trough, and stopped at sight of a camel shuffling toward me with a rider on board. I emptied the bucket and waited while the camel rider slid from his saddle and approached; tall, sun-blackened and assured.

He shook his head and, speaking Greek, said, "Your situation is worse than I imagined. You will lose many animals before your departure."

Too exhausted for surprise, I just stared.

"Come, your animals cry for us. You control them I'll draw water." He moved to the well and dropped the bucket. I summoned enough energy to release the animals in manageable lots while the Bedu poured water in the trough.

We fell into rhythm, a rhythm still unable to control some of the wandering flock. Once watered, their only thoughts focused on finding grass.

The final animal to be watered lifted its head from the trough as Thaddeus returned.

The stranger walked to his camel, tapped its shoulder, and the animal groaned and knelt. The Bedu mounted and the camel lurched upright.

"Thank you," I said. The Bedu looked down at me, a smile crinkling his face. "I'll be back." He tugged the thong attached to the camel's nose plug, turned about and the camel departed with the same shuffle by which it arrived.

I helped Thaddeus pen his charges and started blocking the opening when he asked, "Who was that?"

"I'll explain later. Sheep first."

Come evening our count showed 16 ewes missing, fourteen lambs and one ram. Too tired and discouraged to discuss our mysterious visitor.

Early the next morning as we struggled to bring order from confusion, the Bedu reappeared with a man and boy trailing the camel.

Before them were 14 missing ewes with lambs. A ram and two ewes remained missing.

Necessity drove us and without words we turned to the flocks. Three Levites and three Bedu.

The Bedu headman assigned the boy to help Avner, the other Bedu to assist Thaddeus, while he stayed with me to help water the remaining animals.

Each shepherd returned that evening with bags holding dried sheep dung and twigs for our evening fire. The boy seemed unfazed by the rigors of the day and chattered away with Avner in passable Greek. Avner's limited response of smiles, nods, and the occasional word betrayed his fatigue.

I realized we had not yet exchanged names, though the boy's bonding with Avner must have included name sharing.

I stood and approached the headman. "My name is Micah." I nodded toward Avner and pronounced his name; then did the same for Thaddeus.

The Bedu nodded and pointed to himself. "Malik," he said; then dipped his head towards the boy, "Dirar," and a final dip, "Zabid."

A smile flashed across Malik's face and I realized we had just skipped the usual exchange of pleasantries around our name exchange, a clear breach of custom.

Malik leaned forward, poked the coals and watched flames blossom before he spoke. "I was approached by a caravan master day before last who's been ordered to accept you as part of his caravan to Egypt. He was not happy, though he'd accepted payment for delivering the flock. And that brings the bad news. His payment included no provision for your needs." Malik paused, letting that bit of news soak in.

Again, he poked the dying coals. "*Jonahs*," he called you. "*Jonahs,* cursed to failure before you begin. *Jonahs,* dragging his reputation in the dust. So, he paid me to remove that burden and assist you in delivering your flocks as ordered."

"Why such interest in our flocks," Thaddeus interjected.

Malik raised his eye brows. "Your people give mine no more attention than the mice of their fields. Mice have ears. They hear and remember words from Jerusalem's innermost circles. The most important of those words are relayed to my ears.

"Do you remember a recent flock inspection by the Levite, Phineas? Do you remember the man with him? A very wealthy man, by the way. As he scrutinized the temple flocks, avarice filled his heart. He could not forget the perfection of color, carriage, size and fat of the tails. As Bedu we know how carefully temple-Levites guard your breeding stock, but, when Phineas found your flocks no longer sacred, he scratched them from the records. As a result, your flocks no longer exist on paper and no bill of sale records a purchase of these missing flocks by a wealthy merchant in Alexandria. Now, I've promised my services in assisting you move these animals to Egypt and I am your only hope."

He paused, and sipped from his water gourd while we three Levites exchanged glances. Avner and I ended with our eyes on Thaddeus, who took a moment before speaking.

"How might you help us?"

"My brother attends his flock a day's journey south and I have cousins, and cousins of cousins, scattered throughout the Negev. We hold secrets to water sources and pastures between here and Egypt known to the Bedu alone. You will lose animals, but you will deliver most of them.

Thaddeus stood, head down, and wandered beyond the fire's glow.

We waited.

He came back, nodded, and thus sealed our immediate destiny.

"Dirar needs experience," Malik said. "He will be guide and contact with other Bedu during your journey."

Remain in this location for three more days. The caravan master will deliver fodder and your animals will gain strength.

5: A Flock for Egypt

The same God who rescued me from the claws of lion and bear will rescue me from this Philistine.

Words of David: circa 1000 bce.

We left for Egypt, day 22 of month Heshvan and traveled through the months of Kislev, Tevet, and Shebet, arriving at Eilat on the Red Sea on day 22 of month Adar.

Leaving Dirar with one of Malik's extended family; maybe a cousin or cousin of a cousin, we began our search for the agent representing the purchaser of our flock.

When we located the agent, it seemed an anti-climax to our journey. He examined each animal, checked for blemishes and conditioning; then paid us our wages. He had counted ten rams, one hundred and eleven ewes with eighty-nine lambs.

He gave Thaddeus a terse summary. "Not all you started with, but more than we expected."

While caring for our flocks on the sacred pasturelands of Migdol Eder we'd lost one lamb and one ewe in the years I'd been there. Now, only about two thirds of the animals we'd started with remained and we knew there would have been none without Malik and Dirar.

During our journey we'd left behind a few injured animals with the Bedu, but each death and injury tore at our hearts. Each lost lamb, though, had given us a better grip on life. As we travelled, we had become more and more dependent on sheep's milk for nutrition. Thus, each lamb lost gave us a full-time milking ewe.

With hearts aching at the sacrilege involved in selling the specially bred stock of the temple pasturelands, we found a high point where we could watch our flock being driven onto a small ship in the Eilat harbor. Driven, not led."

Avner gave a choking sound. I looked his way but he'd turned his head.

Well, if Avner can cry, so can I. Tears wet my cheeks. Even at the distance I could identify each animal once part of my flock. Those climbing the ramp included the lamb born the night before Messiah's birth as well as his mother, *Pride,* and his sire, *Alon.*

We didn't wait for the hoisting of sails; just turned and focused our minds on the immediate future.

Thaddeus divided our wages into three equal parts. "Enough for the return," he said, "if we're careful. But first, I suggest we find an inn and arrange a night's lodging; then purchase new clothing, and receive ritual cleansing from a rabbi before we seek employment with a caravan going north."

Following this suggestion, we sold our soiled and tattered sheepskin cloaks, along with the bits of leather remaining from our sandals. We found an inn removed from the waterfront and arranged space for the night. However, finding a synagogue proved somewhat more difficult than locating an inn. The rabbit nests of streets, some half filled with refuse, bore no resemblance to streets and alleys of Jerusalem. Only the hills around the city with identifying features prevented our being lost.

On reaching a synagogue and explaining our situation to the rabbi, we tithed our wages and received the ritual cleansing along with the rabbi's blessing. Even with the seven-day waiting period ahead before gaining ritual purity, a sense of renewal swept through me.

With most of the streets too narrow for three abreast, I walked behind the other two, my mind focused on Jehovah and his blessings. Losing myself in praise my arms rose and fell without conscious thought. I praised Jehovah for all the miraculous events leading to our safe arrival in Eilat. I praised Him for the cleansing I'd just received. I praised Him for sending Messiah.

Messiah, now that thought sobered me as it always did. I'd seen a baby. I'd heard voices from heaven that declared this baby to be the longed for, promised Messiah.

But what kind of Messiah could a baby be?

Despite my absorption in thoughts of Messiah, I recognized the even narrower street leading to the lodging we'd chosen for the night. With the sun just setting, the streets were largely empty; residences crammed together with narrow doorways opening directly to living space within. Then Avner's exclamation ahead of me intruded on both thoughts of Messiah and the disgusting alleyway odors. Ahead of us, three men blocked our way.

Interrupted by a scream from behind, I twisted about to find three more men rapidly closing and looking very unfriendly and ominous. My heart raced as I gripped my staff in both hands, thoughts briefly turning to the moment I'd found it where it lay lodged in the bank of a small river. Though heavier than usual its weight and balance seemed meant for me. I had always considered it a tool fashioned by God himself since I'd found it and used it unchanged ever since.

Today, with hands on the sturdy shaft, large knotted end with its angled crook just above my eye level, I felt well armed.

Should death arrive this day I will die content. I have seen Messiah. That thought seemed almost a relief before reality returned.

Preparing for whatever lay ahead I remembered how young king David had killed a lion and a bear with knife and bare hands as they attacked his flock. I grasped my staff. With it, I too had killed a lion.

My muscles tightened and energy pulsed through me. Taking two steps forward to gain fighting room between myself and two companions, I waited.

At that moment I heard the woman scream again and saw a face looking from a second story window well behind the three men in front of me. "Stop it you murdering ruffians. Get out of here."

The three men hesitated; then crowded forward again. The one on my right carried a knife on his belt and a short sword in his left hand. The one on the left held a heavy cudgel, while the middle attacker grasped a short spear. With eyes to the weapons and the way each man carried his I calculated the first move to come from sword and knife.

We exchanged no words, nor did we need to. These men weren't about to bargain lives for purses. They sought lives first and coins second.

I felt no fear; didn't even trouble myself in seeking reasons for this attack. I carried the rabbi's blessing and an inner assurance my blood would not puddle in the dust of an Egyptian alley. At least not on this day.

I took another step forward, two faces fixing themselves in memory. The man on my left with an angry scar running forehead to chin. Short, broad, dark features, crushed nose, wearing leather helmet and rough leather cloak, all topped off by large hands on a heavy, knotted club.

The man on my right: tall, pale, skimpy beard, bald, scar-faced, thin lips. His narrow eyes, the greeny-blue of the waters we'd just seen, held no expression at all.

Must be left handed, I thought, observing the sword in that hand. I didn't look at the man in the middle.

I took a deep breath. *You're thinking we're just three shepherds, harmless, unarmed, and confused. You're wrong!*

The club rose first as the man in the middle stepped back to give room for his two cohorts.

Wrong guess, I thought, *but the sword will start moving as the club falls.* Just as the man's club hand tensed on his weapon I dropped the heavy knot-end of my staff and lunged, driving it into an unprotected groin, twisting and falling as the thrust found its mark. I only heard a sword swishing over my head. Missing me, the sword struck the middle attacker whose scream echoed through the alleyway, a counterpoint to the club wielder's groan as he sagged to the ground.

Without stopping the momentum of my still moving staff, I twisted and put all my force behind the staff and slammed it into the swordsman's knee just as I hit the ground. I heard a satisfying crunch and the sword dropped. The swordsman staggered and nearly fell as I leapt to my feet ready to defend myself again. The man who'd carried the sword, bent over, grasped his knee, lizard eyes looking up into mine. Eyes filled with tears, not fear, and full of hate. With eyes still fixed on me, he reached out his arm, picked up his sword and hopped away.

Hearing a whimper behind me I switched attention towards my first attacker and found him just beginning to uncurl and still clutching his club. Anger surged through me and I swung my staff again, striking his temple. He straightened, twitched and went limp.

"He's dead," I heard Avner's voice

Startled I turned to find Avner and Thaddeus staring at me with their own attackers in flight behind them.

"Just helpless shepherds," I commented breaking into laughter.

Their eyes turned from me to the motionless man on the ground. "Is he dead?" Avner asked.

I started to kneel, but Thaddeus stopped me. "Don't bother. We must go."

We reached our crowded inn and began working our way towards a protective corner. Shouldering through the crowd, I noticed Thaddeus scrutinize each man we passed.

We reached the corner and sat with our backs to the wall. Avner whispered. "Those dogs tried to kill us!"

"Yes," Thaddeus whispered back. "Just like Eliezer. And if hunters seek our lives, how about those other shepherds who shared our experience with Messiah." Closing his eyes, he dropped his head and cradled it within the cup of two large hands.

Avner and I waited, stiff and tense in our dark corner, relaxing a little when Thaddeus raised his head, shook it, and said, "We were ambushed near this lodging; therefore, our enemies know our location. We're marked men. We know that now. Someone wants us dead and obliterated like words from a slate.

"We must leave this lodging and trust no one has identified us yet. I will go first. Micah, wait a minute then follow. Avner, order wine for your cup and follow last. We still have three mobile assassins who may yet seek their reward. And they may have friends."

Thaddeus pushed his way towards the door a large, intimidating force. I followed, provoking more aggressive responses from individuals already tipsy from too much drink. Once through the door I spotted Thaddeus some distance off and turned the opposite direction, checking over my shoulder as I walked. When Avner emerged, he looked both ways; then followed behind Thaddeus. Noting no sign of pursuit, I joined the parade.

Pausing beyond the last dwelling of Eilat, we squatted together under a dwarfed fig tree on a small rise. The tree obscured us from onlookers giving us a clear view in all directions.

I looked out on the waters of the Red Sea where the setting sun transformed a blue-green sheen into molten red. Even the square white sails of merchant ships took on the color of blood. I averted my eyes.

"What now?" Avner asked.

Thaddeus looked down on Eilat as I had done, his face scarlet in the twilight. "We could board ship for another Egyptian port; then lose ourselves in a Jewish enclave."

An image of the baby Messiah filled my mind. Danger or not, my journey must end near the place I'd started from.

To that end I said, "Or Dirar may still reside with one of Malik's relatives a day's journey northward. He was our guide coming. He may guide us returning."

Avner agreed and we turned for home.

Dirar, still in the same encampment, ran toward us while we were still some distance from the first tent. He slowed to a walk as we neared, straightened; pretended to be the little man we'd left behind. However, I'd seen the marks of a scared little boy before he'd dropped from run to walk.

"Are you all right, sirs?" he blurted. Without waiting for an answer, he rushed on. "My relative is a very kind man and I'm welcome to stay as long as I want. But," his voice quivered, "I need to get back to my own goats. Are you returning by way of my father? Can I travel with you?"

Thaddeus loomed above Dirar's slight form, but his voice was gentle. "We have come to seek your services again. We will pay you."

Dirar straightened, pride brightening his eyes. He paused for a moment. "My relative will be sad that I go so soon, but I will tell him of your need and arrange for your stay this night."

"Thank you," Thaddeus said while Avner and I hid our smiles.

That night became the first of many where we no longer hid our origins, but explained in detail everything we'd seen and heard that special night at the Tower of the Flock.

Dirar's name opened encampments wherever we stopped. No one either denied us lodging or accepted payment. We repaid them with stories of Messiah, remembering what we could from the prophets, and retelling what we had seen and heard. We took perverse comfort in the knowledge that even an assassin's sword would not reverse the impact of those stories.

With the erratic rhythm between pasturing and travelling it had taken us four months to move our flocks to port at Eilat. Our return journey took fourteen days.

We'd grown fond of Dirar on our trip south. He'd proven tough, resilient and resourceful but also a perennially disobedient risk taker. Going south he'd been our helper. Going north he was our guide, more purposeful and focused. Around solitary campfires at night we talked man to man.

On entering Malik's encampment, he paused to greet his father; then scampered off with friends his own age.

We spent half our night with Malik and the other men of the clan, regaling them with stories of Dirar's exploits. Malik tried looking bored, but his questions proved otherwise. The women remained in the background never out of earshot.

Malik interrupted our stories praising his son. "You embarked on a strange journey, the reasons obscure. Why were you forced from sacred Jewish pasturelands?"

That question unleashed our tongues as Thaddeus, Avner and I recounted our experiences of the previous five months. With day just beginning to break Thaddeus put hand to staff, but Malik placed a restraining hand on his shoulder.

"You will eat with us before you leave."

Finished with eating we approached each male over puberty and embraced in a final farewell. Stopping last at Malik, we bowed; he smiled: we embraced and he took a step away, his face serious. "You are always welcome in my tent." He paused, examined each of us in turn; "I wish to learn more of your Messiah."

Thaddeus answered. "Jehovah willing, we will return. If not us there will be others," and with one last bow we turned toward Jerusalem.

6: Herod's Amphitheatre

When David realized that he had been recognized, he panicked, fearing the worst from Achish, king of Gath. So right there, while they were looking at him, he pretended to go crazy.

From the book of Samuel: circa 1000 bce.

A friendly moon sped our journey north and after one day and two partial nights we sighted the dark silhouette of Jerusalem's walls. Thaddeus led us away from the main track and stopped in a patch of obscuring rock with the rising sun's slow warmth dispelling night's chill.

Perching himself on a large boulder, Thaddeus placed clasped hands behind his head and gazed, blank-faced towards those distant walls. Avner and I squatted on the sand beneath him.

With my eyes focused on distant Jerusalem I doodled in the sand until hearing Thaddeus sigh and his feet strike sand. I looked up to see Thaddeus with his face also directed towards the Holy City, and heard him choke out the words. "O Jerusalem, Jerusalem!" Then, turning toward us, eyes red from tears restrained, he shook his head as a grim smile creased his features. "Pariahs! What more fitting word fits us? Pariahs," he seemed to savor the word. "Well, better pariah than dead."

His eyes paused on each of us. "You are my only friends."

Avner broke in, voice quivering, "I feel so alone. We had such a good life. Friends, work, security. Where has it gone? What will we do?"

Thaddeus' expression hardened, "Better than dead," he repeated, "and it will take a lot of work to keep it that way."

I nodded. "I'm with you Thaddeus. I too have no other friends. No close family. And it's best that way.

Avner straightened, his voice now firm. "As a boy I visited the Great Sea and always wished to return. I did well in Beth-Sefir and have skills with ciphers and in the speaking and writing of Greek. Many Greek merchants would value my skills, so I'm considering building a new life with a Greek merchant at a small sea port, maybe Gaza, and then who knows."

"Good choice," Thaddeus acknowledged, "though maybe it's best we keep our plans to ourselves. Whatever those plans they must take us far from Jerusalem and Bethlehem." He paused, shook his head and examined us from narrowed eyes. "And, we must curb our tongues regarding Messiah's birth and the sights only we have seen."

We embraced; then Avner turned west toward the Great Sea, and Thaddeus east and into mystery. In minutes the rough terrain swallowed them leaving me with Thaddeus' words ringing in my ears. *Whatever our plans they must take us far from Jerusalem and Bethlehem.*

I smiled and turned southward; retracing the route we'd just followed for about four hours and found a stream where I could refill my gourd. One of the last streams for a long, long way.

Instead of crossing the stream I followed it eastward as it twisted and turned on its path toward the Jordan River. The stream meant shepherds, an unwelcome hazard as I wished to avoid all human contact, particularly that of shepherds. They would have descriptions of each man recently hounded away from duties with the sacred flocks. Rewards would have been offered.

When darkness fell, I found a small, flat area, near a rock ledge. Sitting, my eyes turned upward to the stars, I prayed the eighth psalm of David, concluding with the words, *Oh Lord your majestic name encompasses all the earth.* Then, tightening my robe, I lay down, my head toward Jerusalem; thoughts of Messiah encompassing me.

I woke with the moon casting long shadows over a lightening world. I'd memorized my path moving down the stream and now followed the same path back; Jerusalem pulling me northward. Jerusalem and news of Messiah.

With the little money gained from our Egyptian venture, I knew my priority involved work. The kind of work very different from that of a shepherd. Work in which to bury my identity. Few Jews would risk losing synagogue privileges by working for a Gentile, but I'd grown used to absence from those benefits and felt ready to risk everything that I might remain near Messiah's place of birth.

Bypassing Bethlehem to the west, I followed little used paths and arrived near Jerusalem's Joppa Gate well before daylight. Only twice had I been to this side of Jerusalem, but I knew something of its busy traffic pattern. Roman soldiers travelled as they moved back and forth between their main base near ports on the Great Sea. Those ports were also a main source of product coming into Jerusalem, while many Jews travelled this way to worship in the temple even between festivals.

A short caravan of heavily packed donkeys gave me needed cover for entering the city. Once inside the city I would have liked to stop and plan, but a stop would let others examine me. Thus, I kept walking, not sure what I sought, praying Jehovah would meet my needs. Down one street, through another alley, exploring every bazaar and market searching for any way to earn a coin.

Herod's unholy amphitheater, built to honor Caesar, loomed before me. Had I not been so desperate I would have detoured to avoid the contamination oozing from such a structure. I'd heard the stories. Inside, naked men wrestled for dominance. One dissolute Jew, ignoring the elders' scorn, had gained a great reputation for his wrestling prowess.

Not only were lewd sports part of each day's entertainment, hypocrites would climb onto a raised platform and pretend to be someone they weren't. But what could one expect of Greeks and Romans? Pagans.

Conscience tickled me. What did I intend to do but playact? I must practice playing hypocrite, a pretender, if I were to remain alive.

I passed a booth in which six men busied themselves in filling papyrus sheets with words, while a Greek reader supplied the content. I paused, fascinated. Beside each scribe lay several feather quills. At a signal, the scribes paused, wiped quill ends, and placed them in clay jars of water.

This reminded me of my days in Beth Sefer, but I'd never seen adults involved in such a degrading occupation.

Then, again in unison, each man picked another quill, dipped it in ink and continued writing. The reader, an elderly man and frail, hesitated, choked and coughed. Coughed again, and reached for a hollow gourd. He sat down and drank while the scribes stopped, quills poised.

An invisible hand pressed me forward until I could touch the elderly man's shoulder. "Would you allow me to continue while you recover?" Unable to speak, he took my hands and placed them on the scroll. He touched a word and I started reading, silently thanking David, my rabbinical instructor, for his oral reading lessons. Soon, though my face burned, my tongue stumbled, but I continued painting verbal pictures and uttering obscenities never before passing my lips.

The elderly man's coughing eased and he just listened. I shut off my mind and let the words roll.

Darkness threatened before the old man signaled day's end and the scribes put away their quills.

Feeling dirty, inside and out, I rolled the scroll and held it out at arm's length. The old man, still sitting, looked into my eyes and in a voice, still hoarse, said, "My name is Ehud. Yours?"

Bile froze my tongue. Another Jew. Another Jew in this pagan environment. I closed my eyes.

"Your name young man?" The voice now imperative.

I opened my eyes, still stunned and mumbled "Micah."

"Ehud held out a hand and I helped him rise. "Thank you," he said. That coughing weakened me and I may need your help getting home and you have a kind face." Ehud gathered a small basket before setting out. He stopped at a market stall already closed with gates to the old city just ahead. He raised the shopkeeper who seemed prepared for Ehud and placed a few items in the basket. Ehud paid two pence, collected the basket and gave it to me.

We entered the old city and stopped at a house plastered against a city wall. Ehud looked up at me. "You will be welcome in my house."

Desperation overcame scruples. "Adonai bless you," I answered. "I will be your guest."

Ehud called, his words weak. A female voice answered.

Thoughts of roof over my head and a sleeping mat on which to lie over-rode my urge to run.

Ehud ducked his head beneath a low mantle. I had to both bend and turn to squeeze through the narrow entry. A flickering oil lamp and a small mound of glowing charcoal under a dark pot did little for the gloomy interior.

"Ehud, how wonderful. You brought a guest. Welcome young man."

Someone has good eyes, I thought, seeing only two dim shadows.

One of the shadows moved. Half my height and slow moving. The short shadow came forward and disappeared in Ehud's arms. The other shadow remained still.

Ehud turned to me. "My wife, Tabitha and daughter, Ruth."

I assumed *Ruth* to be the other shadow.

"And," continued Ehud, "my friend, Micah." He gave Tabitha his basket. "Here's for the pot."

He knelt and removed his sandals. I removed mine and the other shadow moved, her motions easy and unhurried. The daughter poured water into a basin, knelt, and I felt her hands on my feet as blood rushed to my head.

Finished with me, Ruth did the same for her father and stood, the basin still in her hand. Ehud poured water from a pitcher over my hands and then over his own as Ruth collected the excess. As Ehud directed me to a bench at a small table, I thought of the purse attached to my belt and the coins remaining from my Egyptian journey along with some salt and a little dried meat. I picked out the salt and dried meat and gave it to Ehud. "For the pot," I said.

Ruth served us before she and her mother passed through a curtain into a small annex, too small to even be called another room.

I restrained my hunger, knowing Ruth and Tabitha would eat what we left.

We ate in silence and when finished Ehud called and Ruth came for our plates. She filled two cups with wine and left the pitcher.

I sipped and nearly spat out the sour fluid.

Ehud sipped and said, "You read well."

He paused, wishing a response, but I just waited.

"Thank you for helping me this afternoon. You showed disgust at finding a Jew employed in the loathsome environment to which I've fallen. And I have fallen. I once possessed the respect due a scribe. I enjoyed comfort and influence. And then," he paused, "I earned the enmity of an influential Levite named Phineas. From there I spiraled downward towards starvation. At my most desperate moment I received an emissary. An emissary from Phineas in which he offered to pay my daughter's dowry should she become betrothed to his nephew Caleb. And, should I agree, he would assure I returned to my previous place of honor."

Ehud must have heard my gasp for he straightened and paused; his eyes questioning.

Receiving no response from me he continued, "Ruth promised to kill herself before accepting Caleb as husband. As a final resort I accepted employment from a Greek named Cosmo, the work at which you found me this day. I am well reimbursed and my debts nearly paid. Soon we begin saving for Ruth's dowry.

"You are not yet as desperate as I, but I sense, you too have fallen from someone's favor. I may be able to help. An acquaintance just started another transcription service. He follows Jewish law and customs in most instances; enough, in any case to retain his ritual purity. He employs both readers and transcribers.

Again the questioning look. "Do you know the Talmud?"

"I only attended Beth Sefer," I said. "I am well versed in the Torah, but know little of the Prophets, and other Writings. Oh yes, and the Psalms. In my recent employment I worked with individuals who sought knowledge of the scriptures. Together we pieced together fragments containing most of that blessed scroll."

Ehud's smile nearly disappeared in the gloom. "Your interpretations may be even more useful than what we find in the Rabbinical sayings coming down to us from the time of the prophet Ezra, but, not really useful in the marketplace. And I need to warn you concerning your possible employer, Nathan. He worships the marketplace first and Jehovah second.

Thus, I fell into a new occupation; again sensing Jehovah's

provision.

My need to recount Messiah's story grew within me, until one night it burst forth. We were at table as usual, Ehud and I. My confession began with a small cough, which seemed enough for Ehud to raise his hand and say, "Stop!"

He called, "Daughter and Tabitha come to table."

They seemed hesitant at leaving their secluded corner but ended seated together on a small bench opposite Ehud and I.

And to this audience of three, my first attentive Jewish audience since the amazing night when I heard the voices from heaven, I recounted my experiences while a shepherd at Migdol Eder. The story of heaven's messengers, the birth of Messiah, the burning of the stable and our ejection from the sanctified pasturelands. I described our trip to Egypt including our confrontation with six armed men out to kill us. I probably embellished a little and saw's Ruth's hand fly to her lips as I described my part in the scuffle.

I, of course, made no mention of Caleb.

When I stepped outside in order to reach the rooftop lodgings Ehud provided, I looked to the stars. *Time for second watch*, I thought, expecting memories of open pasturelands and helpless flocks to re-awake my former passion. Instead, excitement, anticipation and release surged through me. Release, since I no longer need play the hypocrite to Ehud and his family.

I climbed to the roof, wrapped my robe tight, and shut my eyes with a few last thoughts. Would my hidden enemies be searching for me? Who were they? Would they even know of our escaping the trap in Eilat? Would they even now be tracking Messiah?

I woke next morning and fear fell over me. Undefined, but powerful.

The feeling stayed with me through the day. Words stumbled over my tongue forcing scribes to pause, puzzled. Over our mid-day meal, Nathan came at me like a hyena. "You will receive no pay for this morning's work. Only the poorest students will purchase the mess you've made."

Then, in mid-afternoon, a crowd surged around our booth, voices drowning out our own. Too angry for words, Nathan signaled closure.

Why the sudden crowd, I wondered, and approached a street vender whose booth lay nearer the main thoroughfare. "Why the fuss?" I asked.

"Roman cavalry cleared the streets and when we moved back, we created a further displacement." He spoke without anger seemingly used to bending at the whim of more powerful forces.

"Why were they clearing the street?"

A resigned shrug preceded words. "Who's to know? Probably an escort for some dignitary."

Maybe, I thought, a diversion will drown this clawing fear within.

I followed the crowd as they moved backward till I reached an uncluttered street. I hurried up the street in parallel to the moving cavalry. *Not much hope of seeing anything,* I thought, *but I've nothing better to occupy my mind.*

I reached an area of large residential homes with less crowded streets and turned toward the main thoroughfare. Here, residents continued rushing toward the clamor and crowds. Caught up in the rush, I found myself cornered behind a large palm. I grasped the rough trunk, pulled myself off the ground and kept on climbing.

Turning my eyes to the right I viewed the armored backs of Roman cavalrymen, while a glance to the left presented reason behind the escort. A small cavalcade. Three men on camels riding single file at the front, relaxed and easy in their saddles, but showing signs of exhaustion. Behind them marched ten bowmen, and behind those ten other men in leather protective garment, short spears, small shields and swords. These men walked with the easy swing of guardsmen used to long marches, but their strides seemed automatic, their faces blank.

Ten packed camels; gaunt and dust-covered but still the most magnificent I'd ever seen, finished the parade.

A murmur ran through the crowd. "Astrologers from Babylon," I heard. Then another voice, "These travelers' question where they might find the new King of the Jews, and they plan to inquire of Herod."

Icy fingers clutched my heart. Are not astrologers wise men? If they know of Messiah, why do they not know Herod? He's a murderer. Murdered his wife and children all to protect his throne. He will murder Jesus before he reaches manhood.

My mind froze. Is Jesus still in Bethlehem? I must warn his parents. But how? I can't walk the streets of Bethlehem without someone calling my name. Even here, I'm playing with fire.

Over the evening meal I listened with one ear to Ehud, my thoughts elsewhere. He finally joined my silence, until I excused myself and moved to the rooftop. There I fell to my knees and prayed. Prayed to Jehovah. Prayed for a way to reach Messiah's parents.

Waking the next morning, I felt frustration overriding my fear. In spite of that I gave full attention to my narration, and the scribes put words to papyrus without pause.

Even through my reading I listened for gossip telling more of the strange visitors from Babylon and heard nothing.

Burning for news, next morning I rushed to the transcription booth, anxious for any useful fragment of information. Again, only snippets of conversation, but I found Ehud waiting when I returned for the night. He seemed ready to burst, but bottled his eagerness until after evening prayer and serving of the meal.

He leaned forward, his meal forgotten. "Your words concerning Messiah are confirmed." He paused, embarrassed. "Now, I never doubted your words, but I'm sure you welcome confirmation. My neighbor, three houses over, is Herod's stable master."

"Yes?" I questioned, wondering at Ehud's direction.

"My neighbor heard news you will welcome. Herod ordered him to supervise care for the Babylonian camels. Two to four of the camel men guard their charges at all times while two others watch luggage. Two of the Babylonians spoke Greek and were as eager to learn of Jerusalem as my neighbor to learn of Babylon.

These Greek-speakers made no pretense at understanding the mystery bringing the astrologers to Jerusalem, only their unshaken belief in a message from the stars. A message proclaiming the birth of a new Jewish King who would change the entire course of history."

Ehud paused, and I heard stirring in the alcove. Ehud's eyes turned toward the curtain before he looked back at me. "Would you mind if the ladies joined us once again?"

With Ehud and the two women on one side of the table and I the other, Ehud continued.

"As a scribe I studied the Scriptures in great depth. I had particular interest in the prophet Daniel. You know of Daniel I'm sure."

"I know a little," I answered, "Though I've never had access to the scroll."

Ehud began, "The story of Daniel begins at a pivotal moment in Jewish history, six hundred years ago, when the Babylonians destroyed Jerusalem. King Nebuchadnezzar took the best and brightest young men to Babylon from among the Jewish nobility and added them to his pool of scholars. Daniel and three of his friends worked their way to the top of that pool, and Daniel in particular influenced the rulers of three different regimes in his lifetime. First, King Nebuchadnezzar, the most powerful man the world has ever seen. Then King Cyrus, a Persian who conquered Babylon, and after that King Darius who continued the dominance of the Medes and Persians in the East.

"We know some things concerning Daniel not included in the Scriptures. Most of his schooling in Babylon involved study of the stars. Part of that observation, scientific, and part, mechanisms for foretelling the future. He started a school for magi and that school has influence even today. Some in that school maintain their ties to Jerusalem, attend our major feasts and bring offerings to the temple. And, as scholars within the Jewish faith, they study the Scriptures as do we.

"So, these magi have come to King Herod who they feel should know the location of any new king."

His voice faltered. "Ruth, please pour more wine." As she leaned over to fill my cup, her garment brushed my arm.

Ehud sipped, eyeing me over his cup. "Those reporting from the stable say Herod claimed no knowledge of any new king and called in Jewish scholars for enlightenment. The magi left for Bethlehem this morning."

Mental agony tore through me, and I stood. "Thank you."

Midway up the ladder to the rooftop, something stopped me. I remembered a discarded papyrus fragment left on the ground by the scribe's station. A fragment quoting words from the book of Job. Another book I'd never seen. I'd heard of Job's suffering after being left in Satan's hands. I remembered how Job had succumbed to misery and questioned God's goodness. The fragment represented a portion of God's answer, though I had no idea as to the scribe's accuracy.

The fragment began, *God answered Job from a whirlwind. Who are you to question my wisdom with ignorant words? Where were you when I laid the earth's foundations? If you know so much, tell me who determined the earth's dimensions and stretched out the surveying line to place it among the morning stars as they sing together?*"

Yes, I thought. Who am I? I heard the God who made the heavens sing at Messiah's birth. That same God should also have power to preserve that Messiah.

I continued up the ladder, agony soothed, but still anxious.

Sleep fell on me as I pillowed my head, but I woke with questions racing through my mind, convinced Messiah's parents might need help. *What shall I do? If I go to Bethlehem and get recognized, I might die and accomplish nothing. If I do nothing, Messiah might die.*

No, God will not let him die I reassured myself, but I should give warning anyway.

At work, I forced myself to read with my normal attention to words, and a clear, emphatic enunciation until lengthening shadows darkened the papyrus sheets of the scribes and Nathan called a halt to the day's work.

I approached Nathan and bowed. "Master, I have an unusual request." He frowned and didn't answer, so I blundered ahead. "I will work tomorrow, but then require three days away. I will return after those three days and once again offer my services in case you are unable to find suitable replacement."

I pictured shekels chasing each other around in Nathan's head and almost smiled. Already he'd begun coddling me, as my reading reduced transcription errors and held the attention of those holding their quills.

Nathan forced his words through clenched teeth. "You may go, but you will sacrifice today's wage."

Pretending not to hear, I just held out a hand. Nathan held my gaze for only a moment before reaching into his money pouch.

Stowing the coins, I moved onto the street and paused at the sound of distant cheers from the Roman amphitheater. My feet, it seemed, took on a life of their own and directed me towards the source of that cheering, strange thoughts running through my mind. To have any hope of entering Bethlehem safely, I must take on a new identity. Act the hypocrite, just like the pretenders in the theatre. Professional pretenders from whom I might learn.

The man collecting fees for the performance showed little surprise that a Jew would enter such a Gentile world.

Once seated my eyes nearly popped from my skull at sight of two half-naked performers twisting into impossible contortions, leaping like antelope, and displaying the reflexes of the cobra.

The athletic performance completed, professional hypocrites took the stage, one of them a woman in scant clothing, face painted and eyes as darkly shadowed as some Egyptian women I'd seen in Eilat.

But even my limited knowledge of Greek theatre brought another thought to mind. *Women never perform in theatre, so this must be a man performing as a woman*

As the performers disappeared behind a curtain, I left my seat, and, with all eyes directed toward the next troupe, followed the performers through a tunnel and an open door into a dwelling outside the amphitheater walls.

I observed from the shadows as a robed woman of medium height and a husky servant entered from a side room and approached the sweating performers. The servant set a water bowl on a table near the hypocrites into which the woman dipped a cloth and began removing makeup. The husky servant turned his hands to disrobing the actors as another servant came with a new wardrobe to replace clothing just removed.

The scantily clad woman was indeed a man.

It took but a few minutes for the two *make-up artists*, a term I coined on the spot, to transform two beautiful human beings to grotesque demons.

The gruesome nature of the creatures before me broke a spell. I shivered, cold fear enveloping me. I'd withstood hunger, thirst, raging heat, freezing sleet, attacks of wild animals, and just recently human assassins but felt naked before a new and undefined danger.

An urge to run almost turned me about, but I knew it to be too late.

The transformed hypocrites seemed ready to return to the stage. I stepped further into the room, away from the door opening but still in shadows, and moved to one side. The performers paid me no heed as they walked past and re-entered the tunnel almost as though their masks hid me from sight.

The woman and muscular servant who appeared to be transformation specialists drew stools to the table and poured wine from a jar. The woman raised her cup and drank long. She set it down and looked at the servant. "Ah, Isaac, what have we fallen to?"

"A dream, my love, a dream. A dream to become what we were not."

"And what are we now?"

They sat for a while in silence, eyes on the table.

I coughed and moved out of the shadows. The servant, or whatever he was, lunged to his feet and drew the knife at his belt.

I held up empty hands and watched the woman's eyes run up and down my body.

"A thousand pardons," I said. I have one drachma to pay for your skills. Should you deny my request, I will depart."

Isaac moved a threatening step forward, jaw muscles bulging.

"It's ok, Demetrius. Let the boy have his say."

Boy! My temper flared even as my mind digested this man's two competing names. *Isaac! Demetrius! Jew? Greek?*

"Desperation brings me. Men seek my life. I know they wait for me in Bethlehem, yet I must go there. I wish to play the hypocrite myself. Can you help me?"

The knife twitched in Demetrius' hand, and again the woman calmed him.

"Place this man in the costume room. We'll talk when the last performer leaves."

Sitting there in the dark, airless room, with smells of sweat and unwashed bodies defiling what little air could penetrate, panic coiled through my entrails. I couldn't even take a deep breath. I searched my memory for a calming word from God and found it in the words of Moses. Words spoken to him by God when he faced impossibilities much greater than mine.

Do not be afraid or discouraged for God will go ahead of you. He will neither fail nor forget you.

And, at that moment, the coil in my gut loosened. I pressed against the nearest wall and slept.

I woke as the curtain snapped open and looked upward into a candle's glow with the shadowed form of Demetrius filling the doorway.

The woman sat as she had before and again eyed me up and down as though I were a camel in the market.

She nodded to a third stool and I sat with Demetrius hovering behind.

"Your name?"

"Micah."

She frowned. "You say someone wishes you dead?"

"Yes."

"And what makes that so unusual?"

I just looked at her and she looked up at Demetrius. "Have we ever turned a civilian into a hypocrite?"

Bitterness tinged a short laugh. "Most times they do a better job than we ever could."

She dropped her eyes to mine and I interrupted whatever train of thought she had. "What's your name?"

Her head jerked. She paused. "Call me Dinah."

"No, the name when you and Demetrius are alone, together!"

Her laugh carried no humor. Again she looked up at Demetrius. "Not such a simple boy after all."

Her eyes came back to me. "Rahab's as good as any."

I looked at Rahab, then up to Demetrius and back to Rahab. "I have an obligation in Bethlehem. My death would be small payment for its completion, but, if identified too soon, I die a failure."

My voice cracked at the possible results of that failure. I swallowed as Demetrius moved towards Rahab whose eyes narrowed and lips thinned. Isaac's hand brushed her shoulder as she spoke.

"One of our clients heard a report circulating in the market regarding a ten-shekel reward being offered by a temple Levite named Phineas. He seeks news of three runaway shepherds who abused their positions as caretakers of the sanctified flocks near Bethlehem.

Her eyes snapped wide. "Are you a shepherd?" she asked.

The blood rushing to my face answered for me.

"Remember Phineas," Isaac spoke for the first time.

Rahab's hand flew to a scar at her hairline. "A rock from Phineas' hand did this," she said.

This is too much, I thought. Phineas, Phineas, Phineas. He dogs my every step or I dog his.

Isaac, proving he could talk, took over the conversation, "Our story is quite simple. At one point I wrestled in the amphitheater." A smile touched his lips. "I was very good. Jews began crowding the amphitheater to watch another Jew best the best of the Greeks. I met," he hesitated, "Rahab and I went to her father seeking betrothal. I requested no dowry. He accepted, but changed his mind when religious leaders objected to her marrying a wrestler, defiled by the heathen amphitheater.

"So, we began meeting in secret." His face reddened. "Rahab became pregnant and someone reported her to the temple authorities. At our next meeting in the marketplace, Phineas appeared with a number of the Jewish leaders, grabbed Rahab and hauled her away to be stoned. Temple guards surrounded me with spears, but a number of the shopkeepers objected. One of them drove a mule cart into the guards and I escaped. I knew the place of stoning and reached it as the first rock flew. I roared and charged. They dropped their rocks and scattered like pigeons before a falcon."

Rahab finished with, "I lost the baby, and we became permanent fixtures at the amphitheater." She smiled, "Now we are living hypocrites and, if you wish, we'll make you one too."

Icy fingers clutched my gut once again. Only months previous I might have been one of those holding a stone.

7: Magi

Nebuchadnezzar the king of Babylon said to Daniel, "You are chief of the Magi, and because you possess the spirit of the Holy Gods you are able to solve any mystery. Now tell me what my dream means.

Words from the book of Daniel: circa bce 570

Unrecognizable! Me, the next morning. An ancient Bedu on a flea-bitten camel I called Methuselah, figuring him to be the oldest of his species in Judea. He had a hitch to his gait as though a cord ran from the wooden saddle to his left hind leg. Every step tossed me about.

I'd rented Methuselah from a friend of Isaac's, an animal suited to limited funds.

My departure from Jerusalem coincided with the start of the third watch according to the tail position of the sky-borne Great Bear. A three-quarter moon drizzled light on the barren trail leading down from Jerusalem towards Jericho.

The camel stumbled and I wondered if eyesight and gait were of the same standard.

Methuselah stumbled again as I came to a secondary track angling towards Bethlehem from the east.

With the moon dropping toward the still visible Mount of Olives I looked for a stopping place. Then a fire's glow led me onward. *Probably shepherds who might welcome an elderly bedu wandering the night.*

Flames flickered into view as Methuselah rounded one of the many twists defining this trail's course. Several, indistinct figures moved about the flames. Then a camel's complaining bellow lifted Methuselah's head. I pulled the rope attached to his nose peg bringing him to a stumbling halt.

I couldn't see anything other than figures around the fire so urged Methuselah forward. New details emerged as I neared and a camel's complaint again split the night. The figures around the fire rose as one and a voice just off the trail ordered me off my mount.

The Magi, I thought. What are they doing here? They should be on their way to Herod.

Shivers ran through me as I swung a leg over the saddle's front peg, but before even reaching the ground a rough hand grasped my arm and propelled me toward the fire. I did not have to guess, I knew. Soldiers of the magi.

The soldier holding my arm, jerked hard, and I tensed. "Something strange here," he said in heavily accented Aramaic. This is not the arm of an old man. Maybe one of Herod's spies. Wake El Shazzar. He won't let us kill this prowler, but he may join our baggage until we've crossed the Jordan."

I saw a soldier walk into a canopy covered shelter where a figure rose from a sleeping mat to follow the soldier towards where I sat, cross-legged, on rough gravel near the fire. I moved to rise but a spear shaft pressed me down until El Shazzar stood over me, meeting my gaze with a set of thoughtful, penetrating eyes. Not the kind of eyes one would lie to.

El Shazzar nodded towards the soldier restraining me, and the spear butt fell away. I stood, bowed and examined this studier of the stars and who knew what else. Much shorter than I. Grey-haired with trimmed beard, other features obscure in the firelight.

Following the lead of the soldier who'd grasped my arm, I addressed El Shazzar in Aramaic.

"May God be with you Master as one who bears witness of Messiah. You are the reason for my journey this night. I saw you pass into Herod's palace, heard of your discussion with Herod and your plans to visit our new king in Bethlehem."

Emotion flooded my soul and I fell to my knees, raised my eyes to heaven and prayed King David's words, Thank *you. Thank you with my whole heart, soul and mind. I kneel in humble worship with my face toward your holy temple and say it again, Thank you.* I continued to the end of David's prayer and stood again.

Still those speculative eyes examined me.

He looked to the soldier behind me. "Wake the others," he said, "and bring our stools." The other two magi, once aroused, took positions on the opposite side of the fire to El Shazzar and I with guards all around. “You have a story,” he said. “Tell it.”

“I am a shepherd,” I started. “I am, or was, one of many shepherds caring for the sacred flocks near Bethlehem.”

The sky brightened as I finished with, “I am returning to Bethlehem in order to warn Joseph of imminent danger to his family. Herod will kill them!”

El Shazzar smiled. “Should this babe really be King of the Jews, a King, born of God; a tyrant such as Herod will have no power unless God wills. Go, by all means. Bless the toddler and his parents with your interest, but worry little concerning the fate of our new King. We have done what we could. Joseph and Mary may be spiritually blessed above all humans who have ever walked this earth, but poverty stalks them. Stalked, I should say. We brought gifts suited to a king, and those gifts will change their lives in a different way.

“Your words validate our own observations. You know of the prophet Daniel, chief magician to the Emperor Nebuchadnezzar. We are part of the school he founded centuries before us. A school with its foundations built on observations going back centuries before Daniel, then expanded by him for those magi following Jehovah.

We three are Jews, just as you. We worship Jehovah just as you. We bring, or deliver, our tithes and gifts to the temple just as do you. Our hearts have longed for Messiah just as yours. And now we’ve seen Him.”

He stood as did his companions. They raised their hands and chanted in unison another psalm of David’s. I joined as my eyes fell on guards in the background, weapons lowered and arms raised.

With completion of the psalm, El Shazzar touched my arm. “Your camel may not survive until you reach Bethlehem. We have a better one for you.”

“Thank you. As I’ve told you, should I be recognized, I will probably die. I am not Messiah, you know. I like Methuselah just as he is.”

“Then Jehovah be with you.”

“And He with you.”

They watched me mount, eyes more on Methuselah than me. He lurched upright, creaking and groaning with every stretched tendon. When I looked back from the first bend in the trail the camp I’d entered existed no longer.

8: Decision

After the magi departed, Joseph met an angel in a dream who said: "Arise! Flee to Egypt with the child and his mother. Herod seeks the child to kill him. I will tell you when the time comes to return.

The gospel of Matthew, second chapter, verse 13: circa 70 ce

Following the Magi's instructions, I reached Bethlehem and entered the street leading to Joseph's rented house. As an old bedu on a decrepit camel in this Jewish village I stood out like, well, like an old bedu on a decrepit camel. Better that, though, than looking like a furtive young shepherd.

My eyes searched the street. Children playing one of their never-ending games. A few housewives clustered at the street end. A woman busy fingers at a loom, another grinding flour.

I'd little more than entered the street before it emptied. Mothers called their children; the knot of housewives dissolved and in front of me nothing moved at the house in which Messiah rested. My mind still held the image of a helpless baby though he'd be about two years old by now.

When God created the human heart, He'd never meant it to beat as hard as mine while approaching that closed door. How would the parents of Messiah react on sight of a grubby and aged desert dweller?

What would I say?

A voice from across the narrow street arrested my hand as I prepared to knock. "They left this morning. Very strange. They'd only a donkey when they came and Joseph could barely pay the rent from a builder's wages, but they left with five mules. The little fellow could barely walk, but laughed out loud when Mary settled him in front of her on that mule."

The voice came near and I turned. A tall, skeletal woman examined me with widening eyes. "Why you! You're Bedu. Why in God's name are you seeking a Jewish family?"

Bowing, I replied in the mangled Greek of a nomadic Bedu. "Thank you my lady. You have been kind."

Before she could say more, I grasped Methuselah's halter shank and led him away, mounting well outside the city and returned as I had come. The rental enclosure outside the city walls emerged from the darkness near midnight. There I unsaddled Methuselah, rubbed his unappreciative nose, and re-entered the city through an unlocked side portal.

I approached the back door to Rahab's house and knocked. A viewport opened and after identifying me Isaac opened the door. "Thought it might be you. Come in. I'm sure you have a story or two."

Thus, I spent another sleepless night, and in the process helped empty a large wine jug.

As a shepherd I'd learned to sleep wherever and whenever I found a place to rest my head; thus I felt no surprise when I woke, arms folded on the table, and head resting on those arms. However, the crushing pain hitting me as I raised my head came as a total surprise. I closed my eyes, let the pain settle, reopened and turned my head in a slow circle. No Rahab. No Isaac.

I stood, kept both hands on the table, took a tentative step. My stomach heaved.

A curtain opened to a side chamber and Isaac stepped through, drawing it behind him. He took one look at me and said, "I take it you shepherds of the holy flocks must ration your wine."

"That we do," I answered, "or should I say that we did. And shepherd or no, I will also follow my former custom in future."

Isaac smiled. "You tell a wild story," he said. "And thank God the holy family fled in time. May they travel far."

"What hour is this?" I asked.

"The sixth."

I grimaced. "So late! I apologize for all the trouble I've caused. Thank Rahab."

Isaac interrupted. "No apologies needed. Your stories were well worth the price of admission. Should you ever need help again knock on our door."

I bowed. "God brought me to you, and I thank Him for his providence. God be with you and keep you. We will meet again."

Stepping outside I found myself almost steady on my feet.

Now what? I wondered. Shall I seek Nathan and ask whether I am still employed. Shall I wander the markets and kill time until darkness? Or? I could think of nothing else.

Nathan it is, I thought.

I found a very agitated man. His agitation having obvious impact on the young man reading words for transcription. Nathan saw me through the barrier of several booths and rushed towards me.

"Come!" he said. "Come!" He grasped my arm and tugged. I swayed, eyes unfocused and head spinning. He didn't notice.

He dropped my arm, reached into his purse, rushed towards the young reader and thrust coins into his hand. "Your job is done. Go!"

He pulled me to the podium and the manuscript being transcribed. "We must finish this scroll tomorrow. Do what you can today and we'll start one hour after sunrise in the morning." He pointed to where I should begin reading.

Words popped out at me. Words near the end of the book of Micah. *God has told you what He wishes to see in you. It is really simple. Do what is fair and just to your neighbor. Love kindness and walk humbly in your journey with God.*

I shook my head, wished I hadn't and looked at Nathan with his perpetual squint and nervous twitch. I smothered an urge to recite those words to him.

Nathan came to me as darkness approached while the scribes cleaned their quills and rolled the scrolls on which they'd been working. He presented a coin. "This is a full day's wage even though you came so late. After all I am a generous man." A self-satisfied smirk lifted his upper lip.

As I stepped away from the transcription booth a wave of guilt washed over me. I'd not told Ehud of my absence. *I wonder if they will still welcome me.*

Nathan's coin allowed the purchase of a pigeon; bled, salted and kosher, two loaves of bread, and some half-decent wine. I gave a tentative knock on Ehud's door, my heart hammering for some unknown reason.

When Ehud opened the door he showed no surprise, just welcomed me in. When I started to explain, he waved me to silence. We sipped at our wine while Tabitha prepared the meal, both of us unusually silent. I, thinking of what my next step should be. As Messiah had departed the region, my own safety gained new importance and that also meant some new destination.

Those thoughts accompanied me to my dictation podium the next morning. For the first time since beginning work with Nathan I seemed to see danger wherever I looked. *Too exposed here*, I thought, mulling over my degree of danger while continuing my delivery. True, few acquaintances from Bethlehem, except those caring for the inn that sheltered travelling Levites, ever made the short trek to Jerusalem except to celebrate one of the special feasts. But others, right here in Jerusalem, might recognize me. For one, our interrogators who'd pretended concern over what we shepherds had seen and heard the night of Messiah's birth. Real hypocrites those.

Equally dangerous were the temple guards who'd escorted us from the sacred pasturelands.

This bazaar offered no privacy, and Nathan's transcription service often crossed the border into sacrilege. Should one scrap of papyrus containing God's name fall to the ground a mob would swallow us.

Then another face loomed. *Ruth*!

I knew Ehud to be working toward a proper dowry for his daughter and might have already selected an appropriate groom. And I, what could I offer a bride. Yet, eyes under long lashes often glanced my way.

I walked and prayed, mixing words of the psalms with those of Moses and even those of his sister Miriam. Probably nonsense phrases, but I trusted Almighty God to look beyond words to intent.

That afternoon another disturbance interrupted our work. A unit of Roman cavalry rode past, armored and ready for action. I did not view their return.

Noon, the following day, brought news of their purpose. They had hunted out and killed all babies and children under two years of age in Bethlehem. I thought of my cousin, Edith. Her baby would have been a year and a half.

This must be a mistake, I thought. A wild rumor.

However, new reports trickled in with details of brutal slaughter.

A desperate sense of urgency swept over me. I must get away from this center of hypocrites and murderers. I would not tell Nathan, but I must tell Ehud and his family.

On this night I brought home an entire kosher chicken, a loaf of bread, and a few vegetables.

Ruth and Tabitha had just begun serving when a knock interrupted. Then a voice, one I knew well, called. I grabbed my plate, cup and utensils and ran for the women's nook as Ehud moved towards the door.

Caleb's voice, clear as trumpet notes, brought a red haze to my vision. A desire to kill smothered comprehension and I fought for restraint. Finally, I put a finger in my mouth and bit down, hard, shutting out the words from beyond the curtain. Only Caleb's final words came through.

"Thank you for seeing me tonight and blessing me with the presence of the entire family including that of your lovely and delicate daughter."

Could he have sensed another presence? Had I left any evidence behind? Fear displaced my hate. Fear for Ehud and his family. Fear for my own safety and a growing determination to leave Jerusalem this very night.

I would go to Galilee, despised by those of Judea, maybe Capernaum. I would abandon all dreams of taking Ruth to wife.

Ehud interrupted my mental ramblings by sliding back the curtain. "I fed the hyena and barred the door."

I smiled at the thought of a hyena, gorged, and slinking off to shelter and slumber.

Ehud brought his stool to my side of the table with Ruth and Tabitha sitting opposite. "It is time for a family discussion. Our futures balance on a knife-edge and we need the wisdom of Solomon to save us.

He turned to me. "You are a hunted man!"

"Tell me something I don't know."

Ehud seemed to guess my thought. "I mean it. You are a hunted man. Your name is on the lips of every gossip in Jerusalem. You and two other shepherds named Thaddeus and Avner. It seems you stole a sacred temple flock and sold it to the highest bidder, possibly a wealthy Bedu. Phineas, as overseer of the temple flocks, made a special sacrifice in the temple today as contrition for his careless oversight."

"What a devious, evil heart," I shook my head. "Does he not fear God? I can stay no longer in your house and regret the danger I've brought to your door."

"Regret nothing!" Tabitha snapped, surprising me nearly off my stool. She had never yet participated in our discussions.

"Did you not hear the words of that lizard just departed?"

I paused, searching my memory before answering. "I heard and even the sound of his voice filled me with such rage my urge to see him dead almost overcame me; and, may God forgive me."

Ehud broke in. "Danger sleeps at our door. Our visitor proved how dangerous life has become. You have added nothing to that danger."

My face dropped into my hands. Powerless hands in the face of so many dangers. Looking round the table and shaking my head, I said. "You have blessed me beyond all measures and I will be forever grateful. My plans are made and I leave this very night."

Ehud's expression changed. His eyes sought his wife and daughter and they returned his gaze. Then three sets of eyes turned my way.

I felt the blush rise and stammered. "What's wrong?"

"Had you not returned this night, you would have found others living in this house. I sold it yesterday."

Stiff with shock, mind frozen, my eyes wandered from one person to another. Each face held a different expression. Tabitha's speculative glint sent blood rushing to my face again. Ruth looked sad. Ehud, head tilted, questioning.

Silence stretched as we each contemplated our new reality.

Ehud cleared his throat. "Do you have plans?"

"I did consider seeking employment with a caravan master and reaching the Jewish settlement in Alexandria but changed my mind. I may go to Galilee instead."

"Why Galilee?" Tabitha's unexpected female voice robbed me of any half-formulated plans spinning around in my mind.

"I don't know. Impulse maybe."

"Any idea what you might do in Galilee?" Ehud asked.

I paused before answering and thought, *Why waste time with all these questions. They should be packing?*

Returning to Ehud's question, I shrugged and repeated the same old answer common to Jews without answers. "God will provide." The difference this time: I believed it to be true.

Ehud smiled and nodded. "Maybe He already has. We leave for Capernaum on the Sea of Galilee this very night." He paused, took a deep breath. With my savings and a small amount of money from sale of my home, I plan on financing a new venture. I have seen your work and we could make a team. Would you join me?"

I watched Ruth retreat to the women's nook while Tabitha remained, curiosity written on her face.

I hesitated. "Adding my hazards to yours increases risks for all, yet the hand of providence seems to rest on us. Right now we have little time to pack and leave the city before daylight. We'll consider the future when we reach Capernaum. Pray God the night watch proves not over-zealous."

GALLILEE

9 Lake Kinneret

John the Baptist arrived in the Judean wilderness with a message, and preached, Repent of your sins and turn to God, for the Kingdom of heaven is near. Gospel of Matthew: circa 26 ce.

Cool air from Lake Kinneret washed over me. A setting sun splashed orange patterns on the waves and dappled the sails of fishermen's boats.

I smiled to myself thinking of the quarrels raging over this lake's name. Sea of Galilee worked for some. I preferred the old term, Lake Kinneret, and avoided the recent popular abomination titling it Lake Tiberias. In my mind, applying the names of Roman Emperors to Jewish assets might tickle the fancy of Herod Antipas, but stuck to my tongue like burrs.

Herod Antipas! Thoughts of the tyrant pulled me from the divan on which I'd been lying. *Herod Antipas*. Almost as brutal as his father before him with a natural villainy and a foxlike love for intrigue making him as unpredictable as his father and maybe just as dangerous.

A mental picture of Herod the Great rose in my mind and clouded the evening's beauty. I'd been a boy when King Herod rode through Bethlehem after a successful campaign against rebels hiding in the hills of En Gedi. Blood stains darkened his stirrup. He looked every bit a king.

I'd even heard my father express guarded admiration of King Herod. "He's brutal for sure. But he's brought organization to our country. We've more unity as a nation under Herod than we've had since the Maccabees; very helpful for Messiah when he comes to rule our nation."

I wondered now what my father's thoughts of Herod would have been as he lay crushed and dying under one of the heavy stones intended for the Herodian strong hold.

I sighed. *Messiah? Where was he?* And now the nation created as one by Jehovah Himself had three Herod's not one; all lucky survivors of the first Herod's fears, jealousy and brutality.

Then a different mental picture displaced that of Herod. A tiny baby. A baby lying in a carved stone manger, wrapped in cloths intended to warm newborn lambs. I tried remembering the baby's name. *Jesus, was it not*?

Steps on the marble staircase leading to my rooftop sanctuary interrupted my mental wanderings. I turned and watched Ruth and daughter Sara step onto the rooftop.

What a feast! I thought, not meaning the platter and basket of food they brought with them. They paused under the intensity of my gaze, twin blushes mirrored on cheeks.

"You are both so beautiful, and praise Jehovah you are as beautiful on the inside as you are on the outer."

Ruth bent over and kissed my forehead, "And you are a silly old man who's been too long in the sun."

Sara smiled and turned towards the staircase, "I'll bring the wine."

With Ruth's arm in mine we looked out on the darkening sea where sails were but distant specks against a dark horizon. Contentment, swept over me, so intense I felt tears prickle.

Sara's steps on the stairway brought us back from our mental wanderings. Setting the wine pitcher on the table she poured water over our out-stretched hands.

I held Ruth's chair, then Sara's, as we took our places Greek style, rather than the reclining position around a low table common to others of our class.

I gave the traditional blessing on our evening meal; then chose a small fish from the common platter. Before my fingers could lower the fish into Ruth's special sauce, Sara burst out, "I heard about a new prophet today. Sort of a wild man. He lives in the wilderness near Jericho. He has no house or wife. He possesses no animals or land." A flicker of distaste touched her face. "And he eats grasshoppers and wild honey. People call him John."

"Now, now; a man's diet seldom confers prophetic powers," Ruth chided.

"I know that! But he's attracting people by the hundreds and hundreds. I want to hear him too. He might even be Messiah."

I finished dipping the fish and with fingers halfway to my mouth asked, "What separates John from other self-proclaimed prophets multiplying like rabbits around us? I've personally lost count of them all."

Sara pouted, turned silent and left me feeling the guilt of a failed father.

"John's different; I know he is," Sara broke our short silence. "He doesn't even claim to be a prophet and he promises no rewards to those who follow him. Jehovah, he says, forgives sins of the truly repentant without a temple sacrifice.

"And he baptizes people who do repent."

I returned my fish to the common platter, rose from table and walked to the roof edge. A few of night's brightest stars glimmered and the hint of moonrise gave a sheen to both the eastern sky behind me and a light trail across Lake Kinneret's dark waters.

John! Messiah! Could they be one and the same? No! Messiah would not stoop to the role of hypocrite by using a false name. But supposing John is really a prophet as Sara believes, Scripture should mention him?

Then the words of Malachi the prophet struck like a whip.

You will see the messenger sent to prepare the road for me. And Messiah, whom you seek, will come to His temple.

Twenty years old. I was twenty when I saw Messiah, the baby Jesus. And now I'm fifty. That's thirty years. Messiah would now be thirty years old.

But I still couldn't picture that baby in a manger as a grown man.

Returning to table, I found Ruth and Sara staring up at me.

I sat and picked up the fish I'd returned to the common platter. After dipping it in sauce I presented it to Sara.

"Bless you for your wild ideas my daughter. You have always been sensitive to the spiritual and you always activate our minds. I will ponder your request."

That night, lying in the dark, Ruth put a brake to my racing mind. "I wish my father were still with us."

"Yes," I answered, remembering the gentle but troubled man who'd started me on my present path. "Yes, and he never got to see Sara, but he sure loved the boys."

Ruth's next words caught me off guard. "I have not heard you even mention Messiah for the last few years." Her voice quivered.

"Well, I do think of Him. In fact, the very Scriptures we transcribe serve God's purpose."

"Ours too, don't you think? We've built our wealth on people's hunger to feel the Word of God in their own hands."

"Not just scriptures," I said. "We transcribe documents of many kinds."

"Yes, you do." Accusing words.

Heat rose in my cheeks. I knew she made reference to a side business where I employed only men of Greek origin. I paid more attention to their revenue generation than I did to the content being transcribed and Ruth knew it. Her feather-filled mattress whispered as she turned.

With my eyes tired of tracking a moonbeam's slow crawl along the wall opposite the window, I swung my feet to the floor. The moonbeam led me to the door of my library. I lit an oil lamp and looked around the library's spacious interior. I counted ten cabinets containing scrolls, but shelves lined most walls. It was a large room, unique to Judea and maybe even the world. As my employees transcribed religious scrolls for wealthy clients, I would always have one created for my personal use. My income depended on wealthy clients, not all Jewish, but all desiring the words of Torah or the prophets. The many rabbis walking the hills of Galilee never darkened my doors, but the students of those rabbis did and even their pennies added up.

My mind wandered to one such student, Jacob, very poor but very bright, who came to our business often. One afternoon I'd found him examining a transcription booth, head tilted to one side, lips moving. "What do you think?" I'd questioned.

"Amazing!" His head bobbed. "Amazing!"

I probed, "You know our scribes make spelling mistakes, miss words and sometimes even insert a wrong word. We don't match the jot and tittle perfection required by most rabbis."

Jacob, looking down from his unusual height, commented. "My rabbi ridicules this process. One, for its' many inaccuracies, and two, the unsanctified hands handling the word of God.'' Then a frown, "But how will people ever know scripture with nothing to study on their own? Your scribes produce a hundred copies for every one created in the old-fashioned way. Besides, the traditional transcribing process focuses on reproducing Hebrew language scrolls that most young people today neither read nor understand. The languages of our time are Greek, Aramaic and Latin and you create copies in all those languages."

I'd laughed and accused him of thinking like a Greek when he'd started like a frightened hare, his eyes fixed on something inside the booth."

Following his gaze, I'd noted one of our collators carefully arranging finished papyrus squares into a single pile before handing them to a second man who placed the squares between two flat wooden plates.

Jacob puffed out like an overfilled wineskin. "What are they doing? That's crazy! How can you know where you're reading without words on a scroll?"

Attempting to calm him, I'd given him a name for this new product. "We call it a codex, and I wager codices will one day replace scrolls.

Still fixated on the codex Jacob had insisted "No one will purchase such strange products."

Smiling, I'd answered. "This codex goes to a rich client, Joseph of

Arimathea, a Sadducee who's also a member of the Sanhedrin. When his friend, Nicodemus, obtained our first example he insisted on being next in line.

I'd seen a grimace flash across Jacob's face. "One of the Sanhedrin! Are you sure that's a good idea?"

I'd reminded Jacob of his comment about everyone needing God's word to study, whether it be a poor student or member of the Sanhedrin."

Or merchants such as myself, I thought, and returning to the present I selected the codex containing the writings of Micah. Placing the volume on my reading lectern, I loosened two leather straps and turned back the top cover.

I knew the words I sought would be near the back leaf, but started on the first. *This is God's Word as it came to Micah of Moresheth who lived during the reigns of Jotham, Ahaz, and Hezekiah, kings of Judah, regarding the futures of Samaria and Jerusalem.*

Near the end of Micah's writing I reached the familiar words. Words helping justify my absence from the temple for nearly thirty years.

Will Most High God be pleased if I bow myself to Him and offer burnt offerings, even of year-old calves? What if I brought thousands of rams and ten thousand rivers of oil? What if I offered my firstborn son, the fruit of my body as payment for the sin of my soul?

God expects different offerings from me. He requires me to do justice, to love kindness, and to walk humbly in His presence.

The words struck home; my conscience pricked, as I re-stacked parchment pages within their wooden binder. I'd been a running hypocrite for the last thirty years, far from walking humbly with my God.

I prepared to answer Sara next morning.

10: The Baptizer

People came to observe and hear John from Jerusalem, all of Judea and up and down the Jordan Valley, and when they confessed their sins, he baptized them in the Jordan River.
From the Gospel of Matthew chapter 3, vss. 5-6.

People, some shoeless, clothes often ragged and torn, inter-mixed with men wearing rich robes. A few women observed from the margins.

What is this? I wondered.

I looked down on Jacob where he stood by my left stirrup. "Are you sure you brought us to the right place? I see people milling about like ants but where's the Baptizer you and Sara were so eager to see?"

Jacob stared upward, wide-eyed. His mouth opened then closed but his words were polite as usual. "Sir, I believe the Baptizer stands in mid-stream."

I looked again and saw the human mass crowding the water's edge as they began to thin and back away. And there he was. Even at a distance, striking and a little intimidating. Long hair and beard hid his face and he wore only a tightly wound cloth around his loins. I noted a muscled chest burnt nearly black by long exposure to the elements.

He waded towards the riverbank as the crowd retreated. I urged my mule downward, unmindful of those with me.

We reached the crowd's edge as the Baptizer mounted a makeshift stone platform.

"Hypocrites, actors, wolves in sheep skins, abusers of widows, orphans and the poor."

Those words bursting forth from this homeless wanderer shocked and angered me. Angered me to the point of turning the mule, Solomon, and retreating to the hill-top, but when I looked up and saw a cluster of what were obviously priests, temple Levites and Pharisees, my anger faded.

True words, I thought, and turned my attention back to John the Baptizer.

"You sanctimonious traitors to the memory of Abraham, our

ancestor, whose faith in God brought our very nation into being. You, who think the size and frequency of your temple sacrifices will pay for the sins of your souls."

Then the Baptist's eyes seemed to fall on me. "And you who flaunt your riches, comfortable in the arms of wealth and privilege, blind to the sins of your souls. Repent! Humble yourselves. Remember the words of Micah, the prophet."

I swayed in my saddle. I guessed at the words he was about to repeat.

"Your offerings," John shouted," are to be acts of justice, love and compassion. Those acts bring pleasure to Jehovah, Elohim. And what else does Elohim require? Humility! If you desire Jehovah to walk with you, you must humble yourselves. Bury your pride in the waters of baptism as a sign of your submission to Almighty God.

"Do you want to bring pleasure to God? Do you want your sins covered and forgotten? Our religious leaders suggest an easy way out. *Come to the temple*, they say. *Pay your tithes. Offer your sacrifices. Do this and you will earn God's forgiveness.*"

"Those who teach such things are liars and live without remedy for their own sins.

"I bring to you the example of our own King David. Remember? Remember when he stole Uriah's wife and then ordered Uriah's death as a cover-up?" The Baptizer shook his head. "I imagine this guilty king made several special trips to the tabernacle to make extra offerings as payment for this evil. Did Elohim accept these sacrifices? No, He did not. God had to send the prophet Nathan to confront him. David had to pay for that sin, payments resulting from his sin but not covering it. But he knew the offering Elohim would accept and he wrote: *Sacrifice to Elohim a surrendered spirit, and He will not despise a broken and sorrowful heart.*

"Should you choose baptism this day, in these muddy waters, by this ragged preacher you will have earned nothing. Your humility, however, will be pleasant to Elohim; your brokenness a personal symbol of changed life." He turned and stepped into the Jordan.

Jacob caught my arm as I half fell from the saddle. I wished to rush into the water, but others blocked my way. We edged forward as a group, Jacob, the student; my daughter Sara, and son, Benjamin.

11: Caleb

Hatred stirreth up strifes: but love covereth all sins.
Words of King Solomon, Proverbs 10:12: circa 950 bce

I felt no sense of moving till my sandals settled on the muddy bottom of the Jordan River. Feeling totally shattered in spirit, overwhelmed in guilt and longing for cleansing I blindly followed the line of men before me. When finally, the Baptist's eyes met mine, I felt a flowing wave of compassion, an acceptance, a hope. His hands touched mine, folded them to my chest, and the water covered me.

Blinking water from my eyes, I heard his voice. "Jehovah bless you. Remember the water means nothing. It but signifies obedience, humility and a willingness to serve Jehovah with heart and soul and mind."

Before I even stepped onto dry ground the questions began. *Now what? Can my life really change?*

The sound of great, broken sobs erupting from a man beside me intruded on my self-absorption and I raised my eyes and glanced sideways. There stood a man wearing a dripping robe typical of a privileged Levite, shoulders shaking, all hunched over and oblivious to the world around him.

What's he doing here wearing clothes like that, I thought. *A wealthy Levite truly repenting, not likely.*

Then I looked at my own clothes, equally rich but in a Greek style, without the tassels and a new wave of guilt washed over me. *Why am I judging this man by his clothes and lineage, hypocrite that I am. I've been hiding my Levitical roots for thirty years. Obscuring all traces of a shepherding life.*

When the man straightened something familiar awakened memory.

Then the man looked up and I knew the eyes. Caleb, a man for whom I'd nursed hate the last thirty years. A face still part of dreams.

"Caleb!"

He turned, eyes blurred, mind lost in emotion. He shook his head, obviously reluctant to return from the spell cast by recent experience.

"I'm sorry, who are you?"

"Micah." I let the name hang and saw fear flicker across Caleb's face.

Adonai forgive my carelessness, I prayed. *I had no wish to create fear.*

"A friend, Caleb, should you wish that to be so? As Isaiah the prophet tells us, Jehovah's thoughts are not our thoughts and His ways are higher than ours. He has arranged this meeting. Two sinners who've come to God in humility and repentance."

I could not be sure he even heard me as he choked out the words, "My sin is even greater than King David's. I denied Messiah's birth. I sought the approval of my uncle and the temple priests above truth. And I didn't object to the dispersal of the temple flocks."

Then, with his voice strengthening he continued, "My Uncle Phineas on his death bed ordered me to continue the hunt for each and every shepherd with whom I'd worked. I continued my hunt but not to report them to the temple police, but to ask their forgiveness. However, three had already been captured and killed. I feel their blood on my hands."

"We have lodgings in Jericho," I said. "Please stay with us and we will talk more."

Now what have I done, I asked myself, and a cold shiver ran down my spine.

"Do the temple guards still search?"

"They do." Caleb glanced around. "I've seen some in this crowd and none seeks baptism."

Sara, soaking wet and glowing, joined us.

Caleb looked puzzled and even frightened at sight of a girl, especially a girl who'd just been accepted for baptism. He gathered himself. "I've seen you before."

"But I haven't seen you," Sara answered, "and I do not forget faces. Maybe it was someone who looked like me?"

I smiled inside and turned to Caleb. "Will you join us this evening?"

He nodded and we went searching for our mules.

I'd always felt my mule to be special; large, straight legged and straight backed. Intelligent and possessing great endurance. Only Sara had ever sat on his back, and that only once, with my back turned.

We found the mules and I picked up the reins where I'd dropped them and rubbed the animal's nose. Some say a mule lives for his stomach and given a chance will head for any source they see regardless of training. Solomon, as I'd named this animal, proved it a lie over and over again. He had this look in his eye as though he'd absorbed all the truths in the world, and I'd been tuned to him since I bought him as a yearling.

With Solomon's reins lightly held in one hand I turned to Jacob who'd walked with us from Hammat.

"I wish to walk with Caleb while you ride Solomon."

Jacob shook his head. "No sir, I couldn't do that. I've never ridden a mule, let alone your special mount."

"You'll do fine. Here, put your foot in my hand."

"Do it," I ordered, and felt his ragged sole press down. I hoisted and he managed to dodge each of the saddle's four horns without being impaled.

The road up from the Jordan to Jericho is not an easy one and Caleb seemed no more used to walking than I, but the increasing gap between ourselves and the mule riders gave us privacy.

"How will your baptism affect you in daily life?" I asked.

We began talking about our recent experience, though I sought to open a door into more personal matters.

Caleb finally opened that door. "I'm so sorry," he started, but I interrupted.

"I know. Me too. With financial success the parasitic vine of pride has entangled me. Its tentacles dig deep. Am I rid of it? No, but I'm more aware and will fight that pride with my every shekel of energy. And I will not depend on the blood of a sheep or goat to pay for the results of my pride."

Caleb glanced my way, hesitated. "Temple sacrifice is not without merit. Why were you baptized?"

"Not to pay for my sins, that's for sure."

"Performed properly, your temple sacrifice, a communication between you and God, can mean the same."

I started to ask why then had he chosen baptism from John, a man not even a priest. Started and held my tongue.

On reaching our lodging we washed and prepared to eat the meal prepared for us. I turned to Caleb, "Will you lead us in prayers?"

With prayers complete we knelt together on a frayed rug around the low table. I saw Caleb and Jacob both stiffen as Sara knelt beside me, and hid a smile at this reaction to a woman eating at common table with a man. Neither Sara nor I would have dared such an act had we been in the larger common room full of males.

Caleb and I said little as we tore bits of bread from a barley loaf and dipped them in the pot of Lentil soup.

Daniel and Jacob carried the conversation while Sara knelt, tense beside me, lips twitching in a struggle to hold her tongue.

The young men talked first about their experiences of the day then turned to the meaning of baptism. I knew Jacob to be a scholar and deep thinker but experienced both shock and pride at Benjamin's knowledge of scripture.

Returning to thoughts of Sara, gloom swallowed pride as I considered her plight. Like many girls she'd attended Beth Sefer, but withdrew, aged ten as did other girls in her synagogue. Near the ending of this formal instruction I'd been approached by the local rabbi. "Brother Micah," he greeted. "You have a most unusual daughter. She is more advanced than any other student in her group. I would invite her to continue."

But when I'd talked it over with Ruth and Sara we learned Sara, young as she was, had her own plans. "I like Rabbi Reuben, she said. "He is a good teacher but too narrow."

Too narrow. What does she know? The thought seemed a natural reflex.

I didn't have time to voice that thought before she continued. "My friend Hanna's been talking about a new school in town. It takes in both Gentile and Jewish girls."

Ruth fought the idea, but after much persuasion and a few tears, I agreed.

I glanced down at her, proud and fearful at the same time. Proud of her achievements; though she sought her own way too often.

Benjamin, from across the table, broke into my mental wanderings. "Master," he addressed Caleb. "How can John's baptism compare with our Jewish custom of ritual cleansing by submersion? And where did John's baptism come from?"

All this talk, I thought. All this talk throws dust on the real meaning of the day. I will not dissect the sanctity of this day.

I stood. "Excuse me. I need fresh air."

Caleb looked alarmed. "Be very careful. Jericho is no safe place."

I nodded my understanding and made my way outside. Our inn for the night had better sanitation facilities than most, having a large hedged off area for men, and a smaller area for women. Inside the men's facility were several low pots for deposits and a larger pot in which to empty the smaller ones.

I smiled, thinking of the wine being swallowed in the common room inside. *This will be a busy place come morning.*

I relieved myself and took position just outside the inn door. My thoughts wandered back to the Jordan River and the Baptizer. John's focus on the word *Repent* filled my mind.

Repent! The same word repeated to my wayward nation over and over by every prophet in our long history.

But John's words seem to have focused on me, one person, not the whole nation. I slowly went to my knees in the moonlit dust. I tented my fingers and bowed my head. Words swirled through my mind and maybe off my tongue, I do not know. I only know a hand touching my head brought no welcome.

I looked up into Caleb's face, noting how moonlight highlighted the grey of his beard. "You've been long," he said.

I stood and we re-entered the inn.

The next morning after our morning meal, I had a moment alone with Caleb while the young people readied the mules. My words gushed out, "God brought us to the Jordan and he unburdened us from a load of guilt. I don't know how, but I feel He did. Further He brought you and I to the Jordan at the same moment.

"Why?"

Caleb waited.

"Number one," I said. "He wanted to tie our repentance to flesh and blood reality."

"And that He did." Caleb said. "Now our repentance requires a turnabout on years of silence."

"A turnabout handled with discretion," I replied. Then something surged up from my inner being, an overflow from the ecstasy of the night before and I felt happiness break out on my face.

"Discretion. Maybe not. Could be discretion led to some of our guilt, mine at least. We're in this together, you and I, discretion or no. Come with us to my home if you're free for the next few days. I will give you a mule on which to return."

He shook his head. "Can't. I have one week of temple duty coming up."

"Then promise you'll come to Hammat as soon as you're done. Coming from Jerusalem you'll reach it just before entering Tiberias. Ask for Micah the transcriber."

"Transcriber?" puzzlement etched itself on Caleb's face. "Why transcriber?"

"Here's the short answer. I've adopted the Greek system of producing multiple copies of documents by having an experienced lector read from an original while several writers transcribe the words. The business just keeps on growing, and after the last few days I've plans to expand. Many people have had no opportunity to hear John. I plan on hiring a scholar to follow him, memorize his words and bring them back for transcription and distribution."

Caleb's eyes narrowed, opened. His nose twitched. His brow wrinkled, and his lips moved as conflicting emotions fought for supremacy.

Redirecting his indecision, I broke in. "Right now I'm having difficulty obtaining sufficient papyrus or parchment for use by my scribes. How I might meet this new demand, only Jehovah knows?"

12: Comes One After Me

...someone soon comes, so great I have no right to carry even his sandals... Words of John the Baptist from the book of Matthew.

One of the Baptizer's words played over and over in my mind on our return journey, *Repent*! However, I remembered other, more puzzling words as well.

He'd talked about someone coming after him. Someone so great he would feel privileged to be that man's slave and carry his sandals. *That can only be Messiah.*

Solomon's smooth stride encouraged my mind to wander. It stopped first at that night on Migdol Eder, with angelic beings making announcements, singing; then the sight of the tiny baby in a manger. My eyes closed and emotion flooded in. Emotions of fear, anticipation and wonder with the words of Heaven playing again through my mind.

Don't be afraid, I bring joyful news for all peoples. A baby, Messiah, has been born this very day in the city of David; One who is to be Ruler and Rescuer of all.

A sneeze intruded on my side trip into the past and I returned to the present. My eyes focused on the dusty path, on Sara beside me; and ahead, Benjamin leading his animal and walking beside Jacob. Those mundane sights took me from visions of the past to what might be present reality. *Joseph and his family escaped Herod's jealousy by fleeing Bethlehem about thirty years ago. Why have I heard nothing since?*

Many counterfeit Messiahs had surfaced and subsided since we'd settled in Galilee. Each new rumor had set my heart racing. After that, *Messiah fatigue.*

Ah Galilee. Strange and wonderful Galilee. Most Jews poor; just scraping out a living in every way possible. Galilee, more rabbis per square mile than any other corner of the domains ruled over by the three Herods. Galilee, constantly giving birth to Messiah sightings and rumors.

I turned to Sara, half asleep on her soft-stepping mount, "What have you heard about a new rabbi-in-waiting from Nazareth?"

"Only a little. Many say he has more perfect knowledge of Scripture than any other rabbi alive today."

"Have you heard any news of his gathering disciples. After all it takes disciples to merit the title of Rabbi."

Sara pursed her lips, thought for a moment, and shook her head.

"Has he made any claims to being Messiah."

A violent headshake answered.

My thoughts focused on this young teacher and my next words were more to myself than Sara. "I've been thinking of sending Benjamin to Nazareth to begin recording this young man's words. Tractates from this teacher in Nazareth should sell well."

"And John, the Baptizer?" Sara questioned.

"I've already given Jacob that assignment."

"But…" Sara started and stopped.

Solomon's rhythmic pace combined with the emotional overload of the last few days brought sleep to my eyes. A sleep interrupted by a hand touching my arm.

"Are you ok father?" Sara asked.

Gathering my thoughts took a few moments. "Well, I think so." I patted my arm, chest and thigh. "Can't find any missing parts."

A smile replaced her worried look. "Good. When I saw you swaying around like a drunken Cretan, I moved closer so my mule could at least cushion your fall. You frightened me."

When, in mid-afternoon on the second day of travel, I first saw our house on the hill, I wondered what might pass through Ruth's head when we told her of our baptism and its meaning.

On reaching the courtyard gate, I passed my reins to a servant and looked up to see Ruth rushing toward me, eyes red from weeping. Sara, Benjamin and I gathered her in our arms, felt her body quake, and sobs erupt.

As she quieted, I looked up to find Jacob, the groom and mules gone. I held Ruth's hand and led her inside to our private family space. Just before joining her on the divan with its seating for two I spotted my oldest son Daniel standing in a corner, face strained.

Benjamin and Sara took seats on low stools and we waited for words to replace her tears.

Ruth choked, voice barely audible, "Pilate's gone too far." She glanced up. "Even Daniel talks insurrection."

Sara got up from her stool and filled a cup with water. She passed it to her mother.

Ruth drank before continuing, her voice gaining strength. "Remember when Pilate put images of Caesar near the temple courts."

My memory raced, her next words almost lost in the remembrance of turmoil, of the dead in Pilate's court and the fierce anger of the young men in Galilee. I glanced towards Daniel as Ruth continued. "Several young men from Capernaum travelled to Jerusalem, fasting and praying as they went. Praying for Jehovah to send His liberating Messiah. They'd done nothing to hide their commitment and piety and were culminating their journey with sin offerings at the temple." She choked, collected herself and blurted, "Pilate's soldiers murdered them at the altar of sacrifice."

Daniel fled the room as a red haze blurred my vision. In a moment Benjamin followed his brother.

My mind whirled and turned dark, overcome with memories of the past and a horror of the future. The room dissolved around me as the floor fell away. I felt myself swaying and teetering on the edge of an open pit. A pit filled with flame and debris, emitting the powerful stench of burning sulfur. Across the chasm's opening the ground convulsed, bulged, and gave birth to giants in Roman armor. Fully formed, they stepped toward the abyss; eyes, dark tunnels in chiseled faces, crests on helmets reflecting red- gold from the fire-filled pit, left hands grasping baskets. Indistinct sounds, too faint for identification, drifted over seething flames.

With feet at the chasm's edge, the giants, paused, all in a row. Several seconds seemed to pass before each giant reached into his basket, withdrew an object and flung it into the flames. I could now identify the sounds. Groans, screams and pleas. Flailing arms and legs. Faces with open mouths; all swallowed by flame. One face expanded. Benjamin's."

I cried out, gripped by horror, and lost the vision when two hands grasped my shoulders.

"Father! Father! Please! Please! What's wrong?"

I looked down and saw decorated tile, not a fire-filled pit.

Terror still roiled as I turned to grasp Sara's hands. I staggered as she led me to the divan while Ruth grasped one of my trembling hands in hers.

"Water please," I croaked. Sara filled a cup with wine. Looking down into the liquid I saw blood and my tremor multiplied. I held out the cup. "Just water please."

I emptied the cup and tried smiling, but Sara's tense expression didn't change.

After a few deep breaths I gained enough self-control to say, "Do not fear my dove, Jehovah is with us. Let us remember our baptism. We know, Messiah, creator of all, to be on our side and more powerful than any giant."

With those words, horror of the recent vision diminished and I turned to Ruth, saw her tears, and smiled again; this time not terror-tinged as a plan sprouted.

"We have work to do. Prepare a meal, a feast. A feast for many guests. Spare no expense. Prepare oil for a hundred lamps or more and distribute them in the open area before our house. I wish to address many guests. Have preparations complete for tomorrow evening."

At the stable, I disturbed Daniel, Benjamin, Jacob and the groom in their conspiratorial huddle by gesturing for the groom to ready my mule.

Riding towards Tiberias my thoughts roamed. I identified with the spiritual, political and economic sufferings of Israel under the Romans and began running over in my mind the sources of our many difficulties.

Jerusalem, the holy city, had moved far from the position of spiritual leadership it once had. A wealthy group of insiders, the Sadducees, controlled temple and priesthood. The high priest and family, the most influential individuals among the Sadducee faction, controlled the Sanhedrin, with the high priest holding his position at Herod's pleasure. I shook my head, wondering how Jehovah could allow a group so lax in their adherence to Moses' teaching, deniers of any resurrection from the dead to wield such influence among our religious leaders.

The Pharisees, with their roots right here in Galilee were rigid in their interpretation of Moses' law, along with other traditions passed down through the centuries. John the Baptizer had condemned this rigidity with its focus on observable actions and not the intent of the heart. But, most of our youth had never seen John and could be incited to riot by the merest transgression of law and tradition. The youth of Galilee furnished a fertile ground for rebellion with little understanding of the harvest to follow.

The Roman Empire itself rested on precarious foundations. The emperor, Tiberius Caesar, had removed himself from the responsibilities of governing, thus leaving a void at head of empire. One of his generals, Sejanus, had stepped into that void; step by step adding to his power. In lock step with growth in Sejanus power had grown hardship for my people. Appointing Pilate as governor of Judea had proven an ultimate cruelty.

With Galilee's reputation as a fomenter of rebellion, any attack on Roman personnel or property might turn our forests, fields and dwellings into desolate wilderness devoid of Jacob's seed.

Our very existence relied on one imperative. Avoid an insurrection that could mean the end of Jews in Galilee and possibly all Judea.

We had a problem only Messiah could remedy. We must wait for Messiah's intervention and I knew one man who might buy us that time. The centurion, Flavinus Dexius, in charge of the Roman garrison in Tiberius and Caesarea.

I'd been shocked to see him at the Jordan River as we'd arrived for our baptism. I'd felt even greater shock to see water dripping from his hair.

A Roman being baptized by a Jew. Pilate will learn of this, I'd thought, and *then what*? Flavinus and I had been acquaintances for some time and I knew he'd found Jehovah to be the deity he wished to serve. In a desire to please Jehovah he'd given a major contribution to the Jewish synagogue in Capernaum. So far, though, we had no such structure in Herod's new city of Tiberias, named by Herod to honor the present, absentee Caesar. Even this had angered the Jews, as this new city had defiled a Jewish graveyard.

Darkness filled the streets as I approached Flavinus' courtyard. I knocked on the gate and a young servant answered. Recognizing me, he opened the door as he'd twice done before.

I met Flavinus in the garden behind his dwelling. Our casual greeting turned into a full embrace and I felt the tears as baptismal emotion overflowed.

Flavinus motioned to a bench, the dim lighting from an oil lamp making us little more than shadows.

"I heard," Flavinus noted, "and my soldiers are armed and ready."

I could guess at the turmoil behind that matter-of-fact declaration.

"There may yet be hope," I said. "The teachings of John the Baptist resonate with our young people. If we can make personal repentance a more immediate, more eternal value than revenge, we may avert a blood-soaked Galilee.

"Also," I paused, seeking words. "Also, another factor stirs our nation. Belief grows regarding Messiah's soon appearance."

Flavinus shook his head in what I took to be a gesture of disbelief until he spoke. "Strange you mention Messiah. Some soldiers of my command have been rotating to the Jordan in case of riots. One of those soldiers returned this afternoon. On the day of our baptism, but after we left, this soldier reported seeing a small man in a patched robe and worn sandals walking toward John through the crowds. He saw John motion those around him to move aside before pointing toward this man. *This is the one*, he announced. *The one coming after me who is much greater than I. In fact, he existed before me.*

"This man appeared not to notice, just kept walking. My officer could not hear the following exchange, but John seemed to be arguing with the man before he went ahead with the baptism. My reporting soldier then hesitated, but continued at my command.

"Here's what he said. When the baptized man rose from the water, something like a white hand or dove, fell from the sky and hovered over his shoulder before another event occurred, something even more weird. With no clouds in the sky I heard sounds like thunder, almost like words.

"What words might you have heard?" I asked.

"Didn't sound like anything, really. More like a grumble, maybe dry lightning.

He seemed evasive on the point, but I didn't press."

My throat constricted. I swallowed, licked my lips, worked saliva onto my tongue. "Christos," I whispered, not doubting.

A baby born in a stable and a man in a worn robe. Two sides of a coin. Unexpected images. Unexpected roles. But why should the Christ need baptism? Had not the prophet Isaiah foretold Messiah to be like a lamb without blemish?

Even in my subconscious I interchanged the Jewish word Messiah with the Greek Christos as used in the Septuagint.

"Christos, maybe?" I questioned. Flavinus nodded.

I drew a deep breath, put aside thoughts of Messiah, and returned to the problem of redirecting insurrection energies.

"Are there believers of Jehovah in your command other than yourself?"

"I have two."

"Would you bring them to my compound tomorrow evening? I am inviting a large crowd of young people to attend a feast. Such a crowd may bring unwelcome attention from other Roman forces. If you advertise your presence we may avoid that danger.

"And?"

The question hung for a moment before I answered.

"*John the Baptizer* and *The Christ* are words on everyone's lips. If we can only change focus from insurrection to those two titles the rebellion may die. As Jews in Galilee we face a strange dichotomy; the most religious among us fan the flames of insurrection and it will be the most religious among us who will be first in responding to those names: Christos, Messiah, and John the Baptizer.

Flavinus didn't hesitate. "I will be there."

"You will be in jeopardy," I warned. "Mob mentality may overwhelm reason."

"A small price. Risking the lives of three to save thousands?"

I stood. We embraced again.

13: Power in Names

I speak truth when I tell you that of all individuals born of woman there is none greater than John the Baptist.
Words of Jesus: circa ce 30

Men, in a seething mass, filled the beach in front of my compound, with the dark waters of Lake Kinneret a winking backdrop.

Black night consumed the shooting orange sparks of a large fire.

Early that morning I'd sent a messenger to Ruth advising her to prepare not just any feast, but one for up to five hundred men. This fire, but one example of her efficiency.

Sheep and goat carcasses twirled on spits over charcoal fire pits. A baker's cart stopped in front of the house and two men began unloading bread.

A raised platform with stairs glowed reddish just a few yards distant from the illuminating flames.

Thoughts of what this night might do to my deposits with the Greek moneychanger in Tiberias nagged me for a moment.

Seething and muttering, the crowd reminded me of an angry sea, with the voices, rising and falling a reminder of distant thunder. I understood the gathering storm behind that thunder and fear filled my heart. Anger, justified, but anger inviting Rome's heavy-handed response. These angry men plus the thousands of others behind them would be no match for even one hundred trained Roman soldiers, the number of the century under Flavinus command.

Then the mass before me began to part like the Red Sea before Moses and three men walked through the gap. As each man reached me, I embraced him; then led the way up the stairs onto the platform.

The arrival of the three Romans brought silence; the silence of fermenting wine in a stoppered vase.

The crowd quieted as I walked across the platform. Speaking into the quiet with all the force I'd exerted when practicing on my flocks thirty years in the past, I raised my arms and shouted,

"You know the words of the prophet Joel," I shouted.

The Lord says, "You still have time

To turn your hearts to me,

To come with fasting, weeping and mourning.

Not with the torn clothing of grief,

But with torn, repentant hearts.

Return to the Lord, your God,

The merciful, compassionate one

Who is slow to anger,

But filled with compassion,

And unfailing love.

Eager to forgive,

And not punish.

I let silence rest, the words permeate.

"You are here," I said, "because these men are here." I pointed to the three, armed men on the platform beside me. "Most of you recognize the Roman Centurion, Flavinus Dexius. He and the soldiers with him guarantee our safety tonight and will protect us from any attack by the forces of Rome.

"Most of you also know how Flavinus has shown himself a friend to the Jews and I know him to be a student of our scriptures and a follower of Jehovah.

"The Baptizer accepted these men's repentance as real, making no distinction between Gentile and Jew in his baptism of these men in the Jordan.

A shiver rippled through the crowd. Whispers resonated.

I spoke over the momentary unease, "Remember Hosea's prophetic words. *I will call some my people who are not my people and she who was unloved, I will call beloved, and in the place where rejected ones were called not my people, there they will be called sons of the Living God.*

Fearing I'd over stretched my prologue, I asked, "Do any of you know anything of John's baptizing a young man named Jesus at the Jordan."

A voice from the crowd answered, "I was there. I heard Jehovah speak the words, *You are the Son I love and you bring me great joy.* I heard it, though some claim it was only thunder.

Murmuring swelled through the crowd.

Thanking Jehovah for this interruption, I waited for the murmuring to diminish before speaking.

"You know me as Micah, a merchant of words etched on parchment and papyrus. Many of you have on you at this moment words purchased from one of my marketing booths.

"As I received the baptism of John four days ago, grief overwhelmed my spirit to the point of death. A feeling still with me today. I feel my offence to be so great against the great God of heaven there can be no forgiveness.

"Thirty years ago, I wore a sheepskin cloak and carried a shepherd's staff. Day and night I cared for the sacred flocks near Bethlehem. I once had occasion to care for a newborn sacrificial lamb. I helped inspect for defects; wash, wrap in warm cloths, and personally place the lamb in a manger until it gained strength."

I began talking sometime during the first watch as the Great Bear Constellation began its rotation above us. Midway through the third watch we paused for food and drink. It was a brief pause before I continued, ending the account with these words: "Until now, even my children know nothing of my experience on the night of Messiah's birth. Fearing death, I have tried covering my silence by disseminating Scriptures. Though I now repent of that silence, the world holds insufficient sacrifice to cover my trespass against most Holy God.

"But my trespass is irrelevant at the moment, for at this precise moment in time, I believe Messiah walks among us and will soon reveal Himself and His mission.

"Also, I believe John to be no ordinary man. I believe he prepares the way for Messiah. A way that moves us away from ritual sacrifice towards purified hearts ready for whatever Messiah intends.

"Until Messiah reveals Himself and explains His mission we must wait and prepare. Prepare repentant hearts, purified hearts.

As one of the few having seen the revealed Messiah, I ask you to return to your dwellings and make yourselves ready for His revelation. Food remains. Build your strength for the days ahead that you be ready when Messiah calls."

14: Papyrus

We bear the brunt of God's fiery anger because our fathers ignored the words of this scroll and God's written promises concerning us.

Words of King Josiah in the second book of Kings. Circa 620 bce

A work crew began clearing the grounds as I turned to Flavinus. He grasped my elbow with one hand, shoulder with the other. "I too, will go home to consider your words and will see you tomorrow at the sixth hour."

Those last words seemed more order than request.

Inside, Ruth waited, an oil lamp burning and remnants of the feast waiting. We embraced, her body as tense as my own. Releasing me, she reached for the wine flask.

We sipped, eye to eye, waiting for the other to speak.

Touching her hand, moved almost to tears, I said, "You are a miracle worker. Whatever good might come from this night you made possible."

Ruth's own tears glistened; her hand squeezed down on mine. "You are my love and strong tower. I could not live without you, but I have many fears. You expose yourself to enemies with long memories who fear rumors of Messiah more than all else."

I had no immunity to fear despite my baptism and repentance. Her words struck home. I knew that many among the Pharisees and the local rabbis considered my handling of Scripture to be blasphemous. My words of this evening might well have opened the door to more open attack and even intervention from Jerusalem. My business and all those in my care were now more vulnerable than ever.

Ruth loosened her hand, came around the table, sat on my lap; buried her head on my shoulder. Words came, her voice little more than a whisper. "I have no wish to question you, my husband, yet some of your words troubled me. They sounded too self-important."

Shocked, I put one hand under her head and raised it until I could look into her shadowed eyes. "How can that be? I've humbled myself before Almighty God. I've repented. I've accepted the baptism endorsing that repentance. What more is there?"

"What more is there?" she repeated before asking another question. "What makes you think your trespasses are greater than those of others. What makes you think your trespasses are greater than mine?"

I searched my mind, puzzled; then remembered my words: "I have repented but the world holds insufficient sacrifice to cover my trespass."

Closing my eyes, I drew her close and leaned my head on hers. We sat thus for several minutes. I could not minimize my sin of past years, but refusing the benefits of repentance belittled God's mercy and power.

We knelt together.

Leaving Ruth, I found Benjamin and Jacob watching the platform being dismantled. "Jehovah be with you this morning, I greeted. "Are you ready to resume your information gathering?"

They mumbled something unintelligible.

With the sun nearing its zenith I met Flavinus just outside his courtyard. We walked down the street an arm's length of space between us.

"Jehovah's blessings on you this day," he said, not turning his head.

"On you as well," I answered, knowing there was more to come.

"In all my life, I've never heard such a story as yours. You, your family, and your business do have my protection while I command the Roman forces here in Tiberias. I know things are tough for the Jews, and could become worse. Ever since Tiberias Caesar placed Sejanus, his Prefect of the Imperial Guard, as de facto ruler of the empire, your plight has grown more difficult. Why Sejanus bears such animosity to this tiny corner of the empire is beyond my understanding.

Even, Pilate, the new Prefect of Judea, reflects this animosity. I have a messenger on the way to Pilate now with an assurance that all remains quiet in the Galilee and we require no additional troops."

"Thank you!" The words inadequate, knowing how Flavinus had just bared his neck to the executioner's sword.

Two Sabbaths passed. Galilean anger seemed tempered by

increased attention to John's message of repentance as well as a new focus on the imminent revelation of Messiah. Still, hidden swords were being sharpened in preparation for Messiah's declaration of war against our Roman occupiers.

I paced. *Where were Benjamin and Jacob*? They'd begun their information-gathering mission ten days previous.

Panic struck. What if Benjamin found it necessary to become one of Jesus' first disciples rather than follow my instructions to record and return? What if Jacob felt Jehovah's call to follow John rather than bring back material for the first of the many tractates I envisioned?

Frustration grew. We, here in Galilee, hungered for the words of John the Baptizer more than most in Judea. We were tired of being looked down on and despised by those living near Jerusalem. Remorse settled over me as I remembered my own contemptuous thoughts on hearing the accents of Galilee the night of Messiah's birth.

Now, I'd become a Galilean and understood how John's words presented *Jehovah worship* with the meaning for which we hungered. Though most Galileans would never meet John at the Jordan, they knew of him. Lacking opportunity to hear John in person, I knew they would make every sacrifice possible in order to obtain even transcripts of his words.

My scribes were too few to meet the demand I knew to be coming, let alone obtain the additional parchment and papyrus required.

Papyrus, I needed papyrus. I still purchased parchment but found it a commodity even harder to obtain than papyrus and more expensive. I'd begun accepting poorer grade product, but found much of it contained oily residue. And oil made ink run. Some recent parchment even carried bits of animal hair. No, I required papyrus, and that in greater volume than ever before.

Another Sabbath passed with no word from Benjamin and Jacob. Day after day I climbed to my rooftop above Lake Kinneret and searched the road below.

On this day I happened to be looking north when I spotted two armed horsemen at the forefront of four mule-drawn wagons with another three riders to the rear.

As I watched, one of the three horsemen separated himself from the small caravan and galloped ahead. Only when he turned from the roadway and up the slope toward me did I recognize Caleb.

Stumbling, almost falling, I ran to the stairway leading down, and reached Caleb as his feet touched ground.

"I didn't expect you. Are there problems?" I gasped.

Caleb's words slurred. "Problems abound, but sleep's what I need." He looked over his shoulder towards the small caravan behind him. "And they need it as much as I."

I took his reins in one hand and steadied him with the other.

A nearby gardener responded to my whistle. "Take this mule to the stable. Get some help and take care of the men and animals you see approaching."

"Ruth," I called as we stepped inside the courtyard. She opened the inner door, saw me helping a stranger, and rushed out.

"My friend Caleb. He's exhausted. I'll bring him inside and we'll give him drink."

She turned and called while I helped Caleb to a stool and propped him upright until Ruth finished pouring water over his hands and washing his feet.

The washing revived him enough to stand on his own. Ruth directed him to the table as a maid brought a pitcher of wine; then left to prepare the guest room. Caleb drank deeply before I helped him to his feet again.

"You're dirty, odorous and probably verminous," I said, "but we'll save the bath for later. I accompanied him to the guest room where he fell onto the bed without undressing.

Ruth won't like that, I thought.

Leaving Caleb, I headed for the stable hoping to find someone with information. Having passed the four, loaded wagons, I saw a stranger and one of my servants laying out fodder for the riding horses and mules. The poor animals stood, heads down, ignoring the offering.

The stranger entered the stable and I followed. He heard me and turned.

"Would you care for food and drink?" I asked.

He shook his head. "Too tired. Just need a place to lie down." He pointed to the straw-covered floor already littered with bodies.

"Food will be ready when you wake," I promised.

I looked towards the wagons, and lacking any other information, decided on a closer look. The wagons had slatted sides and through them I could identify baskets, two layers high, with each basket woven from the hard-outer layer of papyrus stems.

I felt like a thief as I used a wheel-hub to lever myself upward where I could look down on baskets with lids also of the hard papyrus weaving.

It took both hands to raise a lid, set it to one side, and peer in. A tingle ran through my body. Too shocked for clear thought, I stepped carefully back onto solid ground.

Impossible! A dream maybe? Not too much wine for sure. My eyes swept the reality about me. Lake Kinneret. The booths protecting my scribes. Even the faint voice of a reader. The stable. My home. A real world, not an illusion.

I raised myself for another look. Basket contents had not changed.

Roll after roll of papyrus scrolls rested inside. Rolled and ready for quill and ink. I grasped one of the rolls and pulled it free; a foot wide and from the feel about twelve feet long. Another similar layer rested beneath this first one. My position being too precarious to return the roll in my hand I laid it to one side and replaced the lid.

Back on the ground clutching the papyrus roll I checked the other wagons. *There's more writing material there than I've seen in my lifetime.* The thought left me dazed.

When Ruth met me in the courtyard, she noticed the scroll in my hand but didn't question.

"You must eat something," she said. "You will soon be more burden than burden bearer. Wait here. I'll fetch a fruit tray."

We climbed to the rooftop and took seats beneath a canopy. Cool air from the sea drifted over us. Confused thoughts filled my mind. *Why tantalize me with papyrus? Caleb can have no idea of my need. Where did he get it? Why in such volume?*

Then the real question. Where does he intend to sell it, and will he sell any to me?

Not even conscious of eating or drinking, exhaustion crept over me. My head dipped towards Ruth's shoulder.

I woke with a start as Ruth's hand touched my shoulder. "The evening meal is ready."

I asked Ruth to pour water over my head as well as my hands and felt some clearing of mind.

Sara joined us, inquisitive as usual. "That man you met at our baptism. Will he be staying long?"

The words didn't register until Sara spoke again. "Are you listening Father?"

I shook my head, trying to clear my thoughts. "Well, so far, he's been too tired to communicate. He'll wake in the morning ready to talk, I'm sure."

Sara glanced at the rolled papyrus. "That looks like papyrus. "A frown wrinkled her forehead, "but I've never seen a roll like that before."

I didn't answer and noticed her silent appraisal through the rest of the meal.

With darkness settling in and the maid cleaning up, Ruth and Sara stood, expecting me to do the same.

Responding to their silent question I said, "I'll sleep on the roof tonight. With all the thoughts running through my mind I would make poor company." And thoughts did run. Half asleep and half awake, my mind turned in an endless loop. Benjamin, Jacob, Caleb, papyrus.

Daybreak finally broke the cycle. Smoke and aromas reached upward from the outdoor kitchen.

Will Caleb have risen early? A foolish thought, but it drew me down the stairs.

The maid had ready a cup of warm wine, mixed with honey and cinnamon. I took the cup and stepped outside both house and courtyard. Honeybees danced on the tiny flowers of the grapevines clinging to the near courtyard wall.

An errant thought passed through my mind. Words from the fourth book of Moses describing the special gift God intended for the first high priest, Aaron, and others in my tribe of Levites.

Part of that gift included the words, *I also give you the best olive oil and new wine.*" I sipped, Well I have access to the best Galilee has to offer of olive oil and wine, but none of it due to being a Levite.

Someone stirred inside the dwelling. On entering I saw only Ruth.

"Has our guest wakened?" I asked.

Ruth shook her head and led me outside. "Let's eat in the courtyard." I ate, not to appease hunger, but to clear her worried look; then with obligation to my wife satisfied, I moved away from the table. "Time to check on our guest."

Ruth glanced over my shoulder, and I turned to see Caleb standing in the doorway still wearing his dusty, sweat-drenched clothes.

I laughed, "By heavens, you are one filthy Levite."

Ruth rose from table, brushed past Caleb, and came back with a clean robe. "Take this and go to the bath. By the time you return we will have a meal prepared."

Caleb watched Ruth depart, a slight frown on his face. "Follow me," I said.

As we sank into the warm waters of the basin pooling from the hot waters of the Hammat hot springs, I examined Caleb. "Old memories surfacing?" I asked.

He frowned, not understanding.

"You observe something familiar in both my daughter and my wife, do you not?"

He rubbed his chin, hesitated, nodded. "A memory stirs."

"Do you recall the names, Ehud, Tabitha and Ruth?"

He thought for several seconds, his mouth dropped, and he surged upward. "You married Ruth!"

He looked down on me, stiff features finally relaxing into a questioning smile. "I think there are parts of this story I don't need to know." He settled back.

We began talking about the past until I could hold my burning question no longer. "Where did you get the papyrus?"

"Papyrus." He let the word roll around his tongue. "So, you snooped."

I threw up my hands, tossing water in his face. "OK, I snooped. Where did you get it? Papyrus is my business and I've never seen so much in my life."

"Well here's the story." I could tell he was teasing. "I met this fellow a while back who claimed to be a transcriber, or at least own a business with transcription his major source of profit. He let slip plans for branching out and needed more papyrus, so I scoured my contacts and found what you see on those wagons.

"I'll tell you the whole story later, but it centers around a source of papyrus in swamplands on a tributary of the Orontes River in Syria."

"Time to eat," I said and splashed from the bath.

Entering the courtyard, I heard Benjamin's voice among others inside the house. Then Jacob's. Joy bubbled over and I nearly skipped my way inside.

Even Caleb seemed impatient with the prescribed prayers and when I finished, Benjamin and Jacob attacked their food with the same ferocity as Caleb. I nibbled a few grapes.

Sara and Ruth sat with us, unsettling Caleb, who obviously had little experience with women eating at the same table with men.

Finished eating the three men looked my way and saw the untouched dipping loaf in front of me. Benjamin opened his mouth. I stopped him with an upraised hand. "We have three stories for this morning before our real work starts. Jacob, we'll start with your summary of time with the Baptizer."

Jacob, awkward and unsure, stood. "I found John still preaching and baptizing in the same spot as before, but his sermons had taken a new twist, namely focusing on the duties of husband and wife. He'd begun using the example of Herod and the way he'd stolen his brother, Philip's wife."

Midway through one of those sermons Herod's soldiers dragged him off. I returned directly.

"Did you bring back content suitable for distribution?" I asked.

"Yes," he replied. "Enough for many tractates."

I presented the scroll filched from Caleb's wagon. "Here is a new scroll. When you leave, take and record your memories."

He left with a sideways glance at Sara.

I waved a hand toward Benjamin, who, young as he was, spoke with confidence. "After following a twisted trail of rumors as to Jesus' whereabouts I reached the town of Cana where I ran into Reuben, Malachi's youngest son, about my age."

Benjamin looked my way, "You remember Malachi. He's rather like you and proud of being named after a prophet. Also a customer."

I nodded.

"My brother's getting married," Reuben told me, "and my father prepares the marriage feast. I will assure you have seat at the table. Join us and locate Jesus later."

He walked with me to his courtyard gate and introduced me to the master of the banquet before leaving to fill other responsibilities. I followed others toward the banquet room and had my hands washed with water drawn from one of six large ceremonial urns. Being young and one of the last to be invited I was shown a seat far from the groom's table. A providential location as it turned out.

"When it seemed most of the guests were seated a whisper swept through the room and every head turned. A lady and two young men, dressed quite simply, but suitable for the occasion entered the banquet room and were led to seats near the groom. The kind of seating most often reserved for near family. Someone whispered, *Jesus.*

"I hadn't had a proper meal for over a week so took full advantage of both food and wine. The food was good, the wine less so, but good enough to divert my attention from the group around Jesus, though I didn't know yet which of the young men would be Jesus. Neither appeared anything special, particularly the one I took to be the youngest."

"Part way through the meal, I saw a servant approach the lady I assumed to be Jesus' mother and lead her away. In a few minutes she returned, leaned over the one I least expected to be Jesus, and laid an arm on his shoulder, while her lips moved close to his ear. He reached up, put a hand over hers where it touched his shoulder and stood. Doubts filled my mind as this man of slight build, medium height, brown hair and uneven beard left the room. All eyes followed them. With so many eyes on Jesus and his mother, I slipped out of my seat and followed.

"In the courtyard Jesus and his mother appeared to be in debate, but after a short discussion Jesus turned to a nearby servant, pointed to the now empty ceremonial urns, and the servant left. Soon three servants returned carrying water pitchers that they emptied into one of the urns. They kept this up until they'd filled all six.

"From where I stood, I could hear Jesus and his mother talking but try though I might could not distinguish words. However, with the urns full, Jesus spoke to one of the servants who filled a cup from one of the urns and entered the banquet room. I followed, took my seat, and watched the servant deliver the cup to the master of the banquet, who sipped, then sipped again before turning to the groom's father and speaking quite loudly. *What is this? Most hosts bring in the good wine first; then the poor, but you saved the best till last."*

Then the master of the banquet stood, held up his cup, and announced, "Servants will be coming around with empty containers in which you are to empty any wine still in your cups. They will refill those cups with the best nectar of the vine ever passing your lips." Then he lifted his cup and took a long swallow.

"That's being foolish, I thought. The rest might be just water.

When my refill arrived, I swirled the purple fluid, and my nostrils thrilled to the aroma of sweet wine. I sipped, not expecting much, but found the flavor so delightful, I had to force myself away from the table. I could not waste a minute before returning with this news.

"Oh, yes. On my way through the courtyard I saw the ladle used to fill wine pitchers. I dipped into one of the still full urns, tasted; shook my head. Every bit as good as my last bowl in the banquet room."

Benjamin sat down. "We will need confirmation," I said.

"Yes, I know," Benjamin answered.

My eyes turned towards Caleb.

Caleb's eyes ran round the table; stopping on Jacob then Benjamin. After a slow nod, he said, "Those were two great stories. Stories of great significance. I, on the other hand bring only the gift of papyrus. Insignificant papyrus, crumbles with time, turns to smoke and ash at a single spark. Ephemeral it's true, but also the material on which the world will hear your stories."

"How the papyrus comes to be with you makes for mundane listening;" he looked round. "However, all of us together with Jehovah form a very good team.

"Those papyrus laden wagons arriving as though gifted by the angel Gabriel are the conclusion of my story."

Caleb paused, tapped his forehead. "As you know we Jews have very good memories, and I used mine. We consume parchment and papyrus in Jerusalem by the wagonload. Not long ago I noticed a new shipment packed just as the loads delivered to you. Very unusual. Being curious I made inquiries and found the cargo's origin to be Seleucia in Syria and, knowing your need, I just followed my nose."

15: Barabbas

Does God lose His temper? Is this the way He acts? Isn't He on the side of good people? Doesn't He help those who help themselves?"

Words of prophet Micah: circa 700 BCE

"I've been thinking," Caleb said on his third day with us.

"You have?"

"Don't be a donkey. When do you ever let your brain out for air?"

"Air? What brain needs air?"

Caleb waved a dismissive hand. "As I said, I've been thinking. You've been a long time away from the temple and it's time to return."

I shook my head. "I've been baptized by John and that wipes out all need for a temple visit."

"No, it does not," Caleb responded, "The temple provides a special place to worship Jehovah. Remember the song of King David."

Your dwelling places fill my heart with wonder, O Lord of hosts! My inner being hungers and thirsts for the courts of the Lord; My heart and body sing joyful songs to the living God.

Amazingly blessed are those who dwell in Your house, My King and my God!

I pictured the temple as I'd seen it in my one visit as a child. A picture I'd long repressed.

Caleb must have seen my faraway expression and awaited eye

contact. "There is, of course, the long-standing charge of theft and sacrilege hanging over your head," he reminded. "A charge, dormant in the mind of some officials, but alive in others. With you present in Jerusalem, I can refute those charges and clear your name."

His words struck home. In light of my recent admissions to the crowd at our estate, a slate wiped clean seemed more necessary than ever. It would mean another layer of protection for myself, my family and my employees.

"I'll talk it over with Ruth," I said. "Right away."

Caleb turned his eyes to the last papyrus baskets being transferred from his wagons to one of the many caves dotting the landscape near our home. Caves, either put there on the day of creation, or a product of the hot, mineral springs bubbling from the ground at Hammat Tiberias.

I found Ruth, in our courtyard, head buried in her loom. She looked up, called for a maid, and requested two cool sherbets. Leaving her loom she followed me to a bench.

"Is the papyrus well-cared for?"

"It is," I answered. "And I've still no agreement with Caleb on his pricing."

"He's a different person than the insecure, petulant, and over-privileged youth I remember," Ruth said, changing the subject.

"You are right, and he's given me, and us, an interesting challenge. He wishes me to accompany him to Jerusalem where I can worship in the temple.

The maid's entrance with the sherbets, gave me time to pause, and consider my next words. I placed my sherbet on the small table in front of us, turned to face her and took both Ruth's hands in mine.

"He also has evidence to clear my name and those of the other shepherds who've spent over three decades on the run. Caleb learned the real details regarding the temple flocks from his uncle Phineas, and after his uncle's death Caleb made full restitution for the stolen animals for which I and fellow-shepherds carried the blame."

Ruth's face darkened. "No," she said. "No! It's too dangerous! So, Caleb's uncle died. He may have been your greatest enemy in life, but there are others in Jerusalem with memories equally long and still threatened by your story."

Her hands tightened on mine, "Do you think anyone in the temple has forgotten the magi's visit and their strange questions? Do you think they've forgotten the shepherds with their unsubstantiated tales of angels and a baby in a manger? Do you think the high priest and other temple elite really fear God or Messiah? Their God is power and believable rumors of Messiah weaken that power. You, my love, carry Messiah's aroma."

My stomach clenched and old fears surfaced. I swallowed, my

suddenly dry throat seeking moisture. "Caleb will have his answer in the morning, and pray God reveals His will to us this night."

Much as my body sought sleep, my racing mind prevented such luxury. On the bed nearby, Ruth shifted and stirred. At some point active thought dissolved into dream-populated slumber.

A final dream woke me. A dream that saw me walking by a lake shore; aimless, lost, feeling my way through heavy fog; sand invisible beneath my feet, water lapping nearby. Awake, eyes still shut, I retained the image of a hand reaching through the fog, beckoning and hearing a voice whisper, "Come."

My eyes opened. The dim wall of our bedroom announced the first hint of dawn. My feet touched the stone floor with Ruth's following. We changed out of our sleeping robes and made our way to the women's bath. No one would interrupt since this morning bath had become a part of household ritual.

We stepped inside the enclosure, disrobed in the chill air of morning, and sank into the steaming waters.

A gauze curtain, rising from the hot mineral waters, shimmered between us, rendering Ruth's face more angelic than usual. Her eyes, though, questioned.

Allowing myself to sink beneath the surface, I felt a lessening of the night's tensions. I let my head rise above the water, shook it, spraying water from hair and beard. Ruth blinked and rubbed still questioning eyes.

I met her gaze and responded to the unspoken question. "Dreams invaded my night, only the last memorable."

As Ruth processed the possible meanings of that dream, she moved to my side and we stood for several moments in silence, her arm about me, the softness of her body comforting.

A deep breath shuddered through her body, as she removed her hold and floated away until her eyes could meet mine.

"My husband," she paused, sighed, "You must go."

Caleb and I joined a small caravan on its way to Jerusalem. We were twenty-one men, seven Levites, three rabbis of the Pharisee sect, two merchants, Caleb and I, along with five well-armed mounted guards. We'd added two servants with a donkey cart to go before us and make preparations for both an afternoon meal and evening accommodations.

"We don't need guards," I'd protested to the caravan master. We'll be the only small caravan with guards and that brings attention."

The caravan master just nodded and pointed to one of the Pharisees whose rigid face; rich robes and long phylacteries suggested he might be one of the more unpleasant of the breed.

Buried in one of the wagon boxes we'd hidden a small fortune in tithes, including my own; as well other members of the caravan and many more unable to make the trek to this festival, second only in importance to Passover.

Apart from the guards on horseback, we all rode mules save for the rabbis who had large, riding donkeys.

Though a special bond existed between Caleb and I, our interests differed and we soon gravitated into company with those sharing longer-term interests; similar vocabulary, similar stories. I found company with the merchants; Caleb with his fellow Levites.

For some reason we all avoided the three Pharisees, who, even when travelling launched into long, loud prayers.

Our five guards rode the perimeter with spears and swords ready, though we'd had no word of bandits in Galilee.

On this journey I'd abandoned the staff I usually used for walking and resurrected my shepherd's staff. Not a natural accessory for a mule ride, but, tied in place with thongs from the riding pad, awkward but manageable.

Scudding clouds allowed an occasional glimpse of the sun, but a cold east wind smothered whatever warmth it offered. I felt more than ready for our mid-day stop, a warming fire, hot cider, along with some bread and salt fish.

Hands wrapped around a hot mug, thoughts lost in the fire's glow, I jerked at the sound of a strange voice. I looked up into the lined face of the eldest rabbi in the caravan. "Might I join you?" he asked.

I nodded, curious. He took a seat on a nearby boulder; calm, kind, thoughtful eyes examining me. A smile shone through his grey beard. "Your reputation accompanies you. I am not one of your detractors who scoff at your methods of producing and marketing scripture. My students praise you behind my back. They think I will be angry at their bypassing the synagogue and the Hebrew text in order to read and study the books of Moses and other prophets. I've seen your work and its good. Even I, as a rabbi, find it difficult to access Scripture with the concentration and depth I would wish for." He chuckled. "Don't tell my companions, but I've even gained access to some of your product."

"Thank you," I said, as he paused and raised his mug. "I believe you are Rabbi Elias." He nodded.

Finished eating, we mounted and rode side-by side, the caravan's slow progress making it easy for his donkey to stay abreast my mule. I had questions of him and he of me.

My interchange with Rabbi Elias proved distraction enough to almost ignore racing clouds, intermittent sun and a cold east wind that drove spurts of icy rain before it.

When the sun broke through, its beams bright in freshly washed air and sparkling off the water drops on grass and bushes, Elias and I found ourselves at the tail of our caravan with only two armed guards behind us. Elias turned to me, smiled, opened his mouth, but no words came as shouts and the scream of a wounded horse in front of us shattered the moment. Both rear guards set their spears and spurred their horses toward the threat ahead. The guard on my right thundered by, bent over, spear ready.

Abreast Caleb and the other Levites the horse tripped, pirouetted in mid-air and crashed down on its rider.

Old reflexes took over and, grasping my staff, I rolled from my mount, and rushed toward the downed guard. I hadn't taken even two steps when a ragged stranger emerged from the neck of nearby wadi, a long knife in one hand; eyes focused on the downed guard, captive to his kicking, struggling mount.

I shouted and charged toward this knife-wielding bandit as the sounds of fighting continued from the caravan's front.

The robber paused, turned my way and changed direction. I stopped, set myself, lowered my staff; then at the last moment raised the end to belly level and caught my attacker just below the ribs. His momentum ripped the staff from my hands, but as he stumbled by his knife spun upward then down and into my palm. Clenching it in my fist I turned and watched my would-be killer bury his face in the dusty roadway.

Once a knife had been part of my daily life and it felt so this day as I saw my assailant fighting for air and struggling to rise. With no time for charity I fell on him as though he were a hungry wolf attacking my lambs. With his blood puddling in the absorbent sand, I stood to ready myself for another attacker. Seeing none my eyes ran over our caravan; motionless and paralyzed, seemingly unable to assess their danger.

Nearest to me, Rabbi Elias sat frozen to his donkey; but the ongoing sound of attack a short distance ahead meant paralysis and death could be near companions.

I looked for a hiding place and spotted the brush enshrouded wadi mouth once concealing my dead attacker. Still crouching I collected my staff and ran for the cover, expecting a shout at any second, the whir of a flying arrow or buzz of a slung stone.

Can't let fear get the best of me, I thought, with my feet pounding the hard, pebble-strewn slope. *We've been ambushed by someone who knew both our route and our treasure. And they're ready to kill.*

Fear left me as I dove into the brush at the mouth of the water-cut wadi and a new thought entered my mind. *This caravan is my flock and I'm the shepherd and I'll protect it with everything I have.*

Fighting my way upward through the tangle of brush and brambles within the wadi-walls I assessed my options. One thing for sure, somewhere ahead there existed an enemy strong enough to attack an armed caravan, but not strong enough to overwhelm it. *Can I make a difference?* I wondered. *or will I just die for nothing?*

When the curtain of brush thinned and the wadi walls lowered, I paused to assess my next step.

A barren hill lay before me with about one hundred yards separating me from a position where I could look down on the fighting. Fading battle sounds urged haste. With a small rock, about the size of a man's head and about fifty yards ahead, I crouched, left the safety of the wadi, and ran.

Somehow that little rock gave me a sense of security as I fell behind it and looked down on the remnant of struggle.

Strangers already occupied our wagon seats and were whipping the mule-teams away from the beaten track. Our mules and donkeys along with their riders scattered like quail across the landscape. A bandit held the bridle reins of Caleb's rider-less mount; an inert form on the ground beside it.

At what had been the caravan's forefront, three guards had sacrificed their mounts to form a protective wall. Six bandits moved towards them.

With protective leather helmets and small, round, leather covered shields; the bandits edged forward, spread out and swords ready.

Then, merging with the landscape about sixty feet below and midway between me and the advancing thieves, I saw another figure; immobile, a sling dangling by his side. His advancing cohorts blocked any chance to use his weapon.

Those six can't be shepherds, I thought. No shepherd would stand in the way of a slinger. Interrupting that thought another struck me. If I could kill that slinger and gain his weapon, we might yet save something.

The thought had barely crossed my mind when a guard raised himself above cover and flung his short spear, striking the nearest bandit in the throat. The man struck by the spear hadn't hit the ground before the slinger had his arm in motion. I heard the stone strike and watched our guard fall.

With fighters tightly focused on the battle below I had moved, unobserved, into a position above the slinger and to one side. A few more steps brought me directly to his rear and I hurried downslope, believing his sling to be useless against my staff. Not more than ten feet from my target, a stone turned beneath my feet and I stumbled. At the sound the slinger dropped his weapon and snatched up his own staff.

I'd felt little fear since that first scream announced an attack, but I felt it now.

Off balance and plunging downward I still sensed an opening and thrust towards this enemy's throat. My staff found only empty air but his smashed into my knee. I crumpled as though I'd hit a tree stump.

With momentum thrusting me forward I tumbled down the hill, memories and thoughts racing through my mind; certain death imminent. Thoughts of home, family, business, Caleb. Then my head hit the ground and with consciousness fading I felt my hair grasped in powerful hands, my head lifted, saw the butcher's knife raised; and gazed into eyes as dark and deep as the abyss of hell.

"Thaddeus." The grip loosened.

"That name is dead! I am Barabbas!"

16: The Fate of Thieves

Describing Roman practices of putting down riots and insurrections, Eusebius, writing in about 325 CE describes a period in about year 6 CE in which "fresh troubles broke out in Palestine which were suppressed by fire, sword and crucifixions.

With consciousness returning I tried lifting my head. It wouldn't move, but something hairy and wet chafed my cheek. My arms seemed paralyzed. Cruel jolts and accompanying pain gradually pushed me back into oblivion.

It may have been the cessation of pain returning me to the world. A world, still with the unreal sensation of course hair on my cheek. My arms and legs felt numb and paralyzed. Only when rough hands grasped my wrists and my arms fell free did I realize I'd been bound. With bindings loosened I began to slip, only saved from disaster by fingers sinking into my hair and cushioning my journey to the ground.

When opening my eyes through distorted, spinning vision, I looked up into the eyes of a curious mule. I felt a tiny smile grow in concert with the thought; *I bet you're the only friendly face I'll be seeing for the next little while.*

Gradually my vision cleared, and with that receding numbness, waves of pain. I forced myself onto one side and vomited, the resulting relief allowing me to examine the world around.

Forest surrounded us. Men bustled about wagons with wheels

braced against small logs to prevent rolling on a steep downslope. Some of the men were unhitching the teams, some unloading the wagons. Others had already begun sorting through the contents and packing them on the backs of mules captured from our caravan. I recognized the mule I'd loaned Caleb.

The bandits began collecting around one of the wagons as two men climbed over the rear rack, lifted a body and laid it gently on the ground. Following that action, the bandits removed the log brakes and began pushing and pulling on the wagon until it started moving. "Let it go," I heard Barabbas say and as the men stepped away the wagon disappeared, crashing and banging as it dropped. The other wagons followed the first.

Four men collected around Barabbas and I saw coins change hands, then these men turned back and left on foot. While this transaction was underway the other bandits gathered around the body. I saw one wipe away tears.

Barabbas reached the body and stopped. "My friend," Barabbas addressed the dead, "we have seen much together. May Jehovah take your soul and please forgive us in failing to provide proper burial."

Following those words, he selected two of his crew. "Bury the body and follow us." As the men grasped the body, his face turned towards me. The man I'd killed.

Dread filled me.

Then I heard Barabbas say, "Return the prisoner to his mule."

Once more I felt rough hands, this time lifting not catching; hands indifferent to any pain or discomfort brought to their prisoner. Once astride they bound my hands together leaving only my fingers to grasp the mule's scanty mane. To lose consciousness would be disastrous.

We left the forest and dropped down to the Jordan River and crossed at a hidden ford. The water proved deeper than any crossing point I'd ever used, rising past the mule's belly, tugging at my injured leg. The splashing sounds of the mules crossing smothered my groans. On the other side we climbed a steep bank with no sign of previous use and continued into untracked wilderness. The mules travelled at a stiff trot wherever possible, my pain increasing with each jolt until I passed into a pain-induced stupor where I remained mounted but impervious to the world around me.

I realized the mule had stopped moving when uncaring hands grasped me and lowered me to my feet, where my leg gave way and I tumbled to the ground. No sounds of sympathy followed, an omission allowing me to wallow in my own self-pity as I fought to at least find a sitting position.

Darkness surrounded us. We seemed to have reached some sort of cache, as I heard mules munching grain. "Here," a hand touched my arm, and reaching out I grasped a cup and a bread crust. The cup held only brackish water, but even that called out for more. The more not forthcoming.

Silence settled on the camp, broken only by the occasional stomp and shift of a mule and a wolf's howl in the distance. Sleep evaded me, my mind sharp despite the pain as mental pictures of the caravan raid flooded my mind. A growing certainty saddened me as I embraced the meaning of that body lying prostrate near Caleb's mule. That had been Caleb.

Questions flooded in. "Had Ruth heard yet? What would people think when they found neither me nor my body.

Uncertainty as to how my old friendship with Thaddeus would impact my fate. If friendship proved meaningless, then what?

The first glimmer of a late-rising moon brought life to the camp. Packs went back onto mules. Men mounted. My dry throat ached for another drink but none appeared.

At our next dismount my scream reverberated through my head, disembodied, unreal.

We rode for two and one-half days before stopping where a muddy little creek pooled beneath a rock wall. Scrub bushes concealed the opening of what proved a very large cave. Large enough to hold men and mules.

Barabbas helped me dismount beside the muddy pool and jerked off my robe. "Sit!" he ordered. I held out my hand and he eased me down into slippery goo. Warm goo.

Using both hands I plastered my knee with mud and felt pain slip just a little. When sitting proved too uncomfortable I sank deeper into the soothing muck. Nestled in a blanket of warmth and with my back braced against the pool's muddy edge, I went to sleep. Waking, I found several of Barabbas' men lying near me, each cloaked in mud, inhuman, their menacing eyes fixed on me.

I shrank from those virulent stares until Barabbas appeared with two other thieves. He ordered those in the mud to wash and get out; then turned to the other two, "Go! Prepare for the next leg of our journey and then you'll bathe. I need time with the prisoner."

They left without complaint.

Barabbas disrobed, moved into the mud in front of me where he too, covered his body in medicinal paste. Running a mud-smeared hand across his beard he shook his head. "What am I going to do with you?" his voice unexpectedly gentle. He paused. "My men want to leave you here."

I shuddered, gulped and answered, "I know no more than those still living back at the caravan." "They saw you as well. Besides, my pain has been so great, I would never find this place again."

Barabbas smiled. A real smile. "Once a shepherd, always a

shepherd. Anyone with the instinct to find a lost lamb in dark and rain, would find this place blindfolded."

He sighed. "Even more important, you know my name. More than that you know who I once was, but let's leave the present for now and review the past. You no longer appear a poor shepherd."

Scowling, he asked, "You make peace with the anti-Messiah faction in Jerusalem?"

I held up a hand, interrupting his outburst. "I'll tell you my story."

Nearing sunset, I concluded an outline of the past thirty years in which I'd emphasized my subtle opposition to the anti-Messiah factions driving us into exile.

"Transcriber," Thaddeus nodded, chin propped in muddy hand. "Familiar title, but never dreamed it might be you. Good work you're doing. You may find this strange, but I, too, serve Messiah and the true kingdom of God."

I didn't answer and he scowled again, unbridled ferocity barely contained.

"You think I and my men are common thieves and murderers. You're wrong! We fight for Jehovah as do you. We fight for Messiah against the temple thieves, hypocrites who pretend to serve God but make sure much of God's tithes flow into their own purses. The same thieves and murderers hunting us. The same thieves and murderers who would kill Messiah should they find him. You fight your way; I fight mine."

I didn't bother telling him of Caleb's promised reconciliation. In fact, I made no mention of Caleb though my heart bled for the man who probably lay crumpled on the ground at Barabbas' hand.

As silence crept between us, I mourned too for the Thaddeus of old; kind, thoughtful and more intelligent than his bear-like physique suggested. Thoughtful, intelligent and loyal.

Loyal! Fear dried my throat. I'd seen hostility in the eyes of those thieves sharing my mud bath. They wanted me dead. I'd killed one of theirs and they'd earned their leader's loyalty.

Thaddeus raised his eyes to mine, his rugged face lightened by a tiny smile. "You've jumped into my boat, maybe you need to grasp an oar and row."

I frowned, not understanding.

"You don't like those thieves governing the temple any more than I do. Forget your quills and papyrus. Fight with us."

Mouth still too dry for words, I shook my head.

Thaddeus sighed, stood, and looked down. "Time to wash up and move inside."

I hobbled into the cave with Thaddeus as crutch, fear once more raising its ugly head. Thaddeus had thrown a life-line. I'd not taken hold. Sinking to the cave's stone floor, numbness spreading through my body, I curled up like an infant and closed my eyes.

A shout echoing off cave walls shattered my stupor. Running footsteps passed within inches of my head, the sound of shouts and clashing weapons reverberated through the cave mouth. Then a scream. A horse neighed.

My fingers fumbled on unfamiliar stone, mind lost in fog. A torch flared into life at the cave mouth. My hands flew to my eyes, shielding against the brightness, adjusting, and seeing light reflecting off armor. Light, outlining a Roman soldier's helmet. I croaked out my name and the torch lowered. "Centurio," the soldier called and a familiar voice answered. Both soldiers came nearer. "Flavinus," my voice came little more than a whisper.

"Micah?"

My mind answered; my tongue didn't.

He reached down and grasped my arm. "Hold on, I'll help you stand."

"No!" that croak again.

"Later, then," and he pressed a flask into my hand.

Minutes after I shuddered to the sound of blows; accompanied by screams and groans. I almost made it to my feet, but the knee wouldn't cooperate.

Screams diminished while groans, cries, and curses directed at Roman dogs continued to penetrate the darkness.

No more than half an hour after leaving, Flavinus returned with two other soldiers. One held a torch while Flavinus and the other man knelt beside me.

I pointed to my knee.

The man with the torch lowered it and Flavinus probed gently, easing off at my choked-back groan."

"We have to get you out of here."

I heard the apology, and closed my eyes as the two men hoisted me upright, linked arms to form a chair and carried me into the light of a rising sun.

Seeing men crucified and dead had come to be a common occurrence in Judea since Pilate's arrival as prefect, but I'd never observed living men hanging, helpless and suffering.

No crosses here in the wilderness. Just one log, braced against a rock face, high enough to suspend five men, arms spread, nails through wrists. Another log lay on the ground holding each pair of feet together, trapped by a single nail. Voices grown faint from suffering still called on Jehovah to pour out his wrath on the pagan pigs.

I gagged and turned away but not before noting Barabbas missing from among the crucified. I moved my lips in silent prayer for his safety.

Two soldiers carried me to one of the recaptured mules, powerful hands hardly more gentle than those of Barabbas' bandits.

Behind me Flavinus gave the order; "Kill them."

A moment later he stood looking up at me. "We're much nearer Jerusalem than Tiberias. Do you know anyone there who could nurse you back to health?"

It took a moment to move past the horrors of the crucifixions and process the words, longer to consider possibilities. Nicodemus, the name floated through my mental fog. The same fog making Flavinus waver in my vision. "Nicodemus," I mumbled. "One of the Sanhedrin. Famous man in Jerusalem."

My mount sidestepped and Flavinus raised a steadying hand. "Tell Ruth I'll be fine," were my last words before reaching Jerusalem."

17: Nicodemus

And the Lord said unto Moses, gather unto me seventy men of the elders of Israel, whom thou knowest to be the elders of the people, and officers over them; and bring them unto the tabernacle of the congregation, that they may stand there with thee."

Book of Numbers 11:16. Origin of the Jewish Sanhedrin. Circa 1400 bce

Jerusalem may have been nearer than Capernaum, but the pace set by the Roman soldiers turned me into jelly and I furled myself within a pain-induced stupor. Only the occasional steadying arm of a Roman soldier prevented a fall.

Reaching Nicodemus' courtyard, one of my escorts leaned over and struck the gate with his spear butt. A wide-eyed servant stepped out.

The soldier beside me, released his balancing arm, flicked my mule's bridle reins toward the servant, wheeled his mount, and spoke over his shoulder, "A guest for Nicodemus."

"Tell him its Micah," I groaned, and the ground came to greet me.

Grey intervals full of jumbled words and hands; touching, probing, painful, only sometimes soothing reached me through the black night into which I'd fallen.

Full consciousness returned with a vision of rising ground rushing toward my face. I jerked my head and felt a pillow's warm embrace. An unnatural mound rose where my knee should have been, but a simple attempt at motion brought back the darkness.

My eyes opened again to the sound of voices and I noted two men standing in a nearby doorway, my friend Nicodemus and a short, stocky, fair skinned stranger. This other man had a leather bag at his feet and addressed Nicodemus in low-voiced, cultured Greek.

After a brief interchange the stocky man dropped a muscular arm to his leather satchel and departed.

Nicodemus turned and came to my bedside. He touched my forehead, shook his head. "You will have to lie very still until the doctor returns. He wishes your swelling to subside before further intervention."

Further intervention! The words shook me and I asked, "May I see the knee?"

Nicodemus pulled back the coverlet and there it was, swollen beyond recognition. The damaged knee had been elevated with the support of cloth bindings attached to a wooden frame. The frame also kept the coverlet from contacting the wound.

Six black gobs of slime rose above the red skin of the swollen knee. I imagined some new kind of deadly infection.

Nicodemus, noting my alarm, said, "Don't worry. Just leeches. A recent experiment of Doctor Luke's. Now, just rest."

I woke to a soothing coolness on my forehead. A strange man leaned above me holding a damp cloth.

"Thank you," I murmured.

The man smiled. "My name is Jason," he said, dipping the cloth in a basin.

The return of the damp cloth to my forehead brought back another feeling. Hunger.

"I'm hungry," I said, lacking energy for polite interchange.

Nicodemus returned as fading light from an open window signaled end of day. Again, he put a hand to my forehead and checked the leeches. "We'll take them off for the night," he soothed.

After a pause he continued, "We sent a messenger to your family two days ago. Cursed Romans. Without them we would be the ones accessing a network of horse exchanges. I provided two mules for the messenger so he could have at least one fresh mount."

I didn't bother telling him of Flavinus and his access to the "cursed" Roman network, nor of his commitment to my family.

Dr. Luke returned on the third day following his first visit. He ran light fingers over the swelling. I flinched when he touched an area near the kneecap.

"Excellent," he murmured. "Swelling's going down faster than expected;" his broad fingers eased the bulging leeches from their hold. He reached into his satchel and withdrew a covered dish and removed the cover. The quivering, slimy mess of more bloodsuckers made me gag.

Paying no attention to my disgust, Doctor Luke distributed a portion of this new crop to the swollen area. "Jason will replace these with others as needed. Be patient. I am confident of full recovery."

He hadn't been gone long when noises in the courtyard roused me from half-sleep. Minutes later Jason stepped aside to let Sara and Benjamin rush in. I waited for Ruth to follow. She didn't.

Sara, falling to her knees by the bedside, grasped my hand and choked, "Oh, Father."

I looked up at Benjamin where he stood upright and serious. "Good to see you, son. You travelled fast."

Words stuck in his throat.

"Things will be fine," I said, not quite believing. "I have an excellent physician."

Benjamin opened his mouth; then clamped it shut.

Fear struck. Had something happened to Ruth? I controlled my panic. "Go ahead, son. Life's paths give few straight paths. We must trust Jehovah."

"The robbers killed your friend, Caleb."

I nodded. "I saw his fallen body, unmoving, but hoped for the best."

Words burst from Benjamin's mouth. "He's the only one with knowledge of the new papyrus source."

Nodding again, I wondered at this strange diversion.

"There's been a fire."

I raised the palm of my free hand. "Go slow. No panic." I pointed. "Pull that stool in beside Sara. Take a deep breath and start at the beginning."

"Mother woke five nights ago to the smell of smoke and light flickering on the walls of your bedroom. She looked out to see flames coming from a cave above our house so woke us and called the servants. We ran to the fire with brooms, blankets, shovels and anything else we could use to beat out the fire. That's when we noted flames beginning to shoot from other cave-mouths."

His voice cracked, "Papyrus burns well."

Grief and hopelessness shrouded my thoughts and interrupted breathing. A sentence from Solomon's writing in that most enigmatic of all scrolls, Ecclesiastes, came to mind. A sentence matching emotion of the moment.

For what happens to the sons of men also happens to animals; one thing befalls them: as one dies, so dies the other. Surely, they all have one breath; man has no advantage over animals, for all our efforts are but spitting in the wind.

Sara sensed my depression and stood, stubbornness etched on her features. "You've never given up before and things aren't all bad.

We've been into each cave and all your workers have begun sorting out any bit of papyrus large enough for even a few words."

My mind drifted back thirty years to the scene of a burning stable, Caleb holding Eliezer's blood-soaked head, and shadows disappearing in the night.

Sara's voice penetrated, "...one cave with little damage. So many volunteers came to our aid we even turned some away. Then Flavinus came with word of your injury."

Benjamin broke in, "Mother and Daniel stayed behind to direct salvage;" then pausing, looked me in the eye. "And, on another track, you were prophetic when you said Jesus must have begun naming disciples in order to claim the title of *Rabbi.* The process has begun.

A frown wrinkled his forehead, "Strangest thing, though. Instead of selecting zealous young scholars like Jacob, he's chosen five fishermen and a tax collector."

A long pause followed, allowing time for me to assess this radical move.

I raised a hand to my forehead, closed my eyes. *Fishermen.* They would never have attended the advanced studies of Beth Midrash, but then neither had I. As a shepherd among other shepherds we possessed, more than anything, a shared hope in Messiah. That shared hope had turned our minds to Scripture. We memorized every fragment of TaNaKh, as blessed and approved by Sanhedrin of previous centuries. When some fragment of Scripture came into our possession we debated endlessly, quoting what we knew and filling gaps with our own conclusions. Would fishermen be different, considering the fierce adherence to Scripture of Galileans? Would the endless hours together on fishing boats be different than my experiences as a shepherd?

From what I'd observed, no child in Galilee escaped Beth Sefer and its focus on Torah. No area in Judea studied the prophets such as Isaiah, Jeremiah, or Daniel with more intensity than the inhabitants of Galilee. I'd felt like a heathen on first arriving.

Neither shepherd nor fisherman ever before had earned the opportunity of following a rabbi in order to observe, absorb and duplicate his thoughts and actions.

Maybe Jesus had something special in mind for these men he'd selected as disciples.

I looked up, felt shame for my recent weakness, smiled and forced calm.

"You have done well," I said. "Don't fret over me. I have an excellent physician and personal attendant. However, I won't be skipping about the streets of Jerusalem any time soon.

My children gave reluctant smiles and I continued, "I believe both John and Jesus to be Jehovah-sent and keys to the greatest turning point for the Jewish people in all our history."

Their smiles faded and Benjamin said, "It hurts to leave. No one can predict the progress of a wound such as yours. Already discoloration spreads.

"Give my love to your Mother. Tell her not to worry and to expect dispatches. Have Daniel meet with Flavinus. The centurion has influence."

They stood, embraced me; kissed my cheeks.

"Give my love to your Mother," I said again to their departing backs.

Just starting to fidget after a good sleep I welcomed sounds of talk between Nicodemus and Jason. Jason entered the room first with a meal tray for two. Nicodemus followed, his face drawn with exhaustion.

Straightening from a tired slump, Nicodemus asked, "Jason tells me two of your children visited today. Did my messenger get through?"

"Appreciate all you did to bring them," I said, evading a direct answer. "Benjamin and Sara came as soon as they heard."

I went on to report the fire, the attempt to salvage papyrus, and our efforts to monitor Jesus and John.

Nicodemus frowned. "Monitoring the Baptizer will prove difficult. Herod holds him at the castle of Machaarus, across the Jordan and well beyond the Dead Sea."

I hadn't considered such a possibility and wished that news had arrived earlier that Benjamin might carry it back to Jacob.

"John and Jesus. John and Jesus," Nicodemus muttered. "That's all the Sanhedrin talk about these days. Joseph of Arimathea and I seem the only ones on the counsel willing to examine the credibility of these two men. Are they prophets, imposters, delusional wild men, or demon possessed?"

He sighed, sipped his wine. "Herod must have heard the Sanhedrin clapping their hands when he arrested John. Now its members are more than happy to see him isolated at Machaarus where he can't stir the crowds."

Another sigh, "But problems just multiply as those same crowds rush off to see and hear Jesus' leaving the Sanhedrin feeling more threatened than ever."

I struggled to sit up; then sank back, sweat beading my forehead.

"You know I accepted John's baptism."

"No, I did not."

"Do you approve his imprisonment?"

He paused. "You know," he said, "I came in here already exhausted. This talk tires me even more. We will have many more discussions. The Sanhedrin meets again tomorrow and I must sleep."

18: Luke

When Hezekiah, King of Israel, fell ill and about to die he reminded God of his long-time faithfulness and Isaiah, the prophet sent this message. "Have your servants prepare a poultice of figs to cover the abscess." They did and he recovered.

From the book of 1 Kings circa 700 bce

My physician returned as he had promised, and this time Nicodemus remained in the room during the examination. He had not visited since he'd learned of my baptism by John.

Again the probing; again the pain. Doctor Luke nodded. "Your swelling lessens. I will be in Jerusalem for a few days so I'll give you a little more time for healing before surgery.

"Surgery?"

He nodded. "Yes. You have a bone chip floating around the kneecap. Should I leave it, you will never walk without pain, and even surgery holds no guarantees."

Luke straightened on his examining stool. "Now it's your turn," he said.

"My turn! My turn for what?"

"To fill your role as physician. I pour my energies into healing the physical body, but their remains the intangibles of mind, soul and a spirit. Intangibles requiring stimulus and healing.

"For many years I've been intrigued by the Jewish faith, and in payment for treating his wife's illness Nicodemus opened his library to me. And that, my friend, presented the opportunity to study the Jewish scriptures from the very same codex he purchased from you. I also devour your tractates when available.

"All that reading leaves a hunger in my mind, soul and spirit. You have knowledge to assuage that hunger and hope you are ready to tell me more on my next visit."

"Talk of surgery tires me," I said, "but let me tease you with the end of my story. Maybe if the story's good enough, you'll reduce your charges?"

He raised an eyebrow and I began. "John and Jesus have drawn the attention of our whole nation. Nicodemus told me a few days ago that even the Sanhedrin talk about little else. My transcription business has turned its attention to recording and distributing words from these two men. At this moment two of my men are assigned the task of collecting the exact words of Jesus and John from which our transcribers will produce multiple copies for distribution. One of those men is my son. We have two tractates containing the exact words of John the Baptist in production.

"Now, with John in an isolated prison, our whole attention turns to Jesus."

The doctor shook his head. "You Jews. How do you learn anything? Exact words! A few words with no context. What meaning can there be to that? I think I possess better understanding of your scriptures than most Jews, even the educated ones. I probably can't quote five sentences of your Scriptures, but would debate any of your scholars on issues of content and meaning."

Nicodemus frowned in the background, leading me to wonder how long he could tolerate my presence and the kind of conversations I'd brought into his home.

Luke stood to leave and I threw in a final word. "Remember King Hezekiah," I asked. Luke paused before nodding. "Remember when he was about to die and the prophet Isaiah ordered a fig poultice which cured him. Don't you have the formula?"

He smiled, shook his head and departed.

An involuntary wince welcomed the doctor as he stepped into my room on his next visit; the word "surgery," filling my mind.

Settling his bag near the bed the doctor drew out a small, stoppered flask. "Here, *The Milk of Paradise*. Drink it all. God willing, when I return from an hour in the library, I will find you asleep, and when you wake, you will find the surgery complete. A small warning though, this potion brings dreams. Sometimes dreams of angels. Sometimes demons. Drink, and dream well."

I hesitated.

"Drink!" he ordered.

I sipped, then sipped again, looked up and said, "Quite nice. Good wine. Bitter aftertaste though."

He smiled, touched me on the shoulder. "Don't worry. God has work for you."

I smiled back, thinking, *never put words like worry in a message of comfort.*

As I finished the potion, the room swayed and the walls expanded outward. A strange euphoria seized me, lifted me from the bed, raised me above the city and propelled me northward faster than the wind. I passed Lake Tiberias, my estate, the transcription booths, Capernaum. The journey continued along a road I'd never traveled, up a river I'd never seen and left me hovering above a sea of papyrus plants, fronds waving in the breeze.

My thoughts turned to my dead friend Caleb. I gave a silent thank you. *There lies your legacy my friend.*

"Micah," a voice interrupted. I fought the voice, enjoying this new world more than the one I'd left.

"Micah," again. The papyrus field dissolved and the bed rose beneath me. Still swaddled in euphoria I fought the voice. Fought it until I could 90fight it no more.

The room swam. Faces peered through a hazy curtain. I heard my voice, "Good evening to you all. Or is it morning." My words slurred. My laugh a croak.

"Sorry," I apologized. "Long journey. Tired." My eyes closed.

Pain, in radiating waves, woke me, but still I felt alert, refreshed even. Refreshed, but lost in a teeming swirl of images. I began reconstructing memories of the previous few days. Barabbas, and events surrounding him returned with great clarity. The house of Nicodemus, too, but then everything blurred.

A vaguely familiar form appeared at my bedroom door. "Micah, sir." The words came in hushed tones as the face sprang into focus.

"Jason, my friend, no more sirs, just Micah. Not managing a full headshake to rid myself of a ringing in my ears, I managed to stir on the pillow. Though the ringing remained, I questioned. "What has happened? Something seems different.

A puzzled look crossed my friend's face. He walked to the bedside and drew the coverlet from the hump of my raised knee. *Something strange here,* I thought. *When did a bandage replace those ugly leeches?*

Jason lowered the coverlet. "You woke up last evening muttering about a journey. Part of you departed, that's for certain." He lifted a small dish from a nearby table, brought it over, and displayed three bits of hard, reddish-colored material. One about the size of a thumbnail, the others much smaller.

"Dr. Luke removed these from your knee while you traveled the unknown. You'll have a scar, but the doctor's incision is well stitched. He told us to remove the bandage in three days, wash the wound and then reapply leeches. Time will heal," he comforted.

Time! I don't have time. Frustration filled me. How could my family cope with the fire's aftermath? How could my business return to full production without me? How was Ruth managing? I spent the rest of the day groveling in misery, playing out every possible scenario that would get me home.

Each scenario bumped into a stonewall. Tired of playing and replaying my options I gave up, accepting that only God had remedies for my crisis, and might even use it in some good way. The words of King David from early in his book of Psalms came to mind. *You alone, O Lord, can make me both live in safety and then lie down and sleep in peace.*

Tense muscles slowly loosened. I took a deep breath and began relaxing as Jason brought my evening meal. "Where's Nicodemus?" I asked.

"A messenger brought his regrets. The Sanhedrin wishes a closer look at this new rabbi, Jesus. They select a delegation for Galilee this evening."

I nodded, "Not surprising. News of a new rabbi gathering disciples without approval from Jerusalem must have knotted their phylacteries. Tsk, Tsk. Wonder if Nicodemus will go?"

The answer came the next morning. "The Sanhedrin's selected five individuals for an investigation of this new rabbi, Jesus. My not being selected came as no surprise. In spite of my substantial contributions to the temple coffers I seem to have fallen out of favor with Caiaphas."

He paused, his eyes on me and a frown on his face. "I overheard you telling Luke of your wish to record words of Jesus as well as John the Baptizer. I'm sorry about John, though many in the Sanhedrin aren't. However, why your interest in Jesus?"

Oh, God in heaven, what am I to do? I cannot lie and I dare not tell the truth. I knew my confession to the group of young hotheads in Galilee would soon reach Nicodemus if they hadn't already. Though I sensed his growing disillusionment with the Sanhedrin, I perceived how much he valued his position. A position valued even above his wealth and probably more than any feelings for me.

I played with the decorative fringe on the coverlet, not meeting his eyes, wanting to evade a straight response. "Reasons for interest in Jesus?" I ventured. "Similar reasons to those agitating your Sanhedrin. Also interest in Jesus builds naturally from fascination with John the Baptizer. Both are outsiders. Both speak with confidence. Both arouse intense interest, and both confound our religious scholars. An aura surrounds them."

Pausing, I searched for additional words and found them in a question. "Do you feel Jehovah will soon reveal His Messiah?"

He answered without hesitation. "Of course."

"Might John or Jesus be the promised Messiah?"

Nicodemus hesitated, ran fingers through his beard, his reply hesitant. "John stated plainly he was not. So far we have no statement from Jesus and certainly no evidence of plans for kingdom building."

Time for a story, I thought and began with the words. "In my youth I worked as a shepherd in the Judean wilderness."

Nicodemus interrupted, "But you're Galilean."

"Not always, but to my point, predators were a constant threat to my flocks. Wolves, the occasional lion, and even large eagles seeking a lamb. A lion began taking sheep from several neighboring flocks and finally killed a ewe from mine. I joined my flock to those of a nearby shepherd and went after the animal not knowing what I would do should I catch it, but determined to try.

"I began my search from the point of the kill. First I found blood and visible spoor. When that faded, I looked for other sign. Blood drops here, a footprint there. I followed each clue, and found my quarry.

"I relate that as an illustration of our present dilemma. There must be clues suggesting whether or not Jesus could be Messiah. What are they and where are they?"

"Stop!" Nicodemus ordered. "What happened when you caught the lion?"

I shrugged. "That's for another day. I just wished to illustrate the importance of clues.

"For example, a young scholar just entering my employ remembers the story of a boy who sat in the temple with teachers of the law and confounded them with his questions and knowledge of Scripture. That was eighteen years ago and he wonders if that boy could be the same Jesus gathering disciples today.

"Adding to my curiosity is a story from my eldest son. Rather than add a room to our existing dwelling after his marriage he built a house of his own. He hired a builder from Nazareth to lay the stone foundation and walls. The builder, a man named Joseph, worked with two of his sons.

"Strangest thing. Every so often strangers would drop by to ask questions of the oldest boy regarding Torah and other scriptures. He never stopped working but had the most amazing answers. Who was that boy?

"You know better than I the parade of imposters presenting themselves as Messiah in just your lifetime. All have failed the most basic of tests. Should Jesus pass similar, and even more rigorous tests, the world should know. Should he fail, the world should know. And I, above all others, am in position for recording and spreading this man's progress."

Immediately I regretted those last words. I felt both guilt over my self-promotion and concern over what impact that boast would have on my growing friendship with Nicodemus.

Puzzlement clouded my host's features, and not from my comments. His head made tiny movements back and forth.

"Well," he breathed, "I don't live in Galilee so can't base my decisions on rumors. I'll make a more informed decision when our delegation returns."

He stood. "Right now, you better rest."

I watched him leave. A man torn between tradition, the opinions of his peers and new possibilities putting him at odds with the Sanhedrin, the most powerful body in Judaism.

I woke next morning, rested, but desperate for bowel relief. "Jason!" I called. Being a mind reader, or so it seemed, he appeared with the necessary basins.

I'd barely finished with that unpleasant business when another face appeared at the door. Dr. Luke.

"I trust you have good news for me today," I said. "Lying here much longer will have me barking like a mad dog."

"You," Luke replied, "are a lucky man. Most physicians would have removed your leg above the knee, and that's still a possibility should you thresh about and disturb my repairs."

I swallowed and lay very still.

The doctor smiled. "Now that's better."

While he peeled back bandages, I watched his face. About what I'd expect," he said, noncommittal.

I waited for more.

"You're healing well. Swelling is down. The stitches hold. I will discontinue the leeches and leave the wound to the open air during the day. At night Jason will apply a salve."

"Poultice of figs," I assume.

Not answering he drew a stool to my bedside, looked me in the eye and stated, "I am Greek."

I raised my eyebrows and smiled. "I won't hold that against you."

He didn't smile back. "I'm Greek, but a believer in your Jehovah. I've read your scriptures and to me they suggest your Deity to be a God for all peoples."

My mind recoiled. *No! He's wrong. God's promises exist for the descendants of Abraham, Isaac and Jacob.* I tried to harmonize Luke's statement with a lifetime's teaching and study. Nothing matched.

Rituals existed whereby Luke and others could be adopted into the covenant people, but I'd never considered Jehovah worship as open to all.

Luke had paused while I digested his conclusion but he now carried on, "Nicodemus mentioned his talk with you last night and your fixation on clues. He felt you to be incomplete in your sharing."

He paused, examined me again. "Nicodemus earned his place on the Sanhedrin. He could lose it with a single misstep. He's a member of the Sanhedrin. I'm not. As a physician I seek to heal and to find new approaches to healing. As a man I seek truth."

I'd never seen a man's face so intent.

Well, I thought, he'll get the story third or fourth hand soon enough. He may as well hear it from me.

"I have to take you back thirty years," I started, wondering how often I would tell my story in secret.

I began with details of the night at Migdol Eder, the living sky, the voices, and the baby in the manger. Detailing the resistance and threats flowing from Jerusalem I summarized my change in careers.

Looking into Luke's eyes, I questioned, "Quite a string of clues wouldn't you agree? A supernatural message, a baby sent from Jehovah with *Jesus* his God-given name. Then, this story of the boy meeting teachers of the law in the temple, John the Baptist saying he prepared the way for another, and finally a man named Jesus who teaches the Scriptures as no one else before him. I believe Jesus to be the Messiah and look forward to new proofs."

The doctor sighed, straightened from the position he'd held since I began talking, stood and stretched. "Too much for the human mind. I believe you, but will need to study your Scriptures further."

He smiled. "Thank you. I know there are parts of your story you wish to remain private, and I will honor that. Should your healing continue, I will visit once more and you should be done with me."

Turning at the door, he said, "Jehovah's blessing on you."

It was then I saw Jason standing at the door. His eyes followed Luke as he passed.

He came to the bedside and when his eyes wouldn't meet mine, I knew he'd been listening. *No sense pretending,* I thought.

"Quite a story, wouldn't you say, Jason?"

He didn't smile, didn't answer. "Can I get anything for you Sir?"

"A beer would be nice. Oh, another thing. Have you ever played the game of Tau?"

A humorous glint surfaced for a moment. "Yes Sir, I do."

"Call me Micah," I said. Anymore *Sirs* and I'll have Nicodemus assign another care-giver."

"Micah." His tongue stumbled. "Remember though, I'm Greek. I have two years left of indentured service before returning to my family; a family seldom dealing with Jews and a home where Jehovah's name would find no welcome."

Once Jason got the name Micah off his tongue a few times, we concentrated on the game of twenty squares. Nearing day's end, having been beaten in all but this last I said, "Enough."

Jason placed the board in a cotton swath, and tucked it into a small chest decorated with inlaid mother of pearl.

Nicodemus arrived and spotted the box. "What have we here?" He chuckled, "Did not the physician order you to avoid excitement."

With a servant departing carrying remnants of our meal, Nicodemus opened the Tau container, and set out the board with its black and white markers. He sat down, picked up the dice, and sighed. "Best way of relieving tension I know."

For the next two weeks I seldom heard of the furor stirring the nation of Judah. Jason avoided all discussion related to Jewish religion, and Nicodemus seemed to value our stress-relieving evenings.

Jason worked every day on my knee, bending it a little more each day. Three weeks after the injury he provided balance as I took my first steps. On that day Dr. Luke returned carrying a short staff with a cross piece at the top.

He examined the knee, nodded. "Not much more I can do for you. Jehovah willing you may walk again without pain or limp."

19: Matthew

While walking along the shores of Lake Tiberias Jesus saw Levi, the son of Alpheus, busy at his taxation booth. Jesus said to him "come along with me." He came.
New Testament book of Mark ch 2, vs 14

For three days I pushed myself, first walking around the house, then, with Jason beside me, short excursions to the outer world. By third day's end, I'd mastered the crutch enough to take about thirty unaided steps.

My game of Tau with Nicodemus that night lacked its usual intensity. Lifting the final white piece that would win the game, I paused. "It's time," I said. Time for me to go home."

"I'll prepare a cart for tomorrow morning," he said.

His prompt agreement made me feel like I'd outlived my welcome. Not what I would have wanted.

Three days of jaw-clenching jolts followed before I looked up from a straw-filled ox cart to the first hint of home. That glimpse stirred my emotions and aroused hunger for Ruth's arms.

Then the cart turned a corner and the sight of transcription and marketing booths drove away thoughts of home. Did the scribes have papyrus? Had there been further threats to my business?

The oxen turned and began the climb toward home leaving the booths behind. The courtyard gate opened and business thoughts vanished as Ruth abandoned decorum and ran towards me. The driver stopped, allowing me to reach down and pull her upward and into the straw beside me. We embraced and our sobs mingled.

The cart continued, stopping near the still open courtyard gate. Ruth rearranged her robe and scrambled down, her strong arms reaching up to support me. *This is home,* I thought. *I wish to never leave again.*

I have no memory of that afternoon and evening but know we talked, shared and luxuriated in each other's company. The next morning, we moved into the patio's shade for the mid-morning meal.

A few months earlier I'd met an Ethiopian merchant in the Capernaum market. During my visit he'd crushed some dark brown beans into a powder that he poured into a pot of boiling water. After a few minutes he offered me a small cup of dark liquid. I sipped and then drank. I rather liked this new flavor and purchased a full bag. We'd been crushing them, adding the powder to boiling water and drinking the brew ever since.

Midmorning, and Ruth and I were sipping an after-meal drink of what we called kaffee, as pronounced by an Ethiopian merchant, whose market booth I'd passed only a month before. An enterprising fellow that. He'd lured me into his booth where his wife pounded some dark beans into a powder; emptied the powder into a metal bowl of hot water, heated it some more, then poured the steaming drink into a porcelain cup. After, emptying the cup, I'd purchased a small bag of beans. That bag was nearly empty.

Relaxed, with all thoughts of the seething world outside our gate pushed aside, I took simple comfort in just holding Ruth's hand, the twitter of a sun bird, and the coo of a turtle dove a pleasant backdrop.

Then, that turbulent world intruded in the person of my oldest son, Daniel. He kissed his mother and leaned his staff against a wall. I stood, awkward and unbalanced to meet his embrace. "You look well father." His eyes sparkled. "And you appear very well fed."

He saw me redden, smiled, put his hand on the staff he'd brought with him and held it toward me.

Recognition and pleasure came as twin emotions." Why that's mine. Where did you find it?"

"Your good friend, Flavinus found it at the ambush site and sent it to us by one of his soldiers. I would have arranged for a practice session, my staff against yours, which might give me a chance. Instead …" He paused gave a quirky smile and finished with "arranged a pleasant diversion. This afternoon I wish you to meet a tax collector named Matthew."

My face tightened. "Ha! Tax collectors and pleasant diversions can hardly live within a single sentence."

"Daniel shook his head. "Don't be so prejudiced. You'll be glad to meet this one."

The sun hung halfway to the horizon before Daniel brought Matthew into our shaded courtyard. A tax collector's aura surrounded this unwelcome guest. Tall and thin; his rich robes, his confidence, his upright frame and chiseled features, seemed to shout hard-nosed extortionist. Nevertheless, I stood and bowed as I would to any man entering my home.

"Please sit down." I pointed to a bench where a large bougainvillea draped over the courtyard wall. He sat as a maid arrived with a platter of honey cakes, three mugs and a pitcher of fruit sherbet.

Daniel placed a stool beside me and stepped back. Not sitting down and balancing forward on my crutch I looked down on Matthew. He looked back, his eyes bland.

Our awkward silence stretched until Daniel broke in. "I'm interviewing two new scribes this afternoon. There is little more I can offer here so will leave. Only Jehovah could have arranged a meeting between tax collector and merchant and I trust Him to bless your conversation." He stood, unlatched the courtyard gate, and departed.

Matthew remained; seated and silent, his eyes drifting over the courtyard and entrance to our dwelling. I could imagine his tax collector mind evaluating the worth of my property and calculating what additional revenue he might squeeze from it.

"I'm puzzled" I said; "tax collectors seldom bring good news, but Daniel says you're an exception. I'm waiting."

"There are few secrets in Galilee," Matthew's smile was the first I'd ever seen on the face of a tax collector; "and your need for papyrus is common knowledge. His smile slipped. Some have taken advantage of that need, one of them a member of my profession who confiscated fifty percent of one load.

"I... I didn't know." Caleb had delivered no such news of tax collector robbery.

"And then," continued Matthew, "Roman soldiers confiscated this half full cart along with its mules."

I shut my eyes; rubbed my nose, shock running through me. When I looked up, Matthew nodded.

"You didn't even know, but you do know fire consumed at least half of what you had left." Wordless, I just listened as he continued.

"If you would agree to be in a tax collector's debt, I will take one of your servants and collect the items taken through dishonest taxation. I'm sorry, but those goods confiscated by the Romans are beyond my control."

"Take Daniel," I said.

He remained seated. "You know why I'm doing this?"

My headshake answered.

Matthew's eyes closed for a moment; then opened. "I've been following the progress of a young teacher from Nazareth named Jesus along with your efforts to spread his teaching. Even your need for papyrus came to my ears many weeks ago."

I interrupted. "How do you know about missing papyrus and I don't?"

"Tax collectors hear things. Announcements, whispers, idle gossip. My booth once rested on the shores of this very lake below Capernaum."

Once? My question remained unspoken.

"I know you've taken an interest in this religious teacher named Jesus. Well, a short time ago, Jesus passed my booth and said, *Levi, follow me.*

My confusion must have shown and Matthew interrupted himself. "Levi, the name I taxed by, Matthew otherwise and forever."

In a moment he had collected his thoughts and continued, "Jesus gave those words only once, then just stood and waited for my answer. As a young boy I'd dreamed of following a rabbi, but those dreams vanished when I became a tax collector. Tax collectors and rabbis don't usually mix.

Matthew shifted his weight on the bench before continuing, "My heart stirred, but a doubt remained. *Who was this Jesus? I'd heard of no other followers. Would I be the only one?* My eyes looked into his and without a single regret I left my booth in the care of my assistant to follow a man, I now call *Teacher*."

My confusion must have shown for he continued, "I know of your transcription service and believe you serve my teacher just as do I. However, I must emphasize that my teacher, Jesus of Nazareth, pursues truth wherever it leads. He is beholden to no one. Before accepting any aid from me you must promise to never embellish or dramatize his words."

"Jesus, of Nazareth?" I questioned, "Now there's a puzzle. I remember no Scriptures, suggesting either a prophet or the Messiah to originate in Nazareth?"

A smile creased Matthew's face. "Did not Isaiah and other prophets call Messiah *The Branch*?"

"What are…?" I started, before remembering Isaiah's prophecy of Messiah being an inconspicuous branch sprouting from King David's family tree.

"Huh! You are a tricky one," I shook my head, providing my own answer to the half-finished question. "*A branch;* same root letters as Nazareth. Not very convincing but clever."

Matthew sobered. "Not convincing to you maybe, but for me, the coincidence too definitive to ignore."

Inconspicuous branch. Old memories stirred. Familiar memories, replayed over and over. A stable. A newborn baby and circumstances of poverty and ritual impurity beyond anything I could have ever imagined. Beyond even the imagination of our most gloomy prophets. Once more I considered the possibility of mass insanity striking our small group of shepherds and wondered whether such insanity could last a lifetime.

Opening eyes I hadn't remembered closing I noted Matthew's appraising gaze.

Cutting off further questions, I said, "Your conditions create no problems. Even before I'd heard of Jesus from Nazareth, I'd given instructions to my son Benjamin and the young scholar, Jacob, to seek out John the Baptizer and record with complete accuracy his words and actions. Those orders remain in place for Jesus of Nazareth."

Matthew nodded.

"And I intend a wide circulation of those accounts."

Matthew dipped his head again. "I could ask nothing more. Now, your son Daniel and I have work to do."

20: Sara

Jesus began a tour of the cities and towns of Galilee announcing the coming of the Kingdom of God and took his disciples with him. Some women went along...Mary Magdalene...Joanna, Chuza's wife (Chuza being King Herod's business manager) Suzanna and many others who gave from their private means in order to support Jesus and his disciples.

*F*rom the beginning of chapter 8, book of Luke.

But a brief time after Matthew and Daniel returned with their precious papyrus, Flavinus surprised me by delivering the final cart, a treasure I'd considered lost forever.

I hobbled towards this strange centurion where he sat his mount. My voice trembled. "Why do you do these things?"

Flavinus smiled down. "Why you're my favorite Jew. Can you think of any other reason?" He sobered. "You do amazing work. I've read every one of your tracts on the preaching of John the Baptizer and now look forward to your writings on Jesus of Nazareth. How can I do less than make sure you have materials to satisfy my hunger? You Jews just might be losing your exclusive claim to Jehovah's Messiah."

Jolted, I stepped back, but too thankful to question, I could only say, "Thank you and Jehovah's blessings rest on you," while inside my head a thought whirled." *That sounds just like Doctor Luke.*

Turning his mount to leave, Flavinus leaned over and paid the driver.

Thankful for my momentary change in fortune, I knew it couldn't last. The same powerful forces driving me from Migdol Eder decades previous had grown no weaker. A faint desperate plan began taking shape. Concentrating on putting flesh to this mental skeleton I proceeded to my work lectern in the library. Immersed in the process of placing stylus to wax tablet a voice startled me.

"Father."

I jerked, stylus slipping from my fingers.

"I'm sorry," Sara apologized, as I turned to welcome her.

Normally impetuous, usually fearless, and sometimes self-controlled, she seemed flustered.

Noticing a flask in one hand, I smiled. "Yes, favorite daughter. I see you've remembered your father's usual neglect of drink. Thank you."

The flask remained at her side.

Spreading my hands in question, I waited.

Sara released a breath, almost a sob. "Did you know that Jesus and his disciples preach and teach without support from any tithes or offerings. Even worse, none of the twelve standing by him day and night possess an income. So far they are dependent on the charity of women followers, only some of them wealthy.

Again the half sob and a moment to collect her thoughts. "Do you remember Joanna, Chuza's wife?"

"Of course, I remember. You, your mother and I met her as our rabbi blessed our newest transcription booth. He hadn't yet raised his hands before a covered chariot complete with armed guard approached. The chariot paused until the rabbi finished his blessing; then a richly dressed lady stepped down. She approached you and your mother and asked about the purpose of our booths. You explained and she purchased a copy of each tract in our collection as well as a parchment scroll containing the Psalms. I remember because that was the last parchment scroll we produced before reverting to papyrus.

"And then what?" Sara asked.

"Your mother invited the lady for refreshments."

"And?"

"A few days later, this lady, Johanna invited you and your mother to visit her in Tiberias and tour Herod's palace. Where is this conversation taking us?"

"While you were recuperating at the house of Nicodemus in Jerusalem, Johanna visited again and told us she intended to travel with Jesus and his disciples to help in whatever way she could. I volunteered to go with her, but mother wouldn't allow it. Now Jesus is about to go up to Jerusalem and Joanna and others will go too. May I go with them?"

An ache pulsed inside my head. A recurring headache troubling me since my confrontation with Barabbas.

I always worked standing when in the library but, feeling an urgent need to sit, I motioned towards the door and we moved to the courtyard with questions swirling through my mind.

Can a responsible father allow his daughter such freedom?

Sara's smart, practical, resilient. Imagine her contribution to my accounts of Jesus should I agree to her request.

What if my suspicions are correct and this Jesus of Nazareth is indeed the baby of Bethlehem? Will Sara's assistance help erase the debt I owe for my many years of cowardice?

We sat, my decision made. "You may go."

A radiant glow blossomed across her face. She stood, walked over to me, knelt and placed my hand on her head. "Bless me, Father."

21: Sara's Story

Let us go to the Lord's house; let us bow before His throne.
Psalm 132:7 circa 800 bce

My heart fluttered like a newly caged bird as Benjamin and I approached Chuza's house. We had a large dwelling but Chuza's compound dwarfed ours. The opulence disturbed me and I reached for Benjamin's hand.

For a moment unholy thoughts washed over me. *Why she's rich, richer than my father. And me! I've never lacked anything. What help can I ever be to a travelling rabbi who doesn't even enjoy the luxury of riding on the back of a mule or even a donkey.*

I'd been totally shocked at Father's easy agreement with my request to travel with Joanna and the small group of women who supported Jesus and his disciples. I almost wished he'd said, "No!"

Johanna's confidence in Jesus reassured me, but how about his disciples. Matthew had seemed an honorable man, but I knew some of the others to be just ordinary fishermen. Johanna possessed a striking beauty. Jacob called me pretty. Father and mother had never allowed me to be alone with a man. Would I be safe?

In preparation for my upcoming trek, Benjamin and I had walked the four miles from our home to Chuza's palatial dwelling in Tiberias. Benjamin knocked on a courtyard gate that opened to reveal Johanna's beaming face. If it hadn't been for her face, I would not have recognized her. No flowing robes today. No jewelry. Just a plain outer robe falling to her feet and a cord around her waist that supported an apron and pouch. A shawl covered her shoulders, loose enough to draw over braided hair.

My clothing mirrored hers.

I felt tension flowing through Benjamin's body as he embraced me before his departure. He'd shown no approval of my adventure, even quoting words attributed to Jesus, *The birds of the air have nests and foxes dens, yet I have no fixed place to lay my head.*

Benjamin's warning rang through my mind again, as I watched him depart.

Sensing my misgivings, Johanna said, "Come, my dear. We will discuss our plans while the maid serves refreshments." She led me to a low table in the courtyard and we knelt on thick rugs. I followed Johanna's lead and bowed my head for the prayer I knew to be coming.

"Blessed be your name Jehovah, our Redeemer. You have blessed Israel with enduring hope of Messiah. We believe the words of your servant Moses, who informed our ancestors of a coming prophet like himself, but greater. We believe you will soon reveal this prophet, Messiah, to our nation. As Sara and I go this day to assist the rabbi, Jesus of Nazareth, help us live and serve well."

Lifting her head, Johanna smiled across the table; "Jesus stays at Peter's house in Capernaum for the moment," she said, "but he and his disciples plan to be in Jerusalem for the feast of booths. You, I and three other women will assure that he and the men travelling with him eat well and have a place to sleep each night. Sometimes we will need to pay for rooms in an inn. There may be times when we sleep on the ground, though the name of Jesus opens many doors. Do you prepare meals?"

"No," I stammered," but I have money to help pay for food and rent."

That I might be asked to cook had never entered my mind. I stared at Johanna, thinking, *How come a rich lady like you talks of meal preparation?* Then I remembered stories from my mother and her early struggles to avoid starvation.

But I'd never starved; never remembered going hungry.

Father! Father! Why didn't you say No? Then, remembering his sad eyes, eyes full of hidden memories, as he'd said "Yes," I straightened. *I'm my father's daughter, and I'm in this for a reason.*

Taking a deep breath, I waited.

"Now, it's off to the stables. What a joy to have you join us. We've never had anyone so young."

At the stable we found three sturdy donkeys, packed and ready. Each donkey raised its head as though in greeting as Johanna picked up the halter shank on the only donkey wearing such control, and, voice bubbling with enthusiasm, said, "You'll follow behind the other two and should one lag, encourage them with this." She gave me a short stick.

The donkeys tap-tapped over a stone-paved walkway until we

reached the dust-capped road leading to Capernaum where the donkey taps turned into a dust-puffing shuffle. I sneezed once before settling in, my imagination producing multiple unpleasant scenarios.

The growing density of the dusty shroud around me added mystery to the yellow sun's brightness and the intense, shimmering blue of Lake Kinneret. Gradually misgivings faded and a joy of living infused me.

Hindered by the donkey's slow pace, we travelled for over four hours before approaching Capernaum. At first glimpse of the little fishing town, I hesitated, sudden apprehension replacing recent euphoria. Then I noticed a small crowd gathered by the lakeshore. A man stood in a boat just a short distance from the crowd, arms waving as though emphasizing important statements.

"I see Peter," Johanna exclaimed and the donkeys stopped.

"Watch the donkeys while I talk to him."

The donkeys took the liberty of wandering off the road to graze, so I turned to watch Johanna's graceful progress down the slope. *Different than mother,* I thought. *Free-spirited, unafraid of risk.* Then came an unsettling thought. *Where will her risks take me?*

When Johanna, in company with a man, not Peter, broke away from the group below, my normal courage took flight. I pressed my hands together to hide their shaking. Only when I noted the man to be shorter than Johanna did my nerves settle; giving me space to evaluate the stranger. He may have been shorter than Johanna, but his bulk doubled hers. The smell of fish preceded him, but a well-trimmed beard, hair slicked down and maybe even combed, suggested more than normal refinement for a fisherman. A multi-colored headband matched his tunic belt.

Intense green eyes examined me.

"Sara, this is John. He, and his brother James are two of those travelling with us to Jerusalem.

Bowing, I remained silent.

"Very happy to have you with us, Sara." The words caught me with head still bowed. "You will have very few dull moments following Jesus of Nazareth. Or quiet ones either. Our teacher has been rushing through Galilee with a lesson for everyone he meets. And now he's off to Judea and Jerusalem.

"We'll be leaving within the next hour."

Unmoving, heart racing, I felt paralyzed. I didn't even hear his closing words to Johanna.

Below us the crowd began dispersing while another man tugged on an anchor rope bringing the boat to shore.

"Come," Johanna said. She tugged on her donkey's halter shank, and, after encouraging one of the other donkeys with a whack, I followed her downslope.

As we neared the men on the beach a woman's pleading voice stopped us. "Jesus of Nazareth, please help!"

Shifting focus, I saw three women approaching. Two of them half-carrying a third whose contorted face and stumbling walk suggested anguish beyond imagining.

Nearing Jesus, the sick woman twisted free and fell to the ground writhing and moaning. One of the other women knelt to give aid; then drew back at a dangerous, uncontrolled thrashing.

The kneeling woman looked up at Jesus. "Please help. We come from the village of Magdala where an evil spirit came upon our friend Mary. She is a good woman. Please help," she entreated.

I saw the man I took to be Jesus, raise his face heavenward, lips moving; then he too knelt beside Mary. His hand touched hers and she snatched it away.

"Leave her! Do not speak!" The command burst through Jesus' lips with assured authority.

I looked on, mouth open.

The words slammed into Mary like an ox goad. She grunted, screamed and curled into a ball; arms wrapped around her knees. She lay unmoving.

"You must all leave." This time Jesus' voice, calm, conversational.

Searching for an exit path believing those words were meant for me, I paused on hearing another grunt, this time weaker, and saw a tremor pass through Mary's body. Jesus waited.

Five more times the grunt and the twitch before her body grew still again; contorted features smoothing.

I closed my eyes, felt my knees tremble. My stomach churned and I suppressed an urge to vomit. *What have I just seen? Will father believe this?*

Jesus interrupted my thoughts by taking Mary's unresisting hand. "Mary of Magdala, stand." Once upright, Mary looked down at her disheveled clothing and brushed away the clinging sand as the two friends came to her aid.

"Mary of Magdala, go in Jehovah's grace."

With my attention on Mary, I didn't even see Jesus turn his eyes my way.

"Child," his voice drew my attention. "Be strong. You've seen the Father's work and you will see much more."

He turned to a burly man near him. "Peter, lead the way to Jerusalem. There I will worship in my Father's House."

They'd gone but a few steps when Mary of Magdala rushed forward to fall on her knees before Jesus. "Rabbi, please, please let me go with you."

Again Jesus stretched out his hand and raised her upright. "You may follow, Mary of Magdala. The road will be rough; your spirit tested again and again. The demons just departed will seek return."

He turned with a smile for Johanna, "As usual, I press new tasks on you. Attend to Mary and make her welcome. Pray the Father's protection on her."

At this point I felt even younger and naiver than my father believed me to be. And, who I wondered, was this Father Jesus referred to? Had not his own died years before?

The morning following our first day of travel revealed the first ripple of tension in our little group as Peter argued with Jesus. "We always cross to the other side of the Jordan at this point. We can't follow your path; it takes us through Samaria."

Jesus head tilted up towards the larger man. "We go through Samaria."

My feet, unused to walking, grew increasingly tender. I hid my limp until midway through the second day when something on my foot popped and a wet patch appeared on my left sandal. Dust and sand collected in the moisture until my foot refused to endure the pain of another step.

Johanna and Mary of Magdala had been walking beside Jesus, but the moment I stopped Johanna turned and dashed back towards me.

"Child, what is it?"

For a moment that word "child" made me try another step. Instantly Johanna looked down, knelt in the dust and raised my foot. A look of horror crossed her face.

Ahead, despite my misery I noticed, Jael a grandmother with greying hair, take Johanna's place beside Jesus.

I felt like crying, "Jesus, I need you more than they do. Come help." Instead, Andrew, Simon Peter's brother joined Johanna at my feet.

Johanna looked up. "We'll move off the path, wash off the sand and dirt, and wrap your injury." Turning her head toward Andrew she said, "The child cannot walk another step. She will have to ride one of the pack donkeys."

A few minutes later, Andrew and Johanna hoisted me onto a donkey's back and the two brothers, James and John, took up the load I'd displaced.

Shamed and frustrated, and with shawl-covered face, I suffered, not quite in silence due to an occasional, muffled sob.

A humorous chuckle made me jerk back the shawl ready for some overly solicitous comment such as, "Child, how are you feeling?" Instead I looked into the eyes of Jesus.

"Sara, are you pouting?"

I didn't answer.

His face grew serious. "Remember the warning I gave Mary of Magdala. The road ahead will be rough. It will test you, body, soul and spirit. Sore feet and aching body are the least of your worries. Right now, you're salving your physical pain beneath a blanket of soul agony. Your feet will heal and toughen. Be concerned for your soul."

His eyes searched mine. He smiled again. I could not help but smile back.

"Thank you," he said. "Your smile makes my day. It's a gift from God, practice it."

With those words he turned away. A tingle ran through my body. Jesus had noticed me.

With shawl in its normal position over my shoulders I saw Jael moving towards me, worry lines adding to her age. I smiled and her tightened features loosened and relaxed into a broad smile of her own.

Thank you, Jesus, I thought. *That smile worked. Worked for me and worked for Jael.* My lips moved in silent prayer, *Lord God Almighty keep my lips smiling. Thank you for Johanna. Keep her patient with me and help me learn from her so that I can better serve Jesus and his disciples.*

Still on the donkey I reached Bethany and found a large house near the town's edge on the Mount of Olives. Before Jesus and Peter could reach the courtyard gate it swung open and a man and two women burst out. Jesus and Peter both embraced the man and bowed to the women.

Being at the rear of our little caravan, I had opportunity to observe the three who'd been so welcoming. The man, tall, pale, thinning hair and sparse beard. One of the women, also tall, larger framed than the man, thin faced, and efficient in movement. The last of the trio, smaller, face more round, had an attractive fluidity of motion.

Their clothing matched the fineness of the dwelling with decorative stitchery and careful tailoring.

With greetings still in progress, the taller lady whispered to the man, ducked back into the house and left by a side entrance.

Slipping off the donkey's back, I limped towards the group as Jesus began introductions. With his hand on the man's shoulder and face turned towards us, Jesus said, "This is my friend Lazarus, just recovering from a serious illness, and these are his sisters. A puzzled look crossed his face as his head turned. "Where's Martha?"

Stepping away from Jesus, Lazarus said, "Martha left for provisions. Welcome to our home. You are our guests."

Peter protested. "No! No!" We are too many. We just need help in finding accommodations."

Lazarus laughed. "You're here just before festival. Though we've yet to take in guests, some of our neighbors already overflow. "Martha will see that we manage."

Jesus nudged Peter. And with that, it seemed, this one dwelling would host our group of eighteen. When Johanna took my arm and headed for a bench in the courtyard, I held back but she kept going and pressed me to a seat.

So, from that bench I watched as others unloaded the donkeys and brought in what supplies remained following our journey. Sitting there, dejection creeping over me, I saw one of the disciples approaching. He drew up a small wooden stool and sat down eyes level with mine.

The ride had given opportunity to observe each of those in the caravan. Naturally, I paid most attention to the disciples, though women should never look long at any man. Generally, I observed from under my shawl to avoid appearing immodest.

Not having been introduced I'd heard most of the disciples' names in conversation. If I didn't know a name, I made one up. This disciple lacked the special intensity I'd noticed in each of the others. His round face, slight paunch, and jolly laugh reminded me of an old mule we'd pastured far beyond his useful years. We children had named him Hee-Haw, and so I'd tagged this disciple.

He spoke softly, "You make me think of the words of King Solomon when he wrote; Charm can deceive, and beauty vanish, but one admires a woman who fears the Lord.

He gave a quick smile. "Best of all, though, is a woman who fears the Lord and possesses good manners and beauty. The master has done well in selecting you for his service."

Shrinking inside, I couldn't speak. I'd never talked to a man alone other than those in my family and Jacob. "Hee-Haw," the thought rose unbidden bringing a smile.

He seemed to take my smile as appreciation for his compliment and continued, "I realize you have a letter from your father giving you credit in many locations. However, we often run short of funds where no credit exists. We have no idea where Jesus leads from one day to the next. I manage our purse and pay travelling expenses. Should you be able to access funds to place in the general treasury the master would thank you."

I saw Johanna approaching and welcomed the interruption. "Judas," she said, "Sara is tired and sore and everything's new and I should be with her when you explain the communal purse."

Judas flushed, stood and bowed. "Of course, Lady Johanna. The child appeared downcast and I but wished to restore her usual joyful self."

When Johanna's eyes returned to me, she smiled, "There's a room for meal preparation inside. We may be able to put you to work."

Inside, Martha rushed about like a hyperactive honeybee, assigning tasks, organizing supplies, and sending a continuous line of water carriers to the neighborhood well.

Mary started fires in two ovens, a large one of brick with a large firebox, the other smaller and of baked clay.

Martha had just removed the last of the coals from the brick oven and inserted several mounds of dough, closed the opening of the firebox and left the loaves to bake in the trapped heat. The other oven of baked clay and looked like a large, lop-sided urn with an opening at the front for firewood.

Small, stuttering flames glowed within the urn-like oven. Martha exited a back doorway and returned with an apron full of olive branches and twigs. She motioned me over. "Keep the fire burning Sara. We have hungry men to feed."

So, I began feeding the oven, quite proud of the multiplying new flames.

"What are you doing?" Martha's voice interrupted as she reached over my shoulder with a metal rod; then stirred the wood until dancing flames became only glowing coals.

"Those flames are dangerous. A little longer and the oven would have cracked. I'll now have to tend the fires along with everything else. See if one of the other women has work for you."

I stood for a moment; initial tears a prelude to uncontrolled sobbing. Something I couldn't remember doing in my entire life.

"Sara," a soft voice interrupted.

I kept my head turned, tears blinding me.

"Sara, come with me." A hand on my shoulder turned me around, and I followed Mary, the sister of Lazarus, into the courtyard. "Sit here." She pointed to a small rug.

I sat and she placed a platter full of onions, garlic and leeks on my lap. A small bronze knife lay on the tray's edge. "For these to go into the pot they must be prepared thus; she reached for the knife and demonstrated.

When she placed the knife in my hand I felt better. I may not have any experience in food preparation, but I knew knives. Benjamin and I had often carved small figurines and objects.

Mary returned as I finished her assignment. "Wait for a moment," she said and took the platter.

Waiting stretched and anxiety grew.

When Mary came back, she carried something very familiar. *A lyre.* The sight of the instrument in Mary's arms brought a tingle to my fingers.

"The men are wearied in body but not in voice," she said. "I believe you play this instrument, and may be able to calm the level of debate unsettling our roof tiles. Will you do that for us?"

With shaking hands I grasped the lyre's arched arms. *Play for Jesus and his disciples? How could I?*

Jael appeared with a tray of parched barley, some dates, and a bowl of wine and held it toward me. "You may be long on the rooftop so best you strengthen yourself."

Too nervous to eat, I drank the wine while adjusting the strings to my liking.

Jael followed three other women up the stairs to the rooftop each carrying a food-laden tray. When we reached the flat roof and I saw the thirteen men; some seated cross-legged on a mat; others reclining and leaning on an elbow, my strength drained away.

Sensing me sag, Jael reached back a supporting arm. "You can do this Sara."

I gathered myself and we stepped onto the rooftop. Thirteen pairs of eyes turned my way while mine sought Jesus.

Jael paused, her heavy tray balanced in one hand, uncertain as to where to place it. In a flash, Jesus, stood and took the tray. He gave a slight bow. "Thank you."

Before Jesus even turned my way, I thought, *Even my father would not have done that.* Then I heard his voice. "I see you have come to bless us with music. We're a loud bunch and that's for sure. Opinions do differ, though we all seek to serve the Father, creator of all that's good. And what better way to praise the Father than with music as the writer of our psalms says; *Let the earth shout to the Lord in praise and with the harmonies of harp and song.*

He smiled, a quirky little curl of his lips, "And will you be singing for us too?"

While heat rose through my cheeks, confidence enveloped me. I bowed, "If you wish Master."

He smiled again and Jael led me to a low stool in a corner of the protective parapet surrounding the flat roof. I sat, placed the base of the harp on my lap and leaned my shoulder into the top brace. This left both hands free, one on either side of the instrument. My fingers gave a tentative pluck to each of the seven strings and then the lyre caught me in its spell.

Not so caught up in the music, though, that my mind couldn't drift back; back to the scroll of Ruth given to me by my father for my eighth birthday. The story of Ruth, so much more interesting than the writings of Moses.

Looking over to where Jesus, had rejoined Matthew and John in concentrated discussion, I gave an extra trill to the lyre strings wondering if Jesus had ever applied fingers and mind to the lyre. I felt my smile as I thought, *Your ancestor, King David was a master, and I wonder who taught him. I think it was his grandmother, Ruth.*

Next morning, Martha had us up when the first grey of dawn gave just enough light to see moving figures.

I opened my eyes to see Martha kneeling at a fire-making chore, fanning coals into life from the night before. I rose up from the floor, straightened my robe, took some tentative steps to assess my mobility and found very little pain.

Martha turned to Jael, "You know the well's location. Go now before it becomes busy. Take the girl."

Girl, I fretted. *Child.* I am neither. Most of my friends are already married. Some have children of their own. Why don't people just call me Sara.

I regretted more than ever my father's approval of this escapade.

Jael and I reached the well before any of the other village women. With our jars full, I saw Jael hoist hers with an easy swing onto the broad edge of the stone casing surrounding the well. I attempted a similar move and barely escaped dropping both jar and contents.

Jael watched my futile efforts for a few seconds before lowering her own jar. "Let me help you. You must learn to use rhythm as much as strength. It takes time. But we'll just get it on your head and hurry back."

With jar balanced on my head, knees wobbling, and results of dropping the jar filling my imagination, I staggered back. Nearing our destination, I looked up to where the men had come to life. In a corner of the balustrade a man knelt, praying. It was Jesus.

Jael and I made three trips to the well. I didn't drop the jar, though my knees wobbled.

The men ate quickly, broke into groups and left for the temple. We washed and swept and filled water jars. There would, it appeared, be an evening meal.

Mary joined the rest of us in our own day at the temple while Martha seemed too busy in preparations for the evening. Excitement made my steps light, my sore foot no longer an issue. Father's absence from the temple through my lifetime made this my first visit.

We followed a path leading down from the Mount of Olives and on toward Jerusalem passing little shelters occupying every niche of space. The Festival of Booths, booths now emptying their occupants into a stream of pilgrims marching toward the temple. Here and there little groups of people would break into song.

Jerusalem's surrounding wall towered ever higher as we neared; impressive in size and impressive in beauty with its white limestone walls; stones laid with mathematical precision, and topped with a steady march of crenelated battlements. Facing us, beckoning us an open gate ingested the flow of worshippers, it's surface flashing bright in the morning sun.

"The Golden Gate." Johanna's voice penetrated through my awe-struck haze.

We stood, mesmerized, until pressure from behind pushed us forward, through the gates and onto frescoed tiles covering the floor of a large courtyard. City walls were behind us and another low wall rose about 40 feet in front. Massive pillars on either side of us reached for the sky and supported a roof far above.

Buzzing sounds of commerce erased all sense of the holiness I had expected. Pilgrims, many in strange clothing, thronged the tables where they exchanged secular currency for temple coinage. Off to the right, would-be worshippers surrounded more merchants who were selling penned lambs and caged doves.

Johanna, however, never slowed, just turned left, waded through the throngs surrounding the merchandisers and paused near a flight of broad steps leading upward to a higher level. She away from the main traffic flow and pointed, "Beyond those stairs lies the court of the women. From this viewpoint you can actually glimpse the temple."

The stairway shut off much of the view, but I could see the top of a towering gate, polished bronze flashing in the sunlight and through that gate a golden glow of temple dome and a portion of white pillar.

A sign stood beside the stairway. *Foreigners are forbidden further entry. Should a foreigner be found beyond the walls of this outer courtyard, he will die, having earned the reward for disobedience.*

Mary touched my arm, pointed to the sign and turned to the crowds. "Look around you."

I did and saw only massed bodies, some mixed among the commercial tables and booths, others walking ahead of us up the steps.

"What do you see?" she asked.

I shrugged and spread my hands.

"Exactly! Where we're standing should be a space where we welcome foreigners in their desire to worship Jehovah, as do we. Do you see any foreigners?"

I examined the crowd, seeing many shades of brown, a few verging on black, but nothing suggesting a Gentile.

"Why would there be a court for foreigners," I asked. " Especially such a large space? And wouldn't Gentiles make us all unclean?"

Mary gave a gentle smile. "Who designed this temple?"

"King Herod?"

"Wrong answer. Remember Moses and the tent of meeting in which our ancestors worshipped after their deliverance from Egypt. Who provided that design? Remember King David who began collecting material for a temple before his son Solomon was even born. Who gave the design for that first temple? Do you really believe this temple had a different designer than all the others?"

I thought back to words from the book of Exodus. God had spoken to Moses directly. *You must build a tent of meeting using the precise instructions I am to give you.*

I looked round trying to imagine this space filled with Greeks, Romans, Persians, Egyptians, Africans and who knew what other races existed and shivered.

Mary saw my frown and gestured me onward. I paused near the top of the stairs and looked again at the space below.

A man brushed past, glanced at me, and wiped his sleeve where it had touched mine.

Ahead, Johanna sought an open space in which we could collect in mutual worship of Jehovah. A crowd, composed of both men and women, pressed our little group towards the barrier separating the women's court from that of the men. We found a little space near the semicircular stairway leading upwards to the men's court.

A chanted psalm helped quiet the crowd. I looked for the source and found it in twenty-four men arranged on the outer rim of the twelve steps.

I heard familiar words. Words familiar to both my fingers and lips. I hummed along.

The scepter will be torn from the hands of the wicked
That they no longer oppress the righteous of the land.

Feeling pressure on my hand I glanced at Mary to see tear-filled eyes. I smiled, holding back my own emotions and turned attention to the sights around me.

Men passed up and down between the singers, entering through and exiting the enormous gates. Gates taller than ten men standing shoulder on shoulder. From my position I could plainly see one of the open gates and an etching of a beautiful city on the polished brass.

Johanna gathered us and we linked arms to form a tight circle. Overwhelmed by the hypnotic chant in the background and the awe-inspiring size and beauty of the space in which I stood, my face lifted toward heaven. We stood thus until Johanna whispered. "Time to return."

Pausing at this point in her story Sara held out her bowl. "More wine please."

She sipped as a frown wrinkled her brow giving emphasis to her growing maturity.

After a slight headshake, she continued. "I heard this from Jael, who in turn overheard the disciples. It seems Jesus had arrived at the temple after us, along with the brothers James and John. They entered through the Golden Gate just as we had. Jesus led, threading the way through the masses surrounding the merchants. The attention he gave each merchant made James and John more and more nervous. When Jesus began retracing his steps, anger pouring from his every movement, their worry changed to fear.

Near the entry gate where the merchants gathered in clusters, he gave a great shout and kicked in a fence surrounding a group of lambs. He opened a cage holding doves and watched them fly away.

The noisy crowds hushed as Jesus stalked towards tables of the moneychangers.

Not sure what was happening the crowd began separating themselves from the tables. Again, Jesus shouted, and turned over one table after another.

Horrified and frozen, James and John could only watch as Jesus mounted the short wall behind the tables. Their disheveled master stood for several seconds in silence; then spoke in a voice shaking with emotion and amplified by the walls around him.

"You! He pointed to a priest passing by. "You, and you and you;" his finger moved over the merchants. "My Father gave you this place for prayer and worship and you have turned it into a nest of thieves."

Ruth, Daniel, Benjamin and I sat near Sara as she recounted her experiences with Jesus. Jacob stood in the background. After a deep breath she ran her eyes over each of us; "What did Jesus mean to accomplish? Men have been found guilty of blasphemy and killed for less." She paused, her eyes questioning, waiting for an answer.

22: Sanhedrin Chill

Israel's priests have both despised my law and debased my holy things, making no distinction between holy and commonplace.
Words of the prophet Ezekiel: circa 580 bce

And that's all, Sara finished, her eyes passing over the room.

Jacob blurted, "Jesus talked to you?" It seemed Jacob's mind had frozen on that one image, to the exclusion of much else.

Ignoring the unintended insult, Sara turned to her mother. "Jesus spoke to our women's group more than once, reminding us of the special roles played by women in the Scriptures. In one instance he commented on the woman's place in his kingdom. That puzzled me."

She paused as though pondering the statement again before continuing: "He even had a story built around the name of our travelling companion, Jael."

She glanced at Jacob then back to her mother. "I'm sure we all remember the Canaanite general Sisera and how he begged refuge in the tent of a woman named Jael. His chosen place for a nap proved fatal and while he slept Jael drove a tent peg through his temple. That action prevented Sisera from returning to home base and building another army."

That evening alone with Ruth I commented, "Remember my telling of Luke's comment about understanding our Scriptures better than most Jews. Now I know what he meant. Our daughter's account with all its digressions gave me a better picture of Jesus than anything Jacob or

Benjamin could have done. I think Luke builds big pictures as he reads without undue attention to every word."

Ruth looked into my eyes, a glint of humor in her own, "Now that takes a real man to admit such a thing."

She sighed. "But what will Sara do next?"

When Sara woke the next morning with vomiting, fever and diarrhea, we forgot about her future with worries of the present.

With Ruth nursing Sara, I returned to my library and business matters but before getting settled I heard a rapping on our courtyard gate.

Peering down from the library window I saw Eldad, an excellent reader and one of those helping Daniel manage the daily work of production and marketing for our transcription enterprise.

A face overwritten with panic faced me as a maid ushered him into the library. Seeking to soothe him I gestured toward a stool and gave a friendly. "Jehovah's blessings on you this morning, Eldad. Will you come in and share our morning meal?"

My words didn't seem to register.

"Sir, a rabbi and two Pharisees from Nazareth question our transcribers."

The cowardly vultures, I thought, reaching for my sandals and supporting staff.

Limping up to the booths, I saw three men standing in front of the six transcribers and reader in the near booth. One of the men whose long phylacteries and rich robe spoke of Pharisee, perused a parchment scrap. I heard his accusing voice, "This, I found on the ground. Do you treat all the sacred words with which you work in such a careless manner?"

Anger filled me as I stepped between the three men and my workers. "Do not torment these men. I answer all questions relating to my business."

The accuser, still with the papyrus scrap in hand clenched his jaws and stood his ground.

"Move!" I said.

The scribes, hearing my words, laid aside their quills and stood as one.

Not willing to appear defeated they back stepped. I followed, anger bubbling inside. "Who are you that you accost my employees in the midst of their daily work?"

"We are Jehovah's servants, and here on Jehovah's business," the man with the parchment scrap answered.

"Ha! You may be here on business, but not Jehovah's. You only fear that God's word may reach the hands of God's people.

"Leave!"

After uttering those words, a twinge of fear seasoned my anger. These men were religious leaders and could do me great harm. The kind of men who had already done me such harm.

Trying to soften my words, I bowed, "Now blessings on your travels."

Turning back to the men in the transcription booth, I could not hide my unease. "This is a troubling day and I believe we will see more. We must trust God. The words of a Psalm come to mind.

I began, and the others joined.

O Lord save me from evil men, and protect me from evil doers, whose hearts plan wickedness and hands create harm.

The tongues of such evil men are as sharp as those of a serpent with lips spitting the venom of asps."

Righteous men thank Your name, Oh Lord, and honest men live where you are.

The words of King David seemed to have eased the anxiety of those around me replacing unease with a tinge of self-righteousness.

Returning to the house I checked on Sara, then went to the library to ponder the meaning of this unwelcome visit. Too restless to sit I wandered outside. My path led upward until I looked down on Lake Kinneret and my extensive estate. Over the years I'd expanded my holdings, but the recent growth of Herod's new city, Tiberias, had forced surrender of some property.

Surveying the landscape below I pictured the original cottage where the villa now stood. I ran my eyes over our small, terraced orchard, with its adjoining grape and olive grove and remembered the months of work involved in changing a barren hillside into the terraced, verdant garden now lying before me. I remembered the first wine from the vineyard, not the best, but still exciting.

The beauty of the hillside however was as nothing compared to the simple and rather mundane booths near the seashore and the road passing from Capernaum south to Jerusalem. No one knew better than I that the work done within and through those booths made possible all the rest.

Can I save it all? I wondered.

Questions had come to us from many sides over the years about our handling of Scripture and matters related to scripture and we knew our work undercut the authority and prestige of the scribes and Pharisees. Rabbi Hillel in Capernaum supported the work, though he considered himself too unlearned to be called either scribe or Pharisee.

Should those visitors I'd just sent on their way, bring reinforcements from Jerusalem a charge of blasphemy could easily follow.

Once again retreating to my library I commenced planning an exit from our home on the shores of Lake Kinneret. With a sharpened stylus in hand, I began roughing out details of an exit from Galilee.

First, I would need to negotiate the sale of property and belongings; then inform and negotiate with my workers. Another goal floated around my subconscious mind, that of locating Caleb's papyrus site.

The action of planning over-rode the grief accompanying the unwanted change in our lives.

After two weeks of secretive negotiations my worries grew as roughly charted plans met barrier after barrier and for some unknown reason the picture of Flavinus, the Roman centurion in Capernaum filled my mind. I shook my head attempting to refocus but the image persisted. *How can he help?* I wondered, feeling the tug strengthen. *Well, help or not, he's a wise, experienced and disciplined man. If nothing else I may get ideas just from confiding in him.*

Ignoring the hazards I knew to exist when a Jew pursued a close and continuing contact with a Gentile, I set out on the three-hour journey to Capernaum and knocked on the courtyard gate leading into the home of Flavinus.

Expecting the young servant, Timon, to open the door, I stepped back when Flavinus stood there instead. He followed and grabbed my hand, his face drawn and pale.

"What's wrong?"

"It's Timon. He's near death, fighting for every breath. I've had visits from every physician within travelling distance and he continues to worsen. "Your Jesus is my only hope."

Flavinus led me into an antechamber where I saw Timon lying on a sleeping bench; his face, pale as a lily and still as wax.

"Jesus is near," I said. "I will find him. He may be teaching in the synagogue."

Short of breath, heart pounding I burst into the synagogue and saw a man sitting in the chair known as *Moses Seat,* a large scroll open on his lap. The small crowd gathered around him turned, not at all happy at this interruption.

I stopped, empty of words, staring. I'd yet to meet the adult Jesus but knew I looked on him now. He examined me, eyes alight and full of recognition.

It is him, the thought reverberated through my mind. *The baby in Bethlehem fully grown.*

My thoughts were interrupted as Rabbi Hillel stepped toward me, obscuring my view of the Moses chair and the man sitting there.

"What is it Micah?" The kind voice of the rabbi released my tongue. "It's Timon, the centurion's servant. You know both the centurion and his servant. They are good men who have shown themselves friends of our faith. Timon is dying and Flavinus asks for Jesus. We would not even have a synagogue had it not been for this man, so please ask for Jesus' help."

The rabbi approached Jesus who stood and without being asked said, "I will come."

Those words sent me rushing back to assure Flavinus. I found him at Timon's bedside. "Jesus comes," I said.

Flavinus drew in a ragged breath. "Thank you, but I do not expect your Jesus to compromise his ritual purity so near Sabbath. Go to Jesus before he reaches my house. I respect a degree of authority much superior to mine and feel my house to be unworthy of him. Tell him that just as I exercise my authority with sword and legionaries, so he can exercise his with a word. I trust his spoken word to bring Timon back to health. Go!"

I met Jesus and the small crowd with him just outside Flavinus' dwelling, and stopped them with an upraised hand. "As you all know, the centurion is a man of authority. He believes Jesus to be one with a much higher authority than his and feels unworthy to have Jesus enter his dwelling. He requests Jesus but say the healing words that will restore Timon."

Jesus examined me for a moment before turning towards those with him. He gestured over his shoulder towards the centurion's house. "This centurion has shown himself a man of faith such as I have yet to see in all Israel."

Turning back to me, his eyes thoughtful, Jesus said, "Fret no longer, Timon has risen from his bed."

Watching Jesus lead the way back toward the synagogue, I noticed an onlooker, a stranger to Capernaum, well dressed, with the long, impractical tassels on his robe typical of an overzealous Pharisee. I remembered how similar individuals stood on the hill to look down on John the Baptist as he baptized in the Jordan River. *Now they're probably following Jesus,* I thought.

The courtyard gate I'd left open had now been shut. I knocked and stepped backward at sight of Timon, standing, smiling, his cheeks rosy and healthy.

Speechless for a moment; then ashamed at my lack of faith, I found the only words suitable. "Praise Jehovah."

Following a short discussion with Timon and Flavinus I started the dusty walk back to Hammat. Halfway home I remembered my reason for visiting Capernaum; an urgent need to bare my soul to Flavinus. I half turned; then noted the strange Pharisee some distance back. *Devil take him,* I thought and continued on.

The man seemed to be circling like a vulture; his sharp, accusing features hanging over me, destroying what little concentration I had this day.

I passed through my courtyard with just a nod for Ruth at her loom, not even remembering Sara and her sickness.

Reaching the library my head dropped to my hands, strength fleeing and sat thus until Ruth's soft hands touched my neck. "We will prevail, my husband. I feel God's arms around us. Come, you must be thirsty and hungry. My maid has refreshments in the courtyard at this very moment. Shall we see Sara first?"

I nodded.

We approached her bed and she looked up at me through feverish eyes. Her body trembled. I felt her head. Very hot.

A maid entered the room with a basin and cloth.

"We should go," Ruth whispered.

The imprint of those feverish eyes stayed with me as we entered the courtyard. We'd yet to sit when I heard a knock on the gate. I raised the bar and swung the gate wide. Two men stood outside. Matthew and Jesus.

I bowed, voiceless, beckoning them in.

Ruth stood, "I will assist the maid."

"Before we share your meal," Jesus said, "I would see your daughter Sara."

"But she is ill," I protested, "and unable to speak."

Jesus gave me an appraising look and smiled. "I know that. Please lead the way."

Reaching Sara's chamber, I stood to one side, giving Jesus room to stand by my daughter. He walked to the bedside, touched Sara's clammy forehead; and I saw her eyelids flicker. Reaching down Jesus grasped a limp hand and with great tenderness raised it above the bed cloths. After a moment Sara's eyes opened, she drew her hand from that of Jesus and sat up.

She looked around the room, saw me, smiled, examined Jesus and Matthew then turned back to me. "You seem shocked father. Why would Messiah not do for you what he's done for others. You will see even greater things than this."

Jesus placed a finger to her lips. "Hush, Micah's daughter. The word Messiah promotes too much emotion, too soon. Come, your father has invited us to table; it's been long since we've eaten."

The guilt I'd been carrying for thirty years smothered me, numbed my mind and kept me from registering much of the conversation swirling around the meal. Over and over again I pictured Jesus taking Sara's hand as she rose from her bed. I could understand Jesus performing miracles in the abstract, but not in my home; not with one I loved.

Before leaving, Jesus beckoned and I followed him outside. I'm not a particularly big man, but I towered over this individual I now believed to be my Messiah, but size meant nothing. As I looked into his eyes, I sensed his love for me and felt an urge to fall on my knees and worship.

Jesus touched my arm. "Don't," he said. "I speak to you as a man; and, when I've returned to the Father your work as a man will continue.

Your profession, and those like yours will see that My Father's message goes out to the world. You and your children after you will do much good. Be strong. A hurricane approaches."

I looked up, searched the sky.

Jesus smiled again, a wistful smile. "For you and your family's sake I wish it were the weather."

23: Saul

Keep thy heart with all diligence; for out of it are the issues of life.
Words of King Solomon in Proverbs 5:23 circa 950 bce

For the past several years the fame of a young Pharisee named Saul had been spreading through all Israel. Born in Tarsus of influential Jewish parents he was also a Roman citizen. His religious prominence gave him access to any synagogue in Israel and his Roman citizenship provided a protective mantle wherever he went.

When news of Saul's coming to Nazareth on a teaching tour reached me, I sent Benjamin to attend his lectures and collect material suitable for distribution. After four days absence I began to worry; calming myself with the thought. *Benjamin's smart and resilient. He knows better how to care for himself than most men twice his age.*

Then amid my mild worry, emerged thoughts of Benjamin's lack of interest in marriage. I'd been a faithful Jewish father and arranged a number of introductions with marriageable girls from suitable families, but he'd shown no interest.

Thinking of my children and marriage brought back the chill I'd felt earlier regarding our future. So far the plans I'd been making would allow little time for Benjamin and Sara to marry.

Ensconced in my library, I still heard the tentative knock on the courtyard gate. I waited for the maid's announcement.

"Master, Reuben from Cana brings words from Nazareth."

My stomach clenched. "Lord Jehovah," I prayed. "May it not be Benjamin."

I went to the courtyard and waved Reuben to a seat. He sat for moments, head cradled, feeding my fear.

"Is it Benjamin?"

He nodded as choking sobs slurred words that only gradually gained coherence. "As Benjamin and I reached the synagogue for Saul's lecture we saw people exiting. His audience had grown so large the lecture had moved outside.

"While Saul arranged some scrolls and a podium from which to speak, I surveyed the crowd around us. We'd seen so much recent turmoil, so much questioning of Torah, and during all that, fantastic rumors of Messiah." He looked up, his voice tentative and apologetic. "We all wished the calming and authoritative words of a great religious teacher."

"And?" I asked.

"Saul gave no calming words. He began his lecture by taking us back to the ancient writings of Ezra and Nehemiah. He outlined how these two great Jewish leaders led remnants of Israel back from Babylonian captivity in order to rebuild Jerusalem, resettle the land and return to worship of Jehovah. He continued with a description of how these returnees abandoned initial fervor and declined into idolatry and wickedness."

For the first time since he'd entered the courtyard, Reuben's eyes met mine. "We did not have a Moses seat in our out of doors setting but Saul had a high table holding several scrolls. He began his lecture with a silent caressing of the scrolls before him.

"*The Torah. The Torah.* Saul spoke in a hushed voice intensifying the attention of his hearers. Then his fingers lifted a small fragment of papyrus from the table.

This! This is sacrilege! A zealous follower of Jehovah found these words of Moses lying in the dirt. Not, only lying on the ground, but the result of a hasty use of quill leading to poor letter alignment and an ink blotch.

The words of God should not and cannot be allowed to suffer such an indignity. These are God's words to God's people, and God's people must prevent further such defilement.

Reuben paused, took a deep breath, caught my eyes and dipped his head before continuing. "I could feel tension building in those around me as more and more of the crowd turned hostile eyes towards Benjamin. I gripped his arm. "Come with me." I turned and pushed through the crowd. Some pushed back, but Saul's words held their interest more than our departure.

We entered the now empty synagogue and waited until Saul's voice died away.

"We'd best remove ourselves from Nazareth now," I said, looking into Benjamin's eyes, but he set his jaw and his body stiffened. *I must speak with Saul. He misunderstands what we do.*

"No, he doesn't misunderstand!" I insisted. "He knows what he's saying, and what's more some of the hare-brained crowd read more into his words than what he intended. Now, let's go! I'll go with you."

He hung back for a moment then followed out a side door and we circled away from Saul and his crowd, found a little used path and followed that until we reached the main road leading back to Tiberias.

"We made it," I said, looking at Benjamin, but his eyes were focused on something further down the road. Following his gaze, I saw several men blocking the road ahead! A backward glance revealed several others closing in from behind."

My stomach clenched and my mind froze so that I missed some of Reuben's next words, catching only the tail end of a sentence finishing with, "Let's run!"

"Benjamin shook his head, *I know some of those men. Why should I be afraid?*"

"You might not be afraid, but I am." I tugged harder. "Those men haven't come to give you more content for a tractate. Come on, let's go," but Benjamin pulled free and kept on walking."

Another choking sob punctuated the narrative before Reuben's tone changed and he lost himself in images of the confrontation.

Benjamin's hurt, I thought. I wonder who's caring for him?

Returning to Reuben's narrative I heard, "two of those who'd come running up from behind grabbed me and pinned my arms.

The others circled Benjamin, calling him *blasphemer, perverter of Scripture*, *a sacrilegious follower of fake Messiahs,* and *Denier of the Holy Temple.* One of the smallest accusers leaned forward and punched him in the nose. I heard the sound, saw the blood start and the look of surprise flooding Benjamin's face; saw his hand beginning to rise just as rough hands seized him, and began dragging him towards a stone pile. When Benjamin saw the stones, he began struggling. No, he cried at the same time I shouted, "Stop!"

"But they didn't stop. Instead a man ran at Benjamin with a large stone and smashed it into his head. Then other stones flew.

"The thud and rattle of flying stones seemed endless before silence fell, leaving only the breathing of the men grasping my arms. I opened my eyes and saw the murderers standing around heaped stones with only portions of Benjamin's body showing. Those who'd thrown the stones stood silent for only a moment before slinking off.

"With the stone's last clatter my captors slammed me to the ground. Lying there, half-stunned I heard one of my captors snarl, *Should you continue in the company of blasphemers you will meet your own stones*."

"I waited, frozen with fear, as the sound of footsteps disappeared before struggling to my feet. Then…" His voice choked.

At that pause I bent my head and covered my face unable to process what I'd just heard. Sitting thus a seed of anger sprouted into consuming rage replacing the shock and sorrow I'd felt only moments before. *Tooth for tooth, eye for eye and life for life,* so the Law of Moses commanded.

Only Saul's life will pay for Benjamin's. Jehovah willing, he will die at my hand.

Nursing those thoughts and that anger, I lowered my hands to see Reuben, head bowed, shoulder's shaking. *Poor lad*, I thought. *To see all that and then fear for his own life is too much.*

I sought soothing words to help him return to the present, "You have an uncle in Capernaum. Go there. No stoning occurs near the Roman garrison. Where is Benjamin now?"

My question undid the soothing I'd intended and released more intense sobbing. I sat down beside him and put an arm across his shoulders.

When his shaking diminished and sobs grew more controlled, I released him and stood. "There is much to do. We have no more time for tears."

I felt Ruth's presence, turned and held out my arms. She pushed me away. "I heard."

She knelt before Reuben and took both his hands in hers. "Thank you for caring for our son. We would go to him."

Reuben lifted his tear-stained face and pointed to the gate. "Outside. I began carrying him by myself until a stranger came to my aid. Then we met two Roman cavalrymen who stopped and demanded an explanation. When I gave Benjamin's name, I saw tears rise in one soldier's eyes. Turning to his fellow he said, *Go to Flavinus and give him the news*; then helped lift Benjamin to the horse's saddle. Still others joined until a man offered a place for the body in his donkey cart. They all wait outside your house."

I rushed to the gate, paused, pulled myself together as Ruth brushed past, raised the bar and pushed it open.

Near the house stood a high-sided donkey cart. Two sandaled feet projected beyond the cart-bed, the only sign of load.

Ruth gasped, and moved, one slow step after another. My feet followed. We paused, looked into each other's eyes and stepped beyond the blocking side-panels.

Not real, I thought. *Not real!* The crumpled, ragged heap in the cart bed could not be Benjamin.

A startling, sloughing sound, like a wind gust through treetops, made me look up. A large crowd confronted me, silent, respectful of our sorrow. Sharing. It seemed the news had already spread through our community and beyond.

I shook my head, clearing tear-blinded eyes and saw not only the crowd before me, but also others streaming up our path.

Rabbi Hillel stepped from the crowd and came toward us. He placed a hand on each of our shoulders, "This is not Jehovah's way, and I am so sorry."

Lifting my eyes past the rabbi I saw a Roman soldier move forward, meet Reuben at the cart, and then place tender arms under our son's body. They adjusted their holds and carried the slack body towards the courtyard gate. Ruth followed.

As I turned towards the crowd, examined faces expressing a similar shock and sorrow as my own, words from the psalms pulsed in my mind.

I raised my arms and face upward and intoned for all to hear; *Our hearts hunger for Jehovah. He alone is our help and shield. We trust in his Holy Name and there we find joy. Oh, Jehovah let your constant love surround us, we have no other hope but you. Selah.* That one word of praise resonated from a hundred lips.

24: What to Do?

Yea, though I walk through the valley of the shadow of death, I will fear no evil. Psalm 23:4

The funeral procession accompanying Benjamin's bier from our home at Hammat Tiberias to the Jewish cemetery near Capernaum stretched on and on, leaving me more resentful than appreciative. The shrill note of flutes; the shrieks, sobs, and moans of professional mourners seemed inappropriate for a grief too deep for words.

The final mass intoning of the blessing for the dead accompanied the stone being rolled over the tomb mouth: *May he come to his place in peace*. But I felt no peace.

Following those final words, a seemingly endless line of friends and even strangers walked past with words of sympathy and blessings. While appreciating these expressions of shared grief, I knew my family longed for the simple solitude of our own dwelling.

Even my grief could not quell an inner urgency. Benjamin's murder seemed but a prelude of things to come, and that evening I retired to my library to worry in solitude; to plan in solitude.

Visions of Saul returning to Jerusalem kept intruding as I pictured him going to the Sanhedrin with his papyrus fragment and a warped account of my business. An investigation would follow leading to my inevitable trial before the Sanhedrin. Such a thought amplified a growing fear for my own safety and concerns for my family and employees. What happened to Benjamin could not be allowed to happen again! Just as I'd changed from shepherd to merchant, I must now change from seller of words to something else.

The transcription service would have to close. I could blunt the impact of lost employment for my workers, though any compensation would seem hollow. Pausing, I looked around my library with its collection of holy books, most in Greek, but the treasure of a lifetime.

One section full of scrolls in the Hebrew language held a special place for me. It had taken time, but over the years I had gained some proficiency in the language of my ancestors and among those scrolls were ones, copied by my own hand, no transcribers involved. Knowing as I did the rituals accompanying normal reproduction, I had followed Jewish tradition by reproducing in my own handwriting the three scrolls it took to contain the words of Psalms.

Fatigue overwhelmed and a picture of my estate on the shores of Lake Kinneret filled my mind. No, not my estate; Ruth and I had created it together, changing barren, brown hillside into a terraced garden of fruit and olive trees with a vineyard and wine press. Our villa, the only home our children had ever known, and the mark of our community status.

Then those images of the paradise in which I lived faded leaving stark reality behind. I must sell.

I counted off priorities for the next few days.

First, inform and take care of my employees.

Second, sell our estate.

Third, salvage what we could while paying special attention to our remaining papyrus.

And fourth, locate a safe haven for my family.

Early next morning I arrived at the transcription booths. Eldad, the head overseer, always early to work, came to meet me.

After our normal pleasantries, I said, "Eldad, I have a special request. I want you to tell each arriving employee that we are closing the booths for the next two days. And while we usually pay every man at month end, I wish you to provide two days' pay to each employee for the next two they miss.

Eldad's welcoming smile faded; his eyes narrowing and full of unanswered questions. "Yes Sir," he answered.

"Then come to the villa and ask for me."

Turning away, I revisited the conclusions I'd reached the previous evening. Galilee no longer provided a safe place for me, my family and my business. Liquidating my assets seemed my only option.

Preoccupied with initial planning, I opened our courtyard gate, passed Ruth at her loom with but a nod and proceeded to my library.

I found five freshly waxed tablets used for drafting ideas prior to going on papyrus, selected a stylus and paused at a flood of second thoughts. I'm not ready for this. I've never evaluated my assets, just accepted them as a sign of Jehovah's favor. And, suppose I calculate a fair value; who will purchase?

Shaking my head to clear it of all doubts, one name came to mind. *Titos,* Greek moneychanger and merchant in Ptolemais, the nearest port city to our region of Galilee. As a regular visitor to Capernaum and Tiberias, we'd had several business dealings and I'd even shown him through our Hammat estate.

No other property along the shores of Lake Kinneret surpassed the beauty, the gardens, or the baths of our home. Many cast envious eyes at our property, though few had resources to purchase.

On a cool winter day, the year previous, I'd invited Titos to use one of our hot baths, a feature unique to all of Galilee and possibly all Israel. Developed from among the many steaming mineral springs emerging from the rocks above our dwelling, they were the result of much planning and hard work.

Emerging, rosy-faced and looking refreshed, Titos had swept his eyes over the terraced gardens, the large house, separate quarters for animals, and the panoramic view of Lake Kinneret. "Wonderful!" he'd praised. "I could but wish to escape Ptolemais' turmoil for a home such as this."

With Tito's features etched in my mind I began writing, pausing only when a maid delivered a pitcher of weak wine with some bread and cheese. Near mid-afternoon the maid's voice interrupted as I reached for a sharpened stylus. "Master, Eldad is here."

The maid left Eldad at the library door where he paused, uncertain.

I stood, gestured him forward. "Unbelievable, how could you have done what I asked in so short a time? You have been very efficient. How many of the workers did you contact?"

"All but two. One man's wife was in childbirth and another ill."

The maid came in with a plate of raisins, figs and cheese as well as a pitcher of wine with two bowls. She poured wine into the bowls and left. I gave one to Eldad. He sipped, placed it back on the table and looked up ready for my next instructions.

I raised my bowl, sipped, set it down and said, "Drink Eldad, and eat. I have nothing to say until you've emptied your bowl. Relax. Take your time."

His body tension eased and I said, "You are the best overseer a man could ask for and what I say next pains me greatly."

Nearing the end of my explanation my voice broke while tears slipped down Eldad's cheeks. Holding on to my own emotions, I continued. "One more task I ask of you. Go to Nathan in Tiberias and rent his large public room for the next two days; then contact each of those working in the transcription booths and instruct them to meet there morning after next. Tell Nathan who it's for and pay him well."

On Eldad's departure, I reached for the stylus again and paused. I'd made preparations for informing employees but not family. I would do that this very night.

It proved far easier informing employees than family and I walked slowly homeward from Nathan's inn, my mind full of assessments, calculations and figures.

The first thing coming into view as I approached home were the dictation booths near the seashore. Booths absent the normal bustle. Next, I looked up at the small paradise I'd built for myself and family. Sadness seeped into my soul, bringing to mind Solomon's pessimistic words passed down through the centuries.

When one grows old, be happy for every new day, but remember, darker days lie ahead, with your future as meaningless as your past.

Heavy clouds had darkened the sky all morning, but, giving the lie to Solomon's dark words, sunlight broke through to shatter my gloom.

Leaving my library after thirty-six hours of total concentration I carried a scroll containing a list of assets, a modest asking price and a prayer for Jehovah to supply a buyer who would purchase the entire package.

With instructions to have a mule ready for the following morning, I dropped onto my bed.

Not having planned to eat before leaving, Ruth surprised me with a prepared meal and a sack with enough food for two journeys such as I'd planned. With mind somewhat fogged, I struggled to make the meal a pleasant one. We had our normal prayers. We ate at a normal pace. We said our good-byes, and just after daybreak I mounted the readied mule where it stood, tethered, just outside the courtyard gates.

Unused to long mule rides, I arrived at Ptolemais that evening, exhausted, stiff and sore. The mule appeared not much better.

After finding an inn, I slept soundly on a hard-packed earthen floor, paid for a breakfast of fresh baked bread, some cheese and a mug of sour wine. The innkeeper agreed to care for my mule until I returned.

Rested and fed I set off down the main thoroughfare where it passed through the city and down to the sea. My goal, the booth of Titos, the Greek moneychanger and general merchant.

Doesn't look promising, I thought on seeing several clients clustered about my goal but felt better when one of Tito's two sons recognized me and disappeared into the booth's shadowed interior. A moment later Titos rounded the rear corner of the booth and beckoned. We embraced in classical Greek fashion and once again I found myself surprised at the strength in his embrace.

A large man, well padded, looking soft, but I'd found him anything but.

"Come," he said and led me to into shade beneath an awning behind the booth. He sat cross-legged on a mat near a low table gesturing that I join him. We'd no sooner settled than a young boy set down a pitcher of wine and two mugs.

The moneychanger's eyes filled with humor, "I can imagine no other reason for your visiting Ptolemais than a need to see your old friend Titos." Sobering, he said, "News of your son's death spreads. I grieve with you."

Respectful silence grew between us until Titos spoke again. "You have not completed the purification period following your son's death, yet here you are drinking wine with a Gentile. You Jews. I will never understand you."

Shaking my head, I answered, "I will never understand us either. But my circumcision marks my outer man forever, and the expectation of Messiah shapes my inner man."

I spread my hands. "I am what I am."

Titos nodded his head twice. "Those worry-lines etching your features and a visit so soon after your son's death, suggest an emergency." He reached for the wine pitcher and re-filled our bowls.

We both ignored the refills, eyes meeting for a few seconds.

Dropping my gaze, I drank from my bowl before taking a deep breath and laying out my proposition. "You know my business and my estate. I have placed funds with you on several occasions to our joint profit. We have developed mutual trust. The news of my son's murder has reached you and I imagine the details surrounding that death as well. My family, my employees and my business are all threatened. I have determined to move, and you are first to know. Would you be interested in purchasing my assets?"

Titos tilted his bowl, swallowed, and returned the bowl to the table as his eyes lost focus and his fingers set up a tap, tap rhythm on the surface.

Breaking the rhythm, he asked, "What portion of your assets do you wish to sell?"

"All of them." I passed over the list of itemized assets.

After slowly unrolling the scroll and perusing the details, he rerolled it, stood, and without a word, re-entered his booth. Fighting impatience, again I waited.

Sweat prickled, even in the awning's shade.

Well over an hour later Titos returned. The scent of lily infused perfume mixed with sweat sifted over the table as he sank to the rug.

"You are in a hurry," he stated, matter of fact.

"Yes, I am."

"Here's my situation," he said. "I just lost a cargo of grain coming from Cyrene. My ship, my cargo. Nevertheless, I believe we can reach agreement. I would value your property and assets as," and he named a sum.

I didn't grimace, realizing how much emotion impacted the price I carried in my head. I calculated, weighed the odds, considered the options and nodded.

"Half in currency to start," he said, "with the rest payable in either currency or in goods and services over the next five years."

Short of funds. Losing a ship and cargo. What if he loses even two more? Uncertainties.

I stood, stretched, and took a deep breath. "Fair enough."

He responded, "I will arrange a room for you this night and tomorrow morning we affix our seals before witnesses."

Standing, I made a final request. "Two things. Would you keep my library intact, and, please no Jews among your witnesses? My family's safety may depend on your discretion."

MESSIAH

25: Chaff to the Wind

By what way is light diffused, Or the east wind scattered over the earth.

Book of Job-circa 2000 bce

Arriving home with the small scroll defining our change in life, I began loosening the chains binding us to Galilee.

On each of the following three nights Eldad arrived with two wagons driven by his most trusted co-workers. For three nights torches blazed among the caves above us as Eldad loaded his wagons. Then early each of the following mornings those wagons departed carrying straw-covered papyrus urns. With the present dearth of writing materials, enough papyrus for a prince's ransom, and all of it in Eldad's hands. He'd agreed to redistribute that papyrus along with writing materials among those who had worked in the booths.

While Eldad transferred papyrus, Ruth, Sara, Daniel and I organized and packed our remaining possessions.

I came to appreciate my son, Daniel, more during those three days than I ever had before. He leaned into each task with every jot of energy he possessed. With the hours we committed to getting ready, he'd decided to stay in the guest room rather than Capernaum with his wife, Rebecca and their young family.

On this final day before Titos took possession, we four, Daniel, Sara, Ruth and I, sat at table in the food preparation area of our home.

Our last servant had departed, leaving us with cold fish, cheese, and day-old bread. The lamp gave faint and flickering illumination as it inhaled the last oil in its base.

Daniel cleared his throat, rousing us from near stupor. "While you were away, Father, I visited Rebecca's father in Tiberius."

The dim light could not hide a redness creeping into his cheeks.

"I have been a faithful son, have I not?"

"You have Daniel. You have indeed."

"I know you are about to go into hiding as a protection for yourself and our family. I think the fewer accompanying you the easier it will be to lose yourself wherever you choose to go. What I am about to ask can both ease your load and increase your pain. Rebecca refuses to uproot herself and our children from home, synagogue and parents. As you know I am very good with sums and Rebecca's father needs a man such as I in his business. Would you be open to giving me a portion of my inheritance that I might partner with him?"

I looked at Ruth; then at Sara, and back to Ruth, who answered with a slight nod.

"I will, my son, but first we sleep. In the morning I will sign a letter of credit. Take it to the money-changer, Titos, in Ptolemais, and Jehovah be with you."

Sara stirred uncertainly and I turned towards her. "And what about you my daughter?"

Sara seemed to be searching for words and when she spoke, we were none of us surprised. "Over the last several months I have come to realize how intertwined has our family's journey been with that of Jesus. I wish to continue that journey and I would go to Johanna's."

So, next morning we said goodbye to Daniel, packed three donkeys, tethered them one behind the other, and, set off for Chuza's house; Sara to travel with Jesus; Ruth and I to wander who knew where.

My heart near broke as Sara stood beside Johanna, a new confidence flooding her features. That confidence, though, did little for our tears as we said our goodbyes.

Ruth and I then set off into our own unknown, unplanned future; two abreast, our silence softened by the shuffling rhythm of donkey hooves.

My thoughts kept turning to Jesus and I finally spoke. "Sources tell me Jesus plans to celebrate Passover in Jerusalem."

"I know," Ruth answered.

"There are those among the Sanhedrin who wish him dead and even plan toward that end."

When Ruth gave no response, I said, "We too, go to Jerusalem."

Turning her eyes upward she responded. "There is no other choice my husband."

Giving slack to the lead donkey's rope, I moved towards her, put an arm around her. "I love you, Ruth, daughter of Ehud."

That night, at an inn in Ptolemais, I outlined for Ruth the plans formulated as we'd walked. "Tomorrow morning, I intend to book passage for either Joppa or Azotus as either port lies about a three-day journey from Jerusalem. Since the Roman road runs from Joppa to Jerusalem, I would prefer Azotus; less busy and less conspicuous.

Pausing, I gathered my thoughts. "You remember what I told you about the Greek physician, Luke?"

"I remember."

"He has his home in Emmaus, in view of Jerusalem's walls. I wish to seek his help as he already knows much of our story."

The next morning, I went to the port seeking passage, and found few captains willing to risk their ships in the rough seas of the moment. One captain, though, having a cargo of wine jars for the upcoming festival in Jerusalem, planned to brave the waves and deliver his cargo to Azotus, my preferred destination. Not anxious to carry passengers he at first refused until I offered sufficient funds to overcome his scruples. When he found he would have to carry my wife as well, he balked again. "Can't carry a woman. That will make the sea gods angry."

After doubling my original extravagant passage money, he began to bend and finally agreed. "Part of this money will go to a Jewish member of my crew who has no belief in the sea gods. His faith in Jehovah may blind the eyes of those gods and bring us safely through. However, you must remain below deck during the entire voyage, and no-one must know we have a woman with us.

Sabbath, being the next day led me to purchase food we could eat without cooking before returning to the inn. Ruth just had time before sundown, when all work is forbidden, to shorten my beard, leaving some shaggy edges typical of a struggling scribe. Should anyone ask about my profession, *scribe,* would be my answer.

We remained in the inn over the Sabbath and left the next morning with the donkeys and our meager belongings.

The captain had obtained extra rowers to help battle the elements when our square sail would prove useless in the face of oncoming wind.

Even with those extra men heaving on their oars our departure from harbor proved a breath stopping battle against frothing waves and the rock walls lining the harbor.

Regrets over my rash decision peaked within that first half-day as we inched our way southward against ferocious winds and terrifying waves. Ruth fared poorly and on the first full day at sea, grew so sick I feared for her life. We had one consolation, our cargo consisting of huge wine jars on their way to Jerusalem for Passover. The captain had provided a sleeping platform atop the wine jars as well as clearing a small space for the donkeys. While seawaters sloshed beneath our feet, we were at least protected from the constant wind and spray hammering all those on deck.

With waves crashing, masts creaking, sail snapping and rowers cursing, I held onto Ruth lest she be tossed from her pallet while my thoughts turned to Jesus.

Though my life had been one of outer transition: first a shepherd; then transcriber and businessman and now a homeless refugee; my inner identity had grown ever more to be that of follower of a man I knew to be the Christ of promise.

The angel's words rang through my mind over and over again. *I bring you wonderful words bringing joy to all peoples, news of a baby born in Bethlehem, the city of David. This baby is the Messiah, the Christos, mans' God-sent king.*

With the angel's words echoing through my mind I began considering my own relationship with Jesus. A relationship with the about to be revealed King of Israel. I had been one of the first to see this king. I had secretly spread word of what I had seen and heard. In my life following that of a shepherd, I had disseminated more scriptures to more people than any other living man? Further I had already begun documenting his amazing work on earth. Documents Jesus would have already examined. And, last of all, my own daughter travelled with him providing for his daily needs from my own wealth.

Calculating my existing relationship with our future king led me to whisper into the wind. "You, Micah will have a special place near a future king, dwarfing even the splendor of King Nebuchadnezzar."

Favorable winds would have brought us to Azotus in two days. We took four.

The mad dance of waves pounding, lifting, dropping and shaking the ship kept us in constant fear for our lives. When one of our donkeys broke its' leg in the chaos, crew members had to struggle for both balance and footing to get it overboard.

That death grieved me. He'd been born and raised on our estate, trained by our groomsman, and a family favorite.

On reaching Azotus, I purchased another, an animal I soon found deficient in every favorable trait one expects of the species. That donkey added another half day to our travel time and we arrived in Emmaus near the noon hour.

Emmaus proved a busy town being a junction for roads coming from Azotus and Joppa, with the Roman road from Joppa to Jerusalem being the most congested. Commerce in Emmaus flourished.

We located two inns, but none with a vacancy, so turned to knocking on doors. Sincere apologies marked our first inquiries as each homeowner explained the many relatives they would be harboring over Passover.

After many disappointments and with night falling, we accepted shelter from a very poor family. They possessed no guest room, just an adjunct shelter to the main dwelling. A space to be shared with a few goats.

As a shepherd I'd little use for these animals and the smell repelled, but with Ruth unwell I decided to look no further.

I bargained for accommodation along with sustenance for both ourselves and the donkeys. The wife showed real concern for Ruth who still carried aftereffects from her sickness at sea. That housewife's concern gave me freedom to begin my search for Luke, the physician.

The first person I questioned regarding Luke's home, examined me, noted my obvious poverty, sighed, and said, "Come. I will show you."

Considering the size of the village, I expected a short walk to the physician's residence, but my guide reached the last house on the street and continued walking. However, before my misgivings mounted far, he passed a rock outcropping and, there before me, lay a two-storied, whitewashed residence with small vineyard and garden nestled behind.

My guide paused and pointed, "The physician's home."

The man waved aside my offer of payment with the words, "I just follow the laws of Moses who told us to welcome strangers."

"But this is no payment," I argued. "It is a gift from one stranger to another. I bless you for your help, and your wife will bless you for the coin." I thrust it into his hand and turned towards my goal.

With quickening heartbeat, I raised my staff, tapped on the courtyard gate and waited. Would Luke be home? Would he remember me?

At the sound of footsteps approaching the gate I stepped back. The man appearing as the gate swung open examined me with a questioning look. He was not Luke, but still familiar. He wore similar clothing to Luke's, the same short robe with blue sash secured by a clasp with serpent symbol. A similar symbol to that worn by Greek physicians to honor their healing-god Asclepius, a symbol I recalled having a snake wrapped around a staff, head raised and forked tongue flashing. The insignia I examined now had a serpent wrapped a pole with its upper body draped over a cross-piece, hanging and dead.

Clearing my head, I asked, "Are you Luke's brother?"

The man started at sound of my voice. "Who are you?"

"I need to see Doctor Luke. Can you help me?"

"Who are you?" the man repeated.

This time I felt surprise and stared into the face and eyes of the man before me.

"Jason?" I exclaimed, recognizing Nicodemus' servant who,

following my rescue from Barabbas, had been both nurse and competitor in the game of Tau. The man frowned, perplexed.

"Micah. It's me, Micah. You nursed me back to health at the house of Nicodemus. What are you doing here?"

Before replying, Jason's eyes ran from my worn sandals, and patched robe to the rag I used for headband.

"Micah? Micah, the Jew." He shook his head, "After your departure from the home of Nicodemus, I went to Luke with questions regarding the Jewish faith and he showed the many ways in which your Jehovah surpasses all the Greek gods. He explained a deity, not subject to the human lusts and failings of our many gods. And," he paused. "And there is Jesus, Messiah, sent by Jehovah."

The gate moved wider, "I apologize. Please enter. Luke is away for two or three days, but come in."

Again, he appraised me. "It seems we both have stories to exchange."

He led the way into the house where a long table filled the center of the main room. Large enough for ten men to have seating, though only two stools sat along the edge.

A bag similar to Luke's occupied the far end. The tools of a physician formed a neat row beside it.

"We have no servants," Jason sounded apologetic as he poured wine.

The words made me wonder at Jason's present status. A wonder he soon satisfied. "Doctor Luke noticed my interest and skill in treating your wound and persuaded Nicodemus to forgive the debt owed him by my family. I am a free man and a physician in training."

After a short explanation regarding my present appearance, I inquired about possible lodging.

Jason tented his palms, frowned and thought for a moment. "I am acquainted with no available lodging, but I'm sure Luke would welcome you here."

While I did not relish the thought of staying in the home of a Gentile, I'd become somewhat careless in my views of ritual purity. I thought of Ruth and our present accommodations. There we had a roof over our heads but little else. I surveyed Luke's comfortable dwelling and

Wishing to return to Ruth I almost refused the invitation, but reconsidered when I remembered my lack of contacts within Judea.

"Thank you. My wife and I will gladly be your guests."

By the time I reached our temporary lodging, the sun's position indicated the tenth hour. Our donkeys, tethered near the cottage, crunched contentedly on a pile of small branches and rough forage.

Ruth met me with a weak smile as I ducked under a lintel absent its door and stepped inside the stable. I didn't ask how she felt, just held her in my arms.

"We have other shelter," I said as I drew a coin from my pouch. "Will you take this coin to the mistress and explain our departure. Give our thanks and I will ready the donkeys."

As I finished packing our donkeys, I explained Luke's absence and Jason's apprenticeship along with the offer of accommodations in Luke's guest room.

"Jason can offer only scant sustenance, what with Luke's absence and his own erratic schedule, but with what food we carry we'll manage for a day or two."

Ruth brightened at my report, not the least discouraged by the news of food deficiencies.

With the last of our items secured to the donkey's backs I turned to Ruth, "I have no idea what we do next. So far Jehovah has gone before us; though not with the pillar of fire at night, or cloud showing the way as happened with Moses; but I've felt His unseen hand on our journey so far."

Ready to pick up the lead rope on the first donkey in our little train, Ruth touched my hand, "We must find the market."

A seller of woven grass baskets met us as we entered the market. When Ruth had her basket of choice, I said, "You get what you need. I'll stay with the donkeys."

An overflowing basket marked her return; two fresh barley loaves perched atop other produce. She looked up at me, eyes apologetic, "I know our state of poverty makes purchase of ready-made bread an extravagance, but doubt our host will notice."

When Luke's dwelling came into view, Ruth touched my arm again. "Would you ask Jason if I might prepare the evening meal?"

When I passed Ruth's question to Jason, he just chuckled and pointed to a clay oven, firewood already laid and waiting for a flint.

By the time we got around to the matter of sleeping arrangements, Ruth, emboldened by Jason's easy-going manner, broached the subject. "Would it be satisfactory for Micah and I to sleep in the main room rather than the sleeping room you've offered. That way I can begin preparations for the morning meal when we wake?"

Jason thought for a moment. "Seems like the question is really who gets up first, and that would be me. I rise at the first glimmer of light to work in the garden. When you become aware of sunlight in the sleeping room, you can know I've risen."

Then, turning to me, he said, "I go into Jerusalem in the morning and will spend the day with patients. Would you wish to join me?"

"I would like that very much," I answered.

Waking next morning I found Ruth's sleeping mat empty. Smoke from a newly stirred fire tickled my nostrils. I smiled, and rose to join her.

Jason entered from the patio as I exited the guest room. Ruth straightened from her stooped position by the oven and hastened to the water pitcher sitting by the door. She raised it and poured water over Jason's hands.

We ate well, though plainly. Parched barley, dried figs, bread dipped in vinegar, and diluted wine. Ruth wrapped some barley and dried figs in cloth for Jason and I to take with us.

The donkey, with Jason's medical kit and supplies on its back, along with the early flow of traffic, slowed us in the four-mile walk from Emmaus to Jerusalem.

A sea of travelers packed the paved Roman road. We all gave way to Roman soldiers passing in and out of the city. A wide gap in the wall appeared ahead of us. Jason pointed; "Herod's Way," and pulled his donkey off the pavement and away from the human stream filling it.

He examined me, questions in his eyes. "You will manage on your own will you not?"

He thinks I'm too old or out of touch to handle myself in Jerusalem, I thought, but instead of giving a sharp reply to his insinuation just nodded, "There is much I wish to accomplish; more than the sun will permit."

"Very well, then. We will meet right here an hour before sunset." Jason tugged on the donkey's lead rope, passed through the gate, and left me to my own half-baked plans.

I had no certainty of Jesus' arrival time in Jerusalem, or even if he would come for this festival. He might have decided to preach in a needy village or baptize repentant people in the Jordan. I wanted him here, and I wanted to know something of Sara's health and happiness.

There, beside the road leading into Jerusalem, my mind focused on Jesus, my earlier dreams of high position in his kingdom relinquished. I knew him to be Messiah. There had been no mistaking the angels and their words. Though proofs were somewhat vague, I believed this Jesus of Nazareth, this Son of Man, as he called himself, to be the adult expression of Migdol Eder's baby.

So, I thought, *Messiah! What does that mean? A king? A priest? A priest-king? No one told him of Sara's illness, yet he came to my door, asked for her and raised her from what could have been the sleep of death. Why must I remain so divided? Right now, his mother may be the only one knowing more about Jesus than I; yet I fear him.*

I had seen nothing of kingship when he appeared at my door. Nothing of the arrogance and sense of power usually accompanying a priest and he was way too small to be a warrior. Only the eyes. Eyes, thoughtful and compassionate, had burst with the energy and power one would expect of Messiah.

I held out my hands, palms up, frustrated.

Ah well, I've played the role of detached observer so far. Maybe that's my intended role. Detached observer and biographer.

Then my mind turned from Jesus to Sara. I intended to find her if she were to be found. I thought for a minute; then remembered being told of Jesus's friendship with an olive oil merchant named Lazarus and his two sisters who lived in Bethany.

Edging into the traffic flow, I passed through the walls and by a massive structure rising on my left. I imagined this to be Herod's palace, another blemish on our holy territory. Bordering the road on my right stood another substantial building, not as ornate as Herod's palace but filling an equal space with its large courtyard.

Old memories surfaced as I passed through the city, bypassing the temple and exiting at a small gate in the eastern wall. Memories of my father-in-law, of seeing Ruth for the first time, and of Caleb, Ruth's would-be suitor. I felt old hatred stir in spite of our recent reconciliation and untimely death.

Sara had described the home of Lazarus with sisters, Mary and Martha, as one of the largest in Bethany resting near the upper edge of the town where olive groves replaced houses.

The press of Passover pilgrims flooding in from the east slowed my pace, and it took at least an hour and a half to reach Bethany.

Placing trust in instinct and the description provided by Sara, I turned onto a main thoroughfare leading upward. The street narrowed, went by the last house and split into two well-travelled footpaths, one going east, the other west. These lanes separated houses from olive trees. No visible house matched Sara's description. I turned left in the direction of Jerusalem, rounded a curve, and there it was, or else one very much like the one I sought.

Now what? I thought, but, before I could take a detailed look, movement in the olive grove further up the slope drew my attention. Glimpses through tree trunks and branches suggested a man coming down. Not wishing to be noticed, I turned back, but not before sensing something familiar in the descending form.

26: Jacob

Let us go to the Lord's house; let us bow before His throne.
Psalm 132:7 Circa 800 bce

Putting distance between myself and the person behind, I reached the street and started down. Within a few hundred yards curiosity overcame caution and I stepped into a narrow gap between houses.

I waited a few minutes before a man passed, head down, feet moving in a tired shuffle.

Jacob! Might have known. He follows Sara like a puppy.

I stepped onto the street and called. "Jacob."

He turned, slow, his motion that of an ancient, eyes examining me without interest, tracking up and down, pausing on the staff and then his eyes met mine.

"Sir, Sir, what...?"

With a calming wave of my hand I said, "Don't worry I'm here for much the same reason as you and no more, and knowing something of your eating habits, you're probably weakened from hunger and thirst. Here, drink."

Jacob sipped and returned the hollow gourd. I pushed it back.

"Drink!"

With the gourd re-attached to my belt, I said, "We'd best move on, lest someone recognize us, an event which, it seems, we both wish to avoid. Walk with me to Jerusalem. We'll eat and talk there."

Inside Jerusalem we found no inn with even standing room, so we joined a line at a street vendor's booth where I filled my gourd with wine and purchased two pitas wrapped around some greyish substance. After passing one pita to Jacob we began forging our way through a human sea until exiting the Jaffa gate we paused in a quiet place.

I watched Jacob attack his pita, took a bite of mine and passed him the remainder.

After sharing the wine, I questioned, "Did you see Sara?"

Blood warmed his face and, with eyes not meeting mine, answered. "I did. No, sorry, I only heard her laughter."

Knowing I would get little more information from Jacob, I asked. "Where did you sleep last night?"

Again the darting eyes, the blood-warmed cheeks. "In the olive groves."

"I thought you'd answer thus, but you will have better accommodations tonight. A friend will be meeting me outside the gate anytime now."

He seemed not to hear, his eyes growing more alert as he examined me again.

"You seem different," he said. "And not just the clothes. What happened?"

Seeing Jason coming through the gate I avoided an answer. "My friend's coming. We will talk later."

As Jason's eyes swept over Jacob in his stained robe, missing headgear, and worn sandals, a flicker of distaste flashed across his face.

"Jason, meet Jacob my right-hand man. Jacob from Galilee. A brilliant young man. And, Jacob, meet Jason, my host of the moment. He served in the house of Nicodemus, one of the Sanhedrin, and now learns the skills of a physician. I benefitted from his natural abilities as he nursed me, both body and mind after my encounter with Barabbas. He, too, has interests in Jesus."

I watched the interplay between these two men of such different backgrounds. The one, used to bowing to the rich; the other averse to an unclean gentile.

Sighing, I pressed ahead. "Presumption Jason, presumption, a habit to which I am prone. Might we invite Jacob to be a guest at Luke's house?

Poor Jason. Caught between welcoming a vagabond into his master's house, or refusing me, a man having strong ties to that same master.

Beside me Jacob stiffened. He, too, caught in a similar vice. Enter a gentile's house? Even sleep there? Or, refuse me, his master?

Jason examined Jacob again, caught the stiffening and smiled. "Luke would welcome Jacob, especially when his good friend, Micah, makes the request.

An adroit answer, typical of one practiced in the game of Tau. Now the onus for Luke's new guest rested on me.

With that exchange we set out for Emmaus. Three, not as companionable as two.

Next morning, we ate much earlier than normal, not even an hour after sunrise.

Again, Jason had patients in the city. Jacob expressed a desire to visit the temple and pray, obviously ignoring any contamination acquired through entering and even sleeping in the house of a gentile. Ruth and I wished them both well and sat down for a few moments together. I told her what I knew of Sara. We talked of Daniel and his family.

When the discussion waned, I asked, "Will you manage should I go to the city again? I wish to visit Nicodemus."

A shadow prefaced her response. "Had it been proper, I would have accompanied Jacob to the temple this morning, but there will be other days." Her face brightened. "Maybe you, Sara, and I will go together. And yes, I will manage."

Walking toward the house of Nicodemus next morning, thoughts tumbled through my mind each seeking precedence. How to contact Sara without insulting her. How to deal with Jacob, infatuated with Sara and here at a critical moment in time. How to reacquaint with Nicodemus?

And beneath those mixed up thoughts lay an enveloping consciousness, a seed. A seed planted that long-ago night at Migdol Eder when the angel proclaimed Messiah's birth as a blessing to all men. A seed, planted it seemed to sprout and grow in order to bring trouble and crises into an already turbulent world. I felt the imminence of a final harvest.

When the gate at Nicodemus' house opened, strange eyes examined me. Even though I'd just been with Jason, I still felt surprise when a stranger opened the gate.

"Micah from Galilee," I said. "Coming to thank Nicodemus for his hospitality of a few months past."

Having said that, I remembered my appearance. Not the kind of guest to find welcome at the home of a wealthy member of the Sanhedrin.

I expected to be turned away, but the servant's eyes narrowed as he examined me further. "Your name again."

"Micah, from Galilee."

"My master has stories of you. Stories of your stories and his desire to have those stories presented candid and complete."

He opened the gate, bowed. "Clement, at your service. I've taken Jason's position."

Examining my clothes again, he asked "Has misfortune, perchance, fallen upon you?"

"Not really," I answered. "Just a need for secrecy."

We hadn't yet entered an inner room when another knock sounded on the outer gate. "My master!" Clement turned and hastened back.

I heard him say, "Micah of Galilee, waits for you."

"Oh, how nice. Will he wish to stay?"

Shock rippled through me. That voice. Tired, discouraged, lifeless. Not the familiar voice I'd last heard. Back then I'd become accustomed to worry notes not despair.

Entering the room and seeing me, he straightened and his features lightened for a moment before worry lines etched his face again as he took in my appearance.

"Is all well with you?" he asked.

"Better than I look and from your features, better than you."

Nicodemus rubbed his eyes. "Very late for breaking the fast, but I've yet to eat this day and other opportunities may be long in coming."

Clement moved. "I will inform the cook."

Nicodemus led the way to his library and dropped onto a low couch where he lay, head on hand. He nodded towards a similar couch. Thus, we lay facing each other; Nicodemus, half-dead from some present ordeal while I was wide-awake and ready to attack my next obstacle.

Without prompting, Nicodemus began talking.

"Word spreads throughout Jerusalem and the entire country. A very well-known olive-oil merchant living in Bethany, named Lazarus, had been sick for some time. He died five days ago, leaving two sisters, Mary and Martha. Then, day before yesterday, Jesus arrived with his disciples and several women. When he learned Lazarus had died, he went to the tomb, and ordered the stone blocking its entrance removed. With that complete, he is said to have called out for Lazarus to show himself. As Lazarus struggled from the mouth of the tomb still wrapped in grave-clothes, some among the watchers fled.

"Others began praising God. Mary and Martha ran to their brother and unwrapped his bindings. With grave clothes removed, Lazarus stood just as normal as a man could be. Not one spot of leprosy remained.

"Some report his first words as being, "I'm hungry."

Nicodemus paused, eyes closing for a few seconds. "Lazarus and Jesus. Jesus and Lazarus. Those topics filled our night."

Just a hoax! Caiaphas, the high priest, pronounced. *We know Jesus and Lazarus are like brothers. How easy for them to stage such a drama. Any of you who suggest otherwise will be expelled from the Sanhedrin and banned from all synagogues in Judea.*

"Our discussions became ever more heated. I joined Joseph of Arimathea in suggesting we wait, observe, and let matters run their course. 'Besides,' we said, 'should Jehovah be with Jesus as he claims, we are powerless and, to oppose Jesus, may be opposing the very God we claim to serve.'

"Well, that statement killed all further discussion. We were shouted down and Caiaphas stood to give a final summary."

Our nation, and our own positions are at stake. This story of Lazarus being resurrected will infect the ignorant multitudes and the crowds may seize Jesus and crown him king. Such a move would bring the armies of Rome crashing down upon us. The Sanhedrin would crumble, and our people might again become dispersed throughout the whole earth.

It is best that one die for the people, rather than death and destruction befall us all. We must choose the right moment to arrest Jesus secretly, find evidence of blasphemy, and deliver him to Pilate for crucifixion.

Clement interrupted our conversation by returning with two serving maids. Once we'd moved our couches nearer the table the servers passed their trays to Clement to place on the table. Nicodemus recited the ritual prayers. Prayers, I barely heard over my pounding heart.

Now, I thought, Now! I see it all. Passover comes. The moment approaches when Jesus must show himself as the Messiah. Passover, how appropriate. Our celebration of freedom from slavery in Egypt under Moses will prove a mere shadow to forthcoming celebrations of our delivery from Rome at the hand of our very own Messiah. And Jesus will have to remember me.

A loud sigh broke into my fantasy followed by Nicodemus' words. "But at least I have one piece of good news. The Romans finally caught up with that thief and murderer, Barabbas. He will steal no more temple offerings. Kill no more priests."

"Barabbas! You're sure?"

"I saw him myself. The temple guards paraded him through Solomon's colonnade for all to see."

His face lightened, "On a happier subject, I'd like to invite you to share the Passover supper in my house, since you are far away from yours. I follow the practice of the Pharisees regarding the date of Passover. What is yours?"

I laughed. "Strange how we Jews make everything complex. As a Pharisee you follow the Hebrew calendar, based on our date for God's creation of the world. The priests and Sadducees have adopted the

Babylonian calendar common to most cultures of today's world, and with the Babylonian calendar being common in business, that is my normal point of reference."

"Sad, really," Nicodemus said. "The disconnect between the two calendars means the high priest offers the sacrificial lamb two days later than the date set by Moses. It dilutes the significance."

Nodding my agreement, I returned to the offer of shared Passover. "Thank you for the kind offer my friend, but my wife accompanies me, and also a young scholar."

Then, thinking my stay in the home of a gentile might render me unclean, I added, "Besides, we are guests of the physician Luke at his home in Emmaus."

Nicodemus grimaced. "I was about to invite you to come this very night. Tomorrow is the Sabbath and I would not wish you to break it with travel. But surely you can join me for Passover."

Nicodemus expressed no concern of ritual contamination due to our time under a Gentile's roof. On the other hand, I remembered the look on Jason's face when he learned a Jewish woman would be coming into Luke's house. The Greeks, with their loose morals, had no such inhibitions, but any Greek in Judea knew the prohibitions surrounding separation of the sexes.

Jason would have no objections to our leaving.

My lips twitched.

"Yes?" Nicodemus inquired, seeing my smile.

"Just thinking of reasons for accepting your generosity. We will arrive this afternoon, but will also remain your impoverished guests for the time-being."

Nicodemus smiled. "I will feel privileged to have you and your wife as guests regardless of status. Also, your young scholar, should he wish to join us. You probably remember my wife's death just over a year ago. I wish she were here to greet your wife and help us share this celebration." He smiled again. "With your permission I will ask your wife to light the Passover candles."

Back at Luke's house a flicker of relief passed over Jason's face when I described our invitation.

"Thank Nicodemus for including me," Jacob said, "but I beg to be excused."

I examined Jacob over raised eyebrows, but he met my gaze head on.

"Well, if that's your wish, you do have back wages not yet paid."

Jacob, about to say, "No," hesitated, and in that gap, I pressed four silver pieces into his hand.

"A little more than your due wages," I said, "but also an inducement. I believe our present business interruption to be temporary and, Jehovah willing, I will have great future need of your services."

27: The Temple

These are the feasts of the Lord, holy convocations which you shall proclaim at their appointed times. On the fourteenth day of the first month at twilight is the Lord's Passover.

Leviticus 23: Book of Moses: circa 1300 bce

Late that afternoon, Ruth and I, still in our humble robes, walked up the street toward the home of Nicodemus. With our decrepit appearance and followed by three loaded donkeys we felt very much out of place in this part of Jerusalem.

Clement heard my knock, called another servant to care for the donkeys and hurried us into the courtyard.

With the courtyard gates closed Clement took time to welcome us. "Your donkeys are in good hands; I trust you will have no problem in having them stabled outside Jerusalem. Nicodemus maintains only a single animal here. Keeps down flies."

He had yet to lead us into the house proper when another knock came on the courtyard gate. Clement opened it for Nicodemus, who appeared no more alert than I'd last seen him. He seemed to barely see us. "Sorry," his voice stumbled. "Clement will see to your present needs and I will give proper welcome in the morning."

Clement ignored Nicodemus' instructions regarding our care, grasped his arm to steady him, and half-carried him from the room.

Ruth looked up at me as though to ask, "Now what?"

I peered around at the solid, surrounding walls of the courtyard and upward along the walls of the palatial three-story dwelling in which we were guests. A cinnamon scent quivered through the stillness; a reminder of our host's occupation as a merchant of aromatic spice.

Ruth crowded closer, shivered, and I placed an arm around her. We stood thus for many minutes awaiting Clement, who appeared with a rush, slowed as he neared, paused to adjust his robe, then approached with his usual relaxed, everything under control, manner.

"The master mourns your need to eat alone," he apologized. "His burdens overwhelm. Many months past he visited Jesus by night and heard never to be forgotten words. Usually one finds swords dividing, not words, but those words of Jesus wrench him one way, while his position on the Sanhedrin and business success pulls another."

We followed Clement to a second-story guest room, reaching it as a far-off horn announced sunset and commencement of Sabbath night.

A very intense Sabbath Day followed. Food, cold, but plentiful along with pitchers of good wine served as stimulant to conversation. Ruth, quietly listening in the background, rose several times to dilute our drink. We unrolled various scrolls, and even opened his codices, first fruits as it were of my business. We examined scripture after scripture and discussed at length.

In addition to the writings of Moses, the prophets and poetic books; Nicodemus provided added content from the oral interpretations, built up, memorized and passed down through the centuries.

The customary evening hot meal, following the traditional restraint of Sabbath seemed absurdly over compensation for what had been a most enjoyable day.

Peering over a final wine bowl, Nicodemus, lost his glow of the day, "Tomorrow, the Sanhedrin meets again." He sighed, "I will attend again, and suggest you both visit the temple and feel the presence of the God supposed to reside there."

I'd never heard such despair from the mouth of either Sadducee or Pharisee in all my life.

Shock spread across Ruth's face as Nicodemus stood, eyes unfocused, turned and walked towards the stairs leading to his bedroom.

We woke with the following dawn according to our usual custom, planned our day at the temple, and dressed. Clement met us as we entered the large central space on the main floor. "Here," he said, presenting a small sack. "Food for your day."

Ruth gave Clement one of her wonderful smiles. "Thank you."

When I inquired as to the best route to the temple, he said, "Follow me," and led us up a stairway to the roof and across roof tiles to a railing. Clustered rooftops rose before us with the backlit roof of the temple in plain view. My fingers clutched the railing and my knees weakened at this sight about which I'd even given up dreaming.

Thoughts surfaced of Caleb and his wish that I experience the profound emotions of worshipping Jehovah in his temple. But those thoughts opened the deep well of fear I'd carried for over three decades. *Who might recognize me? Even my clothes of the moment suggested the poverty typical of shepherds rather than the wealthy business owner I'd become.*

Clement's pointing finger brought me back to the moment. "The street below leads to a gate in the temple wall. Inside you will find a covered portico upheld by giant pillars and inside the gate an array of tiled mosaics on which to walk. This will be the court of the Gentiles. A little smelly and noisy; much like a market with its sacrificial animals, relics and mementos for sale. And, of course, the din of moneychangers. A fifteen-minute walk will take you there."

With our guest accommodation midway between the Joppa Gate and the temple, we stepped from Nicodemus' courtyard gate into a seething crowd, full of individuals with minds fixed on the holy building before them.

Caught in the current, jostled and pushed, I took a tighter hold on Ruth's arm, leaned over and almost shouted, "Whether it makes me a bad Jew or not, this seems unnecessary torture."

Ruth just gave me a questioning smile.

We reached the gate opening onto the temple grounds and followed the press towards the women's court. Reaching the stairs separating the Gentile court from the women's, we paused as a hushed message rippled through the mass of worshippers.

"He's coming!"

There seemed no need to ask *Who?* Only the question of *Where?*

"He's on a donkey outside the walls but heading for the Eastern Gate," these words flashed from lip to lip, and as iron filings fly away from wood chips in the presence of a lodestone the crowds divided with most seeking an exit.

We joined the exodus and a river of pilgrims swallowed us as we exited the temple walls. Total exuberance exhibited itself in laughter and song. Some went as far as tearing down palm branches in preparation for the royal arrival.

No running, no slowing down, just a human current beyond anyone's control. Ahead, shouting reached a crescendo and the moving current stopped; split. An image of the Red Sea dividing for our people eons before came to mind.

Then, through a gap in the dividing throng, I saw a man sitting on a donkey. A small man, a small donkey; meek and unassuming. Nothing visible to arouse the joyous, almost hysterical reaction around me. The volume of shouts, cries, and pleas increased as the donkey moved forward, stepping daintily on the palm fronds and cloaks being thrown to the ground in front of him.

I heard words such as, "Praise God! Blessed is He who comes in the name of the Lord!" Beside me, and unexpected, I heard Ruth's voice, "Praise God in Highest Heaven. Save us! Save us!"

Forgetting to breathe, I waited. Waited for shouts calling out, *King of the Jews!* It didn't happen in the brief span of my listening and I breathed again, once more conscious of impotence and fear considering the massive forces opposing Jesus and those following him.

Caught as we were in the press, I had no chance for a close-up view of Jesus, only a momentary glance at his face. No exultation. No pride from the praise being showered on him. Just calm, maybe even a faraway look as though contemplating something different than the clamorous crowd around him.

Even that look left me shaken.

With the passing of Jesus, those in the crowd turned their faces back toward the temple. Ruth and I rotated as well and waited. Waited for Jesus to complete his lonely journey, freeing those nearest the temple to move back to their original place of worship or any of the other myriad locations from which the crowd had gathered.

With the dispersing crowd went the mass euphoria accompanying Jesus' passage. My mind, though, dwelt on my own detachment from the crowd's jubilant reaction.

The Christ's entry. Not just Jesus of Nazareth, Christ the Messiah. Few in the crowd would have possessed the same certainty as I, and none the same emotional emptiness. Why such detachment I wondered as I held tight to Ruth's hand and we stepped again onto the mosaic tile of the Gentile court.

With Ruth's hand in mine we again reached the stairs leading to the women's court.

Coming to the doors leading into the men's court, I had to pause before the great brass doors; the Nicanor Gates I'd heard so much about. I could not in my most fevered imagination have conjured a vision of such massive structures, let alone believed in their existence.

I might have remained there, staring, hypnotized, had the crowd not pressed me on.

The memory of the gates remained with me as I moved on, overshadowing even the towering white pillars of the temple proper, or its golden frontage.

I tried praying. Tried to feel Jehovah's presence, but only

envisioned the face of Jesus and his faraway look. Unable to force a worshipful attitude I looked around to see men with upraised hands mourning their sins, some feeling it necessary to reach God's ears by outshouting their neighbor. Others stirred about, jostling and applying an occasional elbow in order to move one step nearer the Holy of Holies. All this confusion lessening the potential for either my prayer or my worship.

Despite all the distraction I once more tried to pray, to worship, and failed on both counts. I didn't wish to rush Ruth whose devotion exceeded mine, but the crush of people about me stirred panic within. My heartbeat quickened and I turned for the exit, beginning to gasp for air as I reached the Nicanor Gates. Arriving at the platform above the twelve steps, I looked downward into the women's court where a mass of shawl-covered heads obscured identity. With increasing panic my sense of weakness increased and numbness crept into my hands.

"Jehovah help," I prayed, and a face turned upward from the massed heads below. *Ruth.*

Stumbling down the steps and pressing forward, panic still at work, I reached her, grasped her hand and led the way towards the nearest opening in the temple walls.

The Gentile's court, with the hustle and bustle of commerce filling the air, returned a sense of reality. I pressed Ruth's hand and paused; took a few deep breaths, let my heart slow; then moved on again.

With the temple walls behind us, Ruth tugged me to a stop. "What's wrong, my husband?"

I looked down on her worried face and shook my head to remove an invisible layer of gauze still inhibiting breath. "I don't know. Crowds maybe. Possibly guilt due to my long absence from the temple. Possibly thoughts of Jesus and the shouts of welcome at his entry. Possibly an attempt to discern the meaning of those shouts. I don't know."

"Just pause for a minute. Relax." Her grip tightened.

We stood there, a little island, with a river of humanity swirling by on either side.

After a final deep breath, I led the way back to the house of Nicodemus. Clement answered my knock and stepped back, surprise washing over his face. "So soon. It's not yet the sixth hour. Are you ill? Paleness marks your features."

Ruth answered for me. "Life's pressures overwhelm my husband. He needs rest."

Clement moved aside and Ruth led the way to the guest room and helped me lie down where I dissolved into dreamless sleep

28: The Spice Merchant

And Hezekiah hearkened unto them, and shewed them all the house of his precious things, the silver, and the gold, and the spices, and the precious ointment. From 2 Kings 20:13

Voices and footsteps woke me. The voice of Nicodemus and another man.

Yawning I opened my eyes and saw Ruth just finished with adding a patch to my robe.

After swinging my feet to the floor and pulling the robe over my head I walked out to the great room where Nicodemus knelt at a low table facing another man.

"Join us," Nicodemus invited. "Baruch," he addressed the man across the table, "My friend Micah a notable scribe. And Micah, meet Baruch a business associate. We are about to fetch spices from my warehouse just outside the city walls. Come with us. Baruch will retrieve his purchase from my dwelling on the day following Sabbath.

After Nicodemus collected the single donkey he kept in Jerusalem, we headed out, exiting the walls at the Dung Gate and then turning right.

The spice warehouse looked an extension of Jerusalem's walls; though not so high and roofed in. The unsettling sight of archers walking behind parapets on the warehouse roof sent a shiver of unease up my backbone, an unease increasing as we passed through two locked and guarded gates, leading into a narrow passageway where we stopped in front of a high table. Nicodemus addressed the man behind the table, "Simon, we require 80 pounds of mixed myrrh and sandalwood. See that its packed in eight separate urns and prepare a bill of sale to Baruch of Jericho."

Nicodemus must have heard my gasp, for he turned with a smile lighting his eyes. "Baruch is a merchant much like me, who supplies burial spice for those in the city of Jericho as well as to others beyond the Jordan. He always requests we pre-mix the myrrh and sandalwood prior to sale. Of course, depending on the ability to pay, he will often mix extenders into the pure product we provide.¶"

Any shock I'd felt surrounding the purchase of such an enormous amount of these precious commodities eased in knowing their specific use. Such an amount would provide all that a city such as Jericho could consume for several months, barring a sudden rash of deaths among the very rich.

Waiting seemed to bother Baruch and with no room to pace he began rubbing his hands together. His anxiety seemed contagious and I breathed easier when Simon returned with a small barrow holding eight small urns. He brought the barrow behind the table, selected a quill, dipped it in a small pot and began writing.

He filled two small parchment scrolls; then passed one towards Baruch who perused it once, twice, three times and added his seal. Nicodemus then added his own. Simon presented the other scroll towards Nicodemus who added his seal and passed it on to Baruch.

Two armed guards met us as we made our exit from the spice warehouse and walked, one ahead and one behind, as we made our return.

Just short of the Dung Gate Nicodemus stopped the loaded donkey and turned to Baruch. "You wish to leave us here, I believe."

Baruch bowed, his eyes straying to the load on the donkey's back, "Strength and favor to you until we meet again following Sabbath."

Your goods will be safe with me," Nicodemus responded, bowing. "Safety and honor be yours during blessed Passover."

Crowds diminished as we approached sundown and I was able to walk by Nicodemus' side. We avoided any mention or talk of Jesus or Messiah, and Nicodemus launched into his plans for adding imported silk from the East to his present trade in luxury goods. Midway through his discussion he paused, looked my way. "You'll be glad to know the Romans caught up to that kidnapping, murderous scoundrel, Barabbas. He's chained in the Tower of Antonia and will be crucified before Sabbath."

Numbed past answering I continued straight ahead.

That night as Ruth and I lay on our palettes in the guest room, I spoke into the darkness. "Remember my tales of Thaddeus who shared with me the angels' announcement of Messiah's birth."

"Yes. He taught you much."

"It was also he who crushed my knee and left me with the limp I still carry."

No response.

After a deep breath, I continued. "He now calls himself Barabbas."

Ruth gasped, and I longed for light that I might view her face.

Following a brief pause I continued, "In the few hours before

Flavinus came to my rescue, Thaddeus explained his reasons for banditry and murder. He, as I, went into hiding after being driven from the pastures of Bethlehem. Twice he escaped capture by temple guardsmen; even killing one of them in the process. Over time he met with account after account of corruption and outright thievery by authorities within the temple hierarchy. He learned more of how the very tithes meant to meet the needs of the poor and support ordinary priests and Levites in their service; instead enriched even some in the Sanhedrin.

"Chance brought him into contact with Avner, another of my fellow shepherds. They shared experiences and determined to return hurt for hurt. They took to heart Moses' direction *to repay an eye for an eye and a tooth for a tooth.*

"Thaddeus and Avner began their career as bandits with a few small thefts and focused mischief, until they met a zealot named Gideon. As you know most zealots focus on unseating the Romans, but Gideon too identified the same culprits as had Thaddeus and Avner. They saw in dishonest priests and Levites a greater threat to the Jewish people than even the heathen Romans.

Other disaffected Jews soon joined. Some just criminals, but others, patriots in their own minds. On Gideon's death, Thaddeus changed his name to Barabbas and assumed leadership."

"And the Romans will crucify him?" Ruth whispered.

"They will and nothing we do will prevent it. A few years ago, maybe, when Pilate ran a balancing act between harassing Jews and generating revenue. Now with Sejanus, Pilate's former commander dead, and Caesar hunting down everyone close to Sejanus, Pilate lives in daily fear. No circumstance will make him defy the Sanhedrin and have them complain to Caesar."

Again, I paused, wishing for illumination. Wishing to see the light in her eyes, the expression in her face. I leaned over and brushed my lips across her forehead.

"It's a twisted story," I said. "Twisted beyond understanding. One thing we know. The Jewish leaders with whom Pilate seeks favor want Barabbas' death more than that of any other man, except maybe for Jesus"

"Oh, that poor man," her voice tremored.

An urge to embrace and be embraced overcame me and I moved towards her and found her sitting. I placed an arm about her shoulder while one of her arms encircled me. We sat thus for several minutes.

"Tomorrow, I will go to the Tower to seek audience with Barabbas."

Ruth touched my hand. "And I will go with you."

29: Tower of Antonio

And there was one named Barabbas which lay bound.
New Testament book of Mark Ch 15, vs 7: circa ce 30

In the borrowed robes of the rich, we approached the Roman garrison housed in the Tower of Antonia, a structure hated by all Jews. A garrison with four high towers, two of them looking down on our temple, and even worse, a stone arch stretching out from the fortress with a malevolent arm of stone and mortar reaching out to grasp the very walls surrounding the temple.

Observing movement behind the battlements of the nearest tower I felt the unspoken threat as Ruth nudged nearer. "Be calm," I reminded, "Keep your eyes focused on the ground and mind on the One able to rescue us from evil-doers."

Two guards, spears in hand, stepped out from their guard posts. Without leaning over, I whispered, "Pray for me."

While my heart flapped like the wings of a snared falcon, I drew myself erect and approached what I assumed to be the senior guard. "Would you inform the centurion in charge that Micah of Galilee wishes to speak with him?"

The guard's eyes passed over me and lingered on Ruth. Holding my emotions in check, I waited. Tilting his head toward his fellow guard, eyes still fixed on us, he ordered, "Take this man's request to Centurion Lucius."

The sun beat down while the guard, standing in the tower's shade, seemed to enjoy our discomfort. A sweat drop tickled my cheek.

A subtle atmospheric change preceded the centurion's arrival and once more I stiffened. A story of military life spelled itself out on this man's face. A lined face, sun blackened and ageless with a scar line running from forehead, down cheek and puckering lips. A face I'd seen once before. A face I'd seen beside the centurion Flavinus, as I walked beside my son Benjamin's bier on its journey to burial back in Galilee.

The centurion's eyes showed instant recognition as he ordered the guards back to their posts. "Micah, of Galilee, and…," he paused, his eyes on Ruth.

"My wife, Ruth and I remember your face. You were with Flavinus in Capernaum a few weeks ago. He probably told you something of my story."

"Ah yes, an interesting story. And you, I imagine, are transcribing a new scroll with which you need some help."

In my mind I clasped my hands and gave a silent prayer of thanks for this unexpected opening. Beside me Ruth's soft sigh provided the Selah.

With greater confidence I continued, "Flavinus, your fellow centurion, told you, did he not, how he'd rescued me from the bandit Th…" I stumbled and recovered myself. "Barabbas?"

Lucius, ignoring my hesitation, said "Flavinus not only told me of his rescuing you from the hands of Barabbas, he gave me hints on how to capture the wretch."

My eyes closed, my stomach heaved. Stifling the urge to vomit I choked out, "How fortunate," even as guilt for Thaddeus' capture swept over me.

Words, stumbled from my mouth. "Scars and disability accompany me to this day, all due to that man Barabbas. I wish to see him before…before his death."

Lucius turned. "Follow me."

We'd taken only a few steps when he spoke without turning, bitterness tingeing his words. "My name as the man who'd captured Barabbas would be on every man's lips in Jerusalem were it not for being upstaged by this man Jesus. Jesus of Nazareth, he calls himself. People on the streets are calling him Messiah."

He stopped and turned. "Nazareth. That's not far from Tiberias. Right?"

He opened his mouth, closed it, turned and continued walking.

Don't let him think too much, I thought.

We entered a large open area, with a dozen soldiers scattered about, each man busy with some task. Sharpening weapons, polishing armor, mending gear.

Lucius called a soldier and pointed. "Take this man and his wife to Barabbas. Note the limp. Our prisoner left that mark. A little more derision, especially from a woman, will add weight to the prisoner's cross."

The soldier directed us to a large archway; then led us down a long, stone stairway. Darkness crept in as we descended. Ruth crowded closer. We stepped off the stairway onto bedrock and into a tunnel of natural stone. I retained enough sense of direction to know the tunnel pointed toward the temple walls.

We stopped where two other guards idled at a post in front of us. Our guide explained the reason for our visit and was directed to the fourth door ahead and to the left. Before taking us further he picked up an unlit torch, ignited it from the burning flame at the guard post and led us onward. We continuing in its flickering light past doors one, two and three. Doors pocking the walls. Doors, re-enforced with iron. Doors with small, barred windows.

The soldier paused at the fourth door, raised the latch and pulled. It opened slowly to the demon screech of rusty hinges. A man, or what used to be a man, sat on the floor in front of us with heavy iron manacles on wrists and ankles, a chain running from manacles to an anchor in the floor. The stench of urine and feces billowed through the open door.

The guard expelled a disgusted grunt and stepped back placing his torch in a soot-blackened sconce. "Look all you want. Taunt all you want. I'll wait back with the other guards." He gave a crude laugh, "Shout if you need help, he's a dangerous man."

Ruth brushed past as I braced myself to face the poor, reeking creature in front of me. She lifted a gourd resting beside a manacled hand, shook it, and raised it to the prisoner's lips. Thaddeus opened his eyes and looked across the few feet separating us. Our eyes met.

In that instant the barrier of odor disappeared and I moved to kneel beside Ruth as Thaddeus sipped, struggled to swallow; then sipped again. After a full swallow a mangled croak escaped his lips. Pointing a trembling finger towards the door he nodded his head several times. A warning.

I touched Ruth's arm. "We must take care or we'll end up in the next cell. Keep watch while I talk with Thaddeus."

As Ruth reached the cell door, I offered the wine-filled flask from my belt. Chains rattled as he reached for it, took several slow swallows, then looked at me with eyes flashing hatred. I almost moved away until I heard a harsh whisper.

Annas! Bloody Annas! Annas son of Obed, led to this. His chain rattled again and his eyes softened. Like a brother he was. A brother turned traitor. He brought word of a large gold shipment coming to Caiaphas from Ethiopia and helped plan our attack, but grew too sick for the raid. We found the caravan as Annas predicted and I deployed our force as we'd planned, but soon found ourselves in the midst of a Roman legion, not just temple soldiers, and here I am.

Thus, I and my men die as enemies of Rome and insurrectionists, not seekers of both truth and the Messiah.

Thaddeus grasped my wrist as Ruth's low cough interrupted. The warning did not loosen the grip nor smother the prisoner's last words, *Swear by the Messiah you will find Annas of Bethany and kill him.*

Standing and with a final look at my long-time friend I could only answer: "I will pray for you."

We exited Thaddeus' cell as our guide in company with another made their way towards us chortling over some interchange. I raised a hand; "Don't come near, the prisoner's stench travels with us. We will be happy to follow well behind as you lead us out."

Leaving the tower, we soon re-entered the human stream filling Jerusalem's streets. Wading our way into its currents we ran into impatient travelers brushing, pushing, jostling and impeding our way. Penetrating my mental fog, I heard the occasional grunt of disgust at the stench issuing from our clothing.

Ruth paused as we neared the courtyard, her face pale and drawn. "Show me the stable!" I stopped, shocked. She'd never uttered such terse words in all our years of marriage.

Pausing at the stable's slatted door I looked over Ruth's shoulder into the dark interior. About enough room for a mule or two donkeys. Today, though, it held only a single donkey and a lamb, the Passover Lamb, destined for sacrifice at nightfall the next evening, and eaten after midnight.

Ruth pointed to the hewn stone manger. "That manger is large enough in which to launder our clothing and for us to bathe. You will remove the fodder and arrange for water with which to cleanse the clothes and ourselves. These clothes should not enter even our host's courtyard and certainly not his house."

I moved back to the courtyard gate and knocked. As footfalls sounded, I stepped back several paces. The gate opened, and when Clement saw me, or probably smelled me, his face puckered. "We need much water carried to the stable," I said, before he could question, "and please fetch clean robes.

By the time Ruth satisfied herself as to cleansed garments and freshened bodies, I believed the house of Nicodemus to be emptied of water down to the last drop.

However, even freshly laundered clothes and clean bodies could not erase visions of Thaddeus; betrayed, confined, chained and wallowing in filth. Could not erase the vision of eyes and face distorted by hate.

The cleaning binge had drained us of any energy remaining after our visit with Thaddeus and we retired to the guest room. Not to sleep, but to stare at the white plastered wall where we forged images from shadows, bumps and creases. Images of manacles, chains, dark stonewalls, locked doors, a huddled form and an unbearable certainty. *He will be crucified.*

We heard Nicodemus' voice with the sun down and the last hints of twilight announcing the beginning of another day. A torch flared in the great room, and knowing our duty as guests we rose from the rug on which we'd been kneeling and abandoned our sanctuary.

Nicodemus ushered another man before him; a man I knew. A tall man, taller than Nicodemus, taller than me. Trim in body and face, austere in clothing, but still wearing the long phylacteries common to influential Scribes and Pharisees. Little about him suggested a man of wealth and influence.

I took Ruth's hand, "This is my wife Ruth, and Ruth, meet Joseph of Arimathea, the first man to purchase a codex from our transcription service.

Joseph directed penetrating eyes on Ruth. "Truly you have been a treasure gifted to my friend Micah from Jehovah above. May Jehovah's blessings rest on you, and fill the gap left by the death of your son, Benjamin."

He turned his gaze to Nicodemus. "I am famished; though all appetite should have vanished in this day of battling that nest of vipers. Jehovah will once more smite our nation with a mighty hand should we not change our ways."

At this point Nicodemus intervened, his eyes on me. I apologize, but I am about to be a poor host. Joseph and I will be eating in the library while we continue this day's work. Thus, we abandon both you and your wife."

"We will not feel abandoned," I assured. "We were going to apologize for being ungrateful guests. Our own day has proven too draining for good conversation."

For just a second Nicodemus appeared startled, but with something more pressing than news of our day, he turned back to Joseph and led the way into the library.

As we sat down to table on chairs in the Greek style we heard their voices, faint, only occasionally intelligible. Those voices grew ever more forceful as our meal progressed. While I wished to shield Ruth from the words coming to our ears, I dared not rise for fear of missing a single syllable. I gradually pieced together enough words to build a gist of their conversation.

Nicodemus appeared particularly disturbed at news of one of Jesus' disciples visiting the high priest's inner circle earlier in the week. "Why, did not this visit by Judas be communicated to the entire Sanhedrin?" he asked.

I missed Joseph's answer and the next words were those of Nicodemus, "Jesus' earlier attack this week on Jewish leadership did go too far. Jesus called us names appropriate only to pagans. *Snakes, vipers, thieves, preening peacocks, abuser of widows and orphans, hypocrites.*

"Was he really so wrong?" This time Joseph's voice loud and clear.

Ruth, on the other side of the table, stiffened and gasped.

Joseph's voice continued, "And I even have some sympathy for that bandit, Barabbas, even though he would have robbed me of all I have, given opportunity."

Shocked silence fell.

Nicodemus broke the silence, his voice chastened. "Will the Sanhedrin really agree to arrest and kill Jesus?"

"They will!" Joseph answered, his voice hard and brittle. "They will, and heaven help us when we oppose our other members. Only fear of the crowds prevents the leaders from killing him openly."

"Does Jesus know of these plans?"

Joseph snorted, "Does he know? Of course he knows. I sent a messenger to warn of the danger before he ever reached Jerusalem. I'm sure others have done the same. And what does Jesus do but show up in the temple and in front of the Passover masses; paint scribes, Sadducees and Pharisees as hairsplitters and fools fit for Hades. He does not run from his enemies, just pours more and more oil on the flames."

Ruth and I ate little, drank less and waited for any excuse to rise from table.

Eventually the library voices faded and our host appeared with his other guest. "I apologize again, but you know as well as I that these are trying times." He paused, and turned to Joseph. "With all the turmoil in Jerusalem, you will, of necessity, remain in the city for Passover. Celebrate it here, in my house.

30: Trial

Without having a strong physique or handsome face that people will see and admire; he has no visible attributes attracting us to him. He knows much of sorrow and grief.

Old Testament book of Isaiah, ch 53, vs2: circa 700 bce

Passover proved a miserable celebration when it came. The meal began after midnight according to custom. We entered into the customary rituals. Ate the roasted flesh of the Passover lamb; tasteless as dust. Drank wine but found no flavor or aroma.

Nearing the last prayer, we heard a tremendous pounding on the courtyard gate. Nicodemus scrambled away from the table and rushed toward the sounds. The gate creaked open. We heard someone gasping for air; then the words, "They've arrested Jesus and now take him to the high priest!"

Joseph's head dropped into cradled hands for a moment before he rose, slowly, like a sunflower lifting its head to the morning sun, except no sun resided here. Without looking our way, sleepwalking steps carried him toward the courtyard.

I remained seated, heart pounding, lungs reaching for air, powerless.

Ruth's hand touched mine. The courtyard gate slammed shut. A hush permeated the dwelling.

It took several minutes before we heard soft footsteps and Clement led other servants into the room to clear the table. We exchanged no words.

What is Ruth thinking? I wondered; then let my own thoughts wander.

If they take him to the high priest, Joseph and Nicodemus will be there too. There will be no chance of killing him as though by accident. We Jews cannot assign the death penalty; only Pilate acting on behalf of Caesar. Maybe Pilate will release him?

My mind rested on Pilate for a moment and I shook my head. No. Ever since Caesar Augustus executed Pilate's patron, Sejanus, Pilate's done everything he can to curry favor with Jewish leadership.

If not Pilate to the rescue; then who or what? I could find no answer until I sensed what seemed a flash of insight. Of course! The Jews take Jesus to Pilate. He gives the orders for crucifixion; thus placing a final seal on both his guilt and that of the priests. With that guilt confirmed, Jesus reveals himself as Messiah, King of the Jews. What better way? What better place? Clearly this must be Jehovah's plan.

I squeezed Ruth's hand and our eyes met. "Jehovah has everything under control; we can only leave matters in His hands and everything will be fine."

After watching me pacing and sitting, pacing and sitting, Ruth stood and retired to the guest room. My agitated pacing continued even when the lamp's flame flickered and died.

With morning light brightening the room I heard a soft knock on the courtyard door. It opened so quickly I knew Clement must have slept beside it, ready to open for his master.

This time I did not see the exhausted, overburdened individual, I expected. He near ran into the room, eyes wide, arms flapping.

I stopped pacing, exuberance energizing me. *Jesus did it,* I thought. *Just as I'd hoped.*

Then the agitated arms sagged and despair washed across Nicodemus' face. Ruth emerged from the guest room as Nicodemus' voice, a mere whisper, shivered through the room.

"They take Jesus to the cross."

"No!" my shout rang through the house. "No, that cannot be!"

Nicodemus' eyes met mine for the first time, all sign of hyperactivity gone. "My eyes did not lie."

His eyes left mine and focused on the doorframe to his home where the blood of the Passover Lamb had been sprinkled on the top and sides just hours earlier.

Without taking his eyes from those blood drops; words, soft and emotionless forced their way through barely moving lips. Ruth and I moved closer to absorb his following words.

> Joseph and I rushed to the large meeting room in Caiaphas house where the Sanhedrin often meet. Jesus was already there. His hands were bound, a guard on either side; questions and insults hurtling at him from every side. Chaos, utter chaos!
>
> Jesus just stood there, disheveled, face bruised, head covering gone, looking shriveled and small in the middle of that packed room. Caiaphas lifted a hand for quiet before pointing at Jesus. *You, Jesus of Nazareth, are accused of blasphemy against most*

high God. How do you answer?
Jesus made no reply.

Then Caiaphas turned to one of the few strangers in the room. *Can you testify to this man's blasphemy*? The man gave vague reply with several others adding their own accusations, possibly twisted and out of context, but basically quoting Jesus own words as evidence. Claims of having God as his Father. Claims of ability to tear down the temple with power to rebuild it within three days. Each claim damning unless it were true.

Intense discussion grew heated among members of the Sanhedrin as to whether the accusations were serious enough to warrant death. Behind the discussion rested fear of the crowds, the very crowds who had, the previous day, given Jesus a king's welcome.

The high priest grew so frustrated he finally turned to Jesus and asked the question. *Are you the Messiah, the Son of God?*
I knew there could be only one answer, but expected that answer to bring down the armies of heaven as proof of Jesus own words. Jesus answered not with yes or no, but with the words, *You said it, and you will see the Son of Man at Jehovah's right hand and sharing fully in His power.*

The resulting uproar drowned his next words but they proved enough to bring the high priest raging up from his own seat of power. With shaking hands he grasped his robe at the collar and ripped it wide. *Blasphemy,* he roared. *Blasphemy and double blasphemy, and for those words you must die!"*

Then, turning to us, his anger under control but not his passion. *We go to Pilate. Only he can order this man's death.*
Jesus' eyes, calm and thoughtful, passed over the crowd around him. Though I'd come to him at night over a year previous, when his eyes met mine he tipped his head in recognition just as his guards jerked him about.

Caiaphas led as we began our short walk to Herod's palace where Pilate resided when in Jerusalem.

I brought up the rear as we left Caiaphas' residence, torches lighting our path across the cobblestone pavement towards Jesus' appointment with destiny. Already shadows of morning danced around us and far away a cock crowed. I saw John, a disciple of Jesus and caught a glimpse of Peter as he exited to disappear in the shadows beyond.

A messenger must have wakened Pilate for he stood on the palace porch behind an ornate dais looking down on us. Torches cast sinister shadows over his features.

Caiaphas stepped forward and voice shaking with anger stated the charge against Jesus. *This man,* he turned towards Jesus, *This insignificant human claims to be the Son of God, and for that blasphemy he must die.*

Moving out from behind his dais Pilate stared down on the high priest. I heard anger in his voice. *Fool, you bring someone to me on a charge of blasphemy. Even you Jews cannot decipher the meaning of your inscrutable and innumerable legalisms. I do not judge charges of blasphemy. Go! Judge him yourselves*!

That's when Caiaphas demanded that Jesus be sentenced to death, and not just for blasphemy but his claim to be King of the Jews.
The words, *King of the Jews,* caught Pilate's attention and he hesitated. Turning to Jesus Pilate asked, *Do you claim to be King of the Jews?*

Jesus answered, *You said it*.

Accusations spewed until one of the so-called witnesses mentioned Jesus being a Galilean at which point Pilate's grim look faded. He made a dismissive gesture. *Well, if he's Galilean, he's subject to Herod Antipas, Tetrarch of that region. I'll turn the matter over to him*. With that he spoke to the two Roman soldiers nearest Jesus; *Take him to Herod.*

With Herod and Pilate both having quarters in the palace,

transferring Jesus to Herod meant no long distance.

Once at the porch leading into Herod's apartments, Caiaphas, Jesus and the two guards disappeared into an interior room. They were there a short time before reappearing, but when they returned at first I didn't recognize the staggering man wearing a worn purple robe, a woven ring of thorns jammed onto his head in a manner that shredded his scalp and sent blood dripping down his face.

Whether or not a message had passed between Herod and Pilate I do not know, just that a Roman soldier had a short conference with Caiaphas who turned to us and announced.

Pilate will meet us at the Tower of Antonia.

Fear rippled through me. From that tower had ridden a continual stream of Roman troops over the years, often leading to death and destruction for some of our people. One word from Pilate and we could again be targeted. Nevertheless, we followed the high priest as a crowd gathered behind us.

Pilate knows the decision will be his, I thought, as we neared the tower where he stood ready and waiting. The Roman soldiers leading Jesus walked him up a stairway to the platform to face the Roman prelate. Pilate nodded towards the back of the platform and the guard moved Jesus further back with Pilate following. Jesus and Pilate talked together for some time with only the guards in earshot.

Leaving Jesus where he stood, Pilate returned to the front of the stage, looked down on us and waited until hush fell. *You brought Jesus to me as a criminal leading a revolt. I have questioned him carefully and find no fault in this man.*

Caiaphas stepped out from the crowd and faced Pilate. In a voice once more ringing with rage he bit out the words. *You heard him and we told you, that man*, he pointed a shaking finger towards Jesus, *claims to be the king of the Jews. You are no friend of Caesar's should you release this man.*

Even I, some distance from the platform, saw Pilate's face pale, but he hadn't yet finished in his effort to release Jesus.

My custom is to release one prisoner to you during your Passover. Shall I release Jesus or Barabbas?

Barabbas! The roar pierced my soul.

Pilate shook his head, *And what shall I do with your king?*

Caiaphas answered for the crowd. We have no king but Caesar. Crucify that man.

With a distancing spread of his hands Pilate surrendered. I find no fault in Jesus so his blood covers your hands not mine.

You perform your duty, we perform ours, snapped Caiaphas. *We take all responsibility for this man's blood. Both we and our children.*

The crowds roar, *Crucify! Crucify!* spiraled louder and louder, until the guards restraining Barabbas stripped away his chains.

Free of constraints Barabbas turned his hate-filled gaze from Caiaphas to Jesus. Their eyes met and Jesus motioned with his head for Barabbas to leave. The criminal, free because of Jesus, walked down the steps and into the crowd.

With my eyes on Barabbas, I'd missed any interchange Pilate may have had with his guards, but turned to see those guards grab Jesus, shove and kick him before throwing him down the stairs onto the pavement. As he struggled into a sitting position the guards jerked him upright and thrust him toward a whipping pole, a common destination for criminals or any man the Romans wished to punish. A soldier had already taken position by the post, casually swinging a multi-thronged, lead-tipped whip.

All the while the crowd chanted, *Crucify! Crucify*!
Panic overcame me and unable to face what I knew to be

coming, I turned, pushed and shoved my way through the pack. My reversal made more difficult by others doing the same.

31: King of the Jews

Pilate had his soldiers nail a sign to the cross reading, Jesus of Nazareth, King of the Jews...written in Hebrew, Latin and Greek.
Gospel of John, ch 19: vss 19 and 20: circa ce 30

Stunned by Nicodemus' narration. Stupefied at Jehovah's failure to intervene in the fake trial; at His abandonment of one calling Him Father, I closed my eyes and my mind filled with vivid images of crucifixion. Darkness welled within me.

When sight returned, I found Ruth and Nicodemus silent and still, eyes empty but focused on me. I shook my head, cleared my mind, and waited for Nicodemus to set a course of action. We were in his house and I looked up to him as a member of the Sanhedrin. Nicodemus returned my gaze with the helpless expression of a cow trapped in quicksand.

His look seemed to say. You're the eldest, now what do we do?

When Ruth's eyes met mine, I knew she had joined me in a different focus. *Where was Sara?*

Oh, God, I prayed, *Protect Sara's eyes from the horrors of this day. She is but an innocent child.* Then, with the prayer still on its way to heaven, I recognized its fallacy. Sara's recent experiences made her anything but a child. That realization, however, did not ease an inner hunger to see, to talk with, and to embrace my daughter.

Drawing a deep breath while suppressing Sara's image, I returned to the moment as tears began flowing down Ruth's cheeks. Moving over, I placed an arm around her shoulders and looked at Nicodemus. "Go to Joseph," I said. "See whether or not Roman nails still hold Jesus to his cross; then return. Possibly acts of service still remain."

Clement exited the room with Nicodemus. We heard bits of low-voiced conversation, the whisper of a gate bar lifting; and then, an exclamation. A few moments later Nicodemus re-appeared with Clement following. "You remember Baruch do you not?" Nicodemus asked. I nodded.

"He may come for his spice order while I'm away. Should he wish to borrow the donkey, it's in the stable." He put a hand to forehead, "So sorry. How can I think of such trivia at a time such as this?"

"We will take care of it," I soothed.

This time the courtyard gate closed to leave Ruth and I in a whirlwind of shared grief, horror and bewilderment.

An exclamation from another room in the dwelling pulled me from my mental fog into a darkness so intense I had to tighten my arm around Ruth to prevent slipping to the floor. A scream echoed from a nearby room.

"What is happening?" Ruth whispered.

"I don't know," my voice no louder than hers.

"Maybe Jehovah punishes us for killing His Messiah?"

Without an answer, I could only tighten my grasp.

An eternity seemed to pass before daylight returned as though it had never been absent. Dazed and fumbling for meaning at the strange phenomena of the past hours, I found none and made my way through the house to make sure all was well.

I found the servants collecting in the food preparation area. A bewildered voice mirrored Ruth's question. "What is happening?"

"This portends darkness falling over our whole nation." The response came from Clement, his voice low and hollow as a tomb. "The master heard the high priest answer Pilate when asked what to do with the man called the Jewish Messiah. The priest answered by screaming, *Crucify, and let his death rest on us and on our children.* With those words our leaders bring disaster to us all."

Fear inked the faces of those gathered around the brick kiln; so, trying to ease the tension, I responded, "The sun still shines. We are living through a dark day, it is true, but in such times, I always turn to the shepherd's psalm of King David and the words, E*ven when walking through the darkest valley I fear not the evil around me, for Jehovah is with me and I walk in the protection of his rod and staff.*"

Those soothing words brought no change in the expressions darkening the face of the household servants. A maid sobbed into her upraised apron almost drowning out a tapping on the courtyard gate.

Clement hurried out and a moment later Nicodemus entered the room.

"Jesus hangs from the cross!"

Nicodemus paused, collected himself, looked beyond us and

addressed the wall.

I met Joseph at the place of crucifixion soon after the darkness lifted. Approaching the centurion overseeing the crucifixions we noticed Caiaphas and others of the Sanhedrin arriving and we stepped back.

We cannot have dead bodies hanging from crosses on the Sabbath, Caiaphas said, *Break their legs and hasten their deaths. So orders Pontius Pilate.*

The centurion turned to the nearest soldier who raised a heavy mallet ready for the task. Another of the guards pointed a spear at Jesus. *Don't have to worry about this King of the Jews, he's already dead, but just to be sure.* He approached the central cross and thrust his spear upward.

Sight of that final thrust seemed too much for Joseph and he fell against me as blood gushed from the piercing. He leaned there for a brief moment before straightening, shaking himself, recovering and becoming his old decisive self. *I will seek Pilate's permission to entomb the body,* he said. *My new tomb lies nearby. You know the location. Bring the necessities for burial.*

In front of us, emptied of words, shoulders slumping, Nicodemus sagged onto a bench. He looked up, drained and mute. Only the necessity for action kept me from joining him. How I would have loved time to prepare Jesus' body, to lay it out tenderly, wash it with care, place the burial spices just so, and join others in shrouding the body, but we had no luxury of time.

Sundown and beginning of Sabbath approached and no Jew could be buried on that holy day.

I placed a hand under my host's armpit and pulled him upright. "We have the spice you intended for Baruch. We should take some of that."

"All of it!" Nicodemus' voice took on life. "I will take all of it. You make haste to Golgotha, the place of execution, where you will meet Joseph. Should Pilate have given permission for Joseph to have the body, help him carry Jesus to my tomb."

Turning to leave I overheard his instructions to Clement. "Pack the donkey with the spices and have two of the maids come with you carrying full water pots. I will arrange the shroud."

Carry Jesus to the tomb. Carry Jesus to the tomb. The words played again in my mind as I rushed toward the nearest gate in the city walls and the path to Golgotha. Nicodemus had used the word *Jesus,* not *Jesus body.*

Jesus! With all I'd experienced I could not accept his death any more than Nicodemus' words suggested. I could not envision his body being just an empty container for his departed spirit.

Exiting the gate, with city walls no longer limiting sight, I saw the crosses, three of them, with the victims facing away and Joseph standing beyond the center cross near a small cluster of Roman soldiers. Another soldier stood on a ladder at the center cross with a long pry-bar in hand. A nail screeched loose from its grip on timber and Jesus' arm fell limp. Joseph moved forward, lifted his arms and took on the full weight of Jesus' body as the other arm released.

The weight sent him stumbling backward, Jesus head resting on his shoulder. I hastened forward to lend assistance as Joseph regained his balance and stepped away from the cross.

Already the Roman soldiers had moved on to the other bodies; bodies with no one to catch them as they fell."

On reaching Joseph I looked up at the empty cross and saw a sign stamped with a Roman seal. *Jesus of Nazareth, the King of the Jews.* The words in three different languages, Hebrew, Greek and Latin. The size of the sign struck me. So large, so conspicuous, and, clearly visible to those passing on the road below. Not many on that road now; idle spectators no longer interested as the crucified ones ceased their struggles.

The enigma of the sign bothered me. Why had Pilate approved such wording? But it bothered me for only a second before my focus returned to our present task. Already Joseph staggered away under his burden.

"Let me carry Jesus," I suggested, catching up to the older man. He managed a step or two further before pausing. Tenderly we transferred the body to my shoulder and I walked on, never having carried a burden so light.

After passing several grave markers we entered a small garden showing signs of irrigation; then I saw the donkey and extended my steps. Nicodemus ran towards us, but one look at the sun kept me from wasting even the few seconds involved in a transfer. Instead, I followed to a level area in the midst of well-watered grass, and with three pairs of gentle hands we lowered Jesus slack body onto a woolen blanket.

Nicodemus dipped a small pitcher into an urn and poured a stream of water onto Jesus' body. After waiting a few seconds for the water to soften congealed blood, he wet a towel and wiped away some of the stain.

When Joseph caught our attention and pointed to the setting sun, we turned the body and looked down on cuts from the Roman whip; open gashes showing bone, gashes too deep for even partial cleansing, but again we poured water and wiped off what little blood we could.

Deep in my heart I knew our washing to be merely symbolic and far from complete; but, having done our best, we lifted Jesus' body onto the grave cloths, covered his body with burial spice and wrapped the linen strips about him.

Joseph lit a torch as the sun touched the horizon and led the way to the open tomb. Nicodemus lifted Jesus' head and shoulders while I grasped the lower body.

We had to bend as we entered the tomb. Standing upright inside the entrance, I froze at the sight before me.

Carved into the rock's living stone, torchlight reflecting from its surface, I saw for a moment what seemed Bethlehem's manger enlarged.

Numb to my burden, the image of that earlier manger overwhelmed me.

Movement from Nicodemus called me back to the present and together we placed Jesus body on the heavy stone cap of the sarcophagus. A cap, we had neither the strength nor the time to remove.

As the torchlight flickered and dimmed, Joseph, Nicodemus and I looked down on the shrouded form of the man we'd hoped to be our King and Savior.

Too drained for tears I exited the tomb; then looked back as Joseph knocked away the wooden block restraining the round, stone wheel designed to close the entryway forever.

The grinding horror of the stone cylinder's descent, the finality of its halt, the totality of its closure, all spelled *finish*. Turning, stumbling away, I left Joseph and Nicodemus with eyes still fixed on the closed tomb.

My subconscious registered a small group of women watching from the shadows. But a question so filled my mind, I paid them no heed.

Who was this Jesus of Nazareth?

BACKGROUND

Every story begins somewhere and whether you come at this story simply from someone who enjoys historical fiction, or from a Christian background it makes little difference. The story, though, follows information from the New Testament as closely as possible.

The story of Christmas gets its details from biblical New Testament authors: Matthew, one of the twelve disciples, and Luke, a Greek physician. Of course, neither of these men were eyewitnesses to any part of the Christmas story, but rather base their gospel accounts on those claiming eyewitness experience or direct knowledge of events surrounding the birth of Jesus.

Both authors describe Mary's pregnancy as a supernatural act.

Luke provides details of angels announcing Messiah's advent to shepherds working near Bethlehem. He further describes how these shepherds followed directions of angels and visited Jesus, a baby, born in a stable and lying in a manger.

Matthew recounts the visit of magi, or wise men from the east who have interpreted a celestial event as announcing a newborn Jewish king of such importance they travel a great distance to worship him.

Both general historical records and Jewish folklore suggest the lands between Jerusalem and Bethlehem to be the sacred pastureland of animals destined for temple sacrifice. General Jewish folklore and historical records underscore a general belief that Messiah would be revealed at Migdol Eder, or the Tower of the Flock, where pasturelands bordered Bethlehem.

From the above skeleton, *A Different Manger,* builds.